DIRTY WOMEN

'A gritty detective fiction at its best, Madhumita's *Dirty Women* is also very much a bildungsroman of a fledgling lifestyle journalist and her steady upswing as a brave crime reporter, moving almost dangerously, in the otherwise restful city of Calcutta. Pacy and nail-biting at times, Madhumita among other things, offers a compelling critique of the news-hungry media and regressive society, and how it can disrupt individual lives.'

– Jane Borges, author of *Bombay Balchão*

'A searing, nuanced, feminist crime novel about loss, memories, and motherhood. Compelling characters, immersive storytelling. Highly recommended.'

– Damayanti Biswas, author of *You Beneath Your Skin*

OTHER INDIAINK TITLES

Anjana Basu	*Black Tongue*
Anjana Basu	*Chinku and the Wolfboy*
Anuradha Majumdar	*Infinity Paper: A mysterious quest, an unforgettable adventure*
Boman Desai	*Servant, Master, Mistress*
Chitra Banerjee Divakaruni	*Shadowland*
Claudine Le Tourneur d'lson	*Hira Mandi*
C.P. Surendran	*An Iron Harvest*
I. Allan Sealy	*The Everest Hotel*
I. Allan Sealy	*Trotternama*
Indrajit Hazra	*The Garden of Earthly Delights*
Jaspreet Singh	*17 Tomatoes: Tales from Kashmir*
Jawahara Saidullah	*The Burden of Foreknowledge*
John MacLithon	*Hindutva, Sex & Adventure*
Kalpana Swaminathan	*The Page 3 Murders*
Kalpana Swaminathan	*The Gardener's Song*
Kamalini Sengupta	*The Top of the Raintree*
Lavanya Arvind Shanbaoug	*The Heavens We Chase*
Madhavan Kutty	*The Village Before Time*
Pankaj Mishra	*The Romantics*
Paro Anand	*I'm Not Butter Chicken*
Paro Anand	*Wingless*
Paro Anand	*Weed*
Paro Anand	*Pure Sequence*
Paro Anand	*No Guns at my Son's Funeral*
Rakesh Satyal	*Blue Boy*
Ranjit Lal	*Bambi Chops and Wags*
Ranjit Lal	*The Life &Times of Altu-Faltu*
Ranjit Lal	*The Small Tigers of Shergarh*
Ranjit Lal	*The Simians of South Block and Yumyum Piglets*
Sanjay Bahadur	*The Sound of Water*
Sanjay Bahadur	*Hul: Cry Rebel!*
Selina Sen	*A Mirror Greens in Spring*
Shandana Minhas	*Tunnel Vision*
Sharmistha Mohanty	*New Life*
Shree Ghatage	*Brahma's Dream*
Sudhir Thapliyal	*Crossing the Road*
Susan Visvanathan	*Nelycinda and Other Stories*
Susan Visvanathan	*The Visiting Moon*
Susan Visvanathan	*The Seine at Noon*
Tanushree Podder	*Escape from Harem*

FORTHCOMING TITLE

Sumedha Verma Ojha	*Chanakya's Scribe*

DIRTY WOMEN

MADHUMITA BHATTACHARYYA

First published in 2021

IndiaInk
An imprint of
Roli Books Pvt. Ltd
M-75, Greater Kailash II Market
New Delhi 110 048
Phone: ++91 (011) 4068 2000
E-mail: info@rolibooks.com; Website: www.rolibooks.com
Also at
Bengaluru, Chennai, & Mumbai

Cover design: Gavin Morris
Layout design: Bhagirath Kumar
Production: Lavinia Rao

ISBN: 978-81-86939-89-5

Typeset in Minion Pro by Roli Books Pvt. Ltd.
and printed at Sai Printo Pack Pvt Ltd, New Delhi.

Prologue

The Loss of Tara

What happens when we lose a child?

What happens when those entrusted with the child's protection stand accused of the most abhorrent acts imaginable?

What happens when a whole town stops to watch?

On 13 June 2002, Tara Sengupta, age four, went missing from her own home, her own bedroom. Kidnap or murder – what had become of the girl in the middle of the night – was a mystery that took the nation by storm. A girl who happened to be the daughter of a single, celebrity mother.

The aftermath of the tragic events wrecked several families. The town that watched, open-mouthed and ugly, emerged unscathed, and walked away nonchalantly, as it always does.

What about the disappearance of Tara brought out the worst in us? It was a scandal to be sure, but at its heart it was an intensely personal tragedy. Coming at a time when the 24-hour news cycle was just emerging, when India was getting a taste for sensational news. After decades of dry Doordarshan, it had discovered the painful pleasure of watching the crises of others from a safe distance. But there was more to its hunger for blood, something sinister and frightening to those who watched closely.

The case had all the ingredients of a hit: tragedy, love, sex, money. It occurred in an upmarket Calcutta neighbourhood which made it feel as though it could happen to anybody, anywhere. But even though Drishti Sengupta, the tragic mother, was People Like Us, she was also Drishti Sengupta, singer with a salacious past, sufficiently different to set her apart. It was everyone's worst nightmare, but at a comfortable distance.

This book is a factual account of the events that unfolded. As the newsmen played judge and jury, I too became a part of the story, and it has stayed with me in ways I did not expect.

Which is why, when I received a request from the most unlikely of sources to write this book, it gave me pause. Was I ready to open up the wounds of all involved again, seventeen years after the fact? Was I willing to relive and recreate the horror of 2002 in 2019?

As I took a closer look, however, I became convinced that there was a need to tell the story, for despite the hysteria of the time, the chilling crime had been largely forgotten by the public. But for those involved, it had never gone away.

Day 0

The Loss of Tara

On the night of 13 June 2002, Drishti Sengupta took the stage at the Blue Banyan, the pub at the Victoria Hotel. It was a Thursday, not a night for a headline act, but Drishti liked playing to the smaller crowd that would assemble to hear her sing at the venue that had launched her career.

The Victoria Hotel was a cozy establishment in the heart of the city's tourist district, what might be called a four-star for no objectively verifiable reason at all, except that the owners had deemed it so. It was a family-run affair that had been around for about forty years, and it catered to locals as well as the Sudder Street backpacker crowd. It had a café, The Alcove, popular for its pancakes and omelettes at breakfast, sizzlers in the evening. Drishti had sung at the Blue Banyan, alongside bars both seedier and more luxurious, for over fifteen years.

In fact, she had, for the most part, taken whatever shows had come her way through the bulk of her career as a singer. It was only in the past couple of years that she had enjoyed the privilege of picking and choosing a little more, since her work had taken flight in directions she had not foreseen. But she still enjoyed the intimate space that the smaller stage afforded, and the loyalty of a crowd that had appreciated her before fame had found her.

And if Drishti was being honest, which she usually was, the routine of a weekly job allowed her to get out of the house. Away from the domesticity that she both adored and abhorred at the same time, often in the same moment. The regular gig meant weekly practice, and that translated to two days a week where she got to hang out with other adults and pretend for a few moments, in the smoke-filled rooms of her youth, that she was the same as she'd always been.

That night, Drishti was late and she was flustered. Her bandmates, who had already done set-up and soundcheck, noticed this because, as they said later, 'little could usually get under Drishti's skin'. She arrived at the hotel in her ancient Maruti 800, ran in to the bar and straight onto stage, dressed in regulation white shirt and tight blue jeans. Her short pixie hair was damp; it had been raining that evening. There were a couple of whistles and catcalls – she was used to that sort of thing, and half the time it was a friend in the audience. She had already discussed the setlist with the guys – the 'guys' being Debanjan Dutta on lead guitar and vocals, Shiv Ahuja on bass and Karna Das on drums. They had also been warned that she was in a rush that evening – she'd be singing for seventy-five minutes and no more.

They started the set at 9.30 pm, with covers as usual. She knew better than to leave them out; she could wait for her chance to perform her new material. She'd also play *Run for your Life* early on: it was her most recent hit, and she hadn't grown sick of it yet. It helped that it was one of the first songs she had written and loved, even though it had taken years to put it out. And the fact that she liked the film that had made it a hit.

But she could also not neglect *Nick of Time*, an audience favourite, and the song that had pulled her out of obscurity. The crowd would sing along to that one without fail, though she herself could take it or leave it.

Was it de rigeur for artists to hate the work that made them famous? Drishti had liked *Nick of Time* well enough when she wrote it. It was a mildly sentimental love song, nothing too offensive, with a lilting, hummable tune that slid off the raspy edges of her voice like water off stone. But in the past two years since it had been out, she had sung it so many times at so many shows, with requests hurled at her from the dark corners of clubs, that she had grown weary of it. However, today she would pull it out so the audience would feel it had got its two-drinks' worth when she cut out early.

But Drishti never did get around to singing *Nick of Time* that night.

At about 10 pm, she saw the pub's manager, Bunty, coming towards the stage. She had known Bunty for the better part of a decade, and they often shared a meal at the end of the night. When she had the time, in the olden days. All the performers got dinner after their set, and she would share hers with Bunty, but only if he added on a beer.

He caught her eye. 'Come now,' he mouthed.

She raised her eyebrows at him, still singing *Ode to My Family*, as if to say, 'Now, mid-song?'

He nodded. Yes.

That was when she knew that something was terribly, terribly wrong.

'Excuse me,' she whispered into the microphone, leaving her bandmates floundering through the rest of the track without any vocals.

Bunty quickly led her to his small office outside the pub, with its entrance through the hotel lobby. 'You have a call from home,' he said.

He averted his gaze as Drishti picked up the phone. He knew it was the maid, Sumita, and she had sounded frantic when he had answered the phone. He was on his way out to give Drishti some privacy, when he thought better of it and stopped. He knew it had to be urgent. Drishti didn't have a cellphone, but this was the first call from home ever on the landline in the past eight years.

'What do you mean?' said Drishti, her face twisting with alarm.

An alarm he mirrored when he heard what she said next.

'If she isn't in her room, where is she!'

He knew her daughter Tara was at home, and that she was not quite five years old. Drishti had only returned to regular weekly gigs over the past year, and she had stayed away before that in large part because it was hard for her to arrange childcare at night. 'Have you searched the house?' she asked.

She heard the reply, and then briefly closed her eyes, head

propped up by her hand, shoulders scrunched together.

'I am coming right away. Take the key and go down. Search as much as you can. Ask the guards to help. Find anyone you can to help.'

Bunty raced the little Maruti 800 down the streets, the twenty minutes to her home taking closer to ten.

They were met by a crowd milling near the entrance of the building. Drishti ignored all the curious looks and located Sumita as quickly as she could.

Bunty didn't need to ask – it was clear that the child was still missing. The maid looked tired and drawn, and petrified.

Drishti, however, was still business-like. 'Where have you looked?'

'Everywhere! The car park, the garden, the playground. I don't know –'

'Have you been back upstairs?' Drishti asked.

'One aunty is waiting in the house in case she comes back.'

'How did she get out of the house?' Bunty asked.

'I don't know!' she said, sounding shrill. 'I was in the bathroom and when I came out, the bedroom door was open. When I went in to check, she was gone!'

'What about the main door?'

'It was closed!'

'Wasn't it bolted? I told you always to bolt it!' said Drishti, her voice raised for the first time.

'Didi, you know I always lock it when I am alone,' she said. 'I don't know how this could have happened!'

The three guards at the main gate all swore up and down that they would have seen Tara had she been wandering around the complex alone. She hadn't left through the main gate; of this they said they were certain.

Bunty had visited the building enough times to know the guards were relatively vigilant. It was an upmarket neighbourhood, one of the older, larger residential complexes in Ballygunge. It was not luxurious, but it was much sought after for its location, and its strong sense of community.

After that, Drishti took off. Bunty trailed behind her as she ran into the building. Seeing that the lift was on the 10th floor, she headed for the stairs. Her flat was on the third floor of B Block. The main door was already open. A lady was sitting in the living room. Drishti did not even stop to speak to her. She charged into her own bedroom, where Tara usually slept, pulled back the sheets, looked under the bed, ran into Tara's playroom, threw open the doors to a wooden cupboard, went onto the balcony. She checked the guestroom, the two bathrooms, the kitchen.

And then she ran out again.

Bunty hesitated. By now, the scenario was clear in his head: he was convinced that it could only have been a kidnapping. It was not as though Tara had disappeared in a crowd, nor had she wandered off while outdoors. She was a small child, so small that nothing else made sense, and Bunty was certain that a search was futile. But it still had to be done.

He could have called the police in that moment. He wondered if he should, but thought it would delay him for too long. Getting through to the right people, even with the right connections, would take time. These first, precious moments would be better spent elsewhere. Bunty called the hotel and told the night manager what had happened, asking him to send whatever spare hands that could be mustered. He then called Drishti's bandmates, asked them to come over, and to inform Drishti's closest friend in town, Mona, who was often at the nightclub during Drishti's gigs. Drishti would need support tonight, and Bunty couldn't think of anyone else to call. He had never met her family.

On his way out, he took a long look at the front door, and though he couldn't be sure, it didn't look damaged, like anyone had broken in. And then he went back downstairs.

There seemed to be at least a dozen random people huddled around in groups – some servants, some residents – in addition to the guards. None of them seemed to be engaged in the search. The complex lights were all on.

He had been to Drishti's home a few times before, but he hadn't really paid attention to the details. He knew that the guest parking was on the ground level, all along the boundary wall, and the resident parking was in the basement. Now he registered that there was a playground off to one side, with a swing, a slide, and a seesaw, adjoining which there was a lawn with a few benches, and a large Radhachura tree with clumps of yellow blooms. There were a few more trees around the complex as well, but it was mostly concrete.

He did not see Drishti immediately, so he went to take a look out on the street. The gate opened out onto the busy main road. Whether or not the guards insisted that Tara had not left, a check would need to be done of the vicinity. There did not seem to be any security cameras in or around the building.

Thirty minutes later, Bunty had handed over the search of the streets to the three boys from the hotel–kitchen staff whose shift had ended and who had arrived on two bikes. He had given them a description of the child and what she was wearing and then returned to the building. There he found Drishti, with her friend Mona by her side. Drishti had clearly been crying. They hadn't found Tara, Mona said, or even come across anyone who had seen her that night.

Her bandmates had also arrived, and had covered all the landings of the 24-floor buildings – all three towers. Drishti and Mona had done the rounds of the neighbours whom Tara had known, in case they had seen anything, as well as the public areas in the complex.

'I don't know where else to look,' she said, her voice hoarse.

And then Bunty heard it. 'How could a child just disappear out of her own home?' asked a man standing in the crowd, somewhere behind him.

He turned. The man, younger than Bunty had expected, closed his mouth quickly, but the expressions of those in the crowd said it all. Shifty, guilty, righteous.

'Okay, thank you for your help,' said Bunty. All eyes turned to him, wondering who he was in all of this. It didn't faze him in the least, but Bunty had seen crowds turn on far less, and he knew it had to be tamped down before it got ugly. 'There is no more that can be done now, at this time.' He said thank you to a few people individually, and stood between Drishti and the assembled residents of the apartment. There were murmurs as they dispersed, but Drishti seemed to barely register any of it. She sat down on a concrete ledge skirting a patch of garden in front of her building. 'Sumita, go home now,' she said to the maid.

Sumita, who appeared to be no more than twenty, looked down at Drishti sitting there, wiping her face with a corner of her dupatta, as though she was waiting for something, some sort of absolution perhaps. But it wasn't coming. After a beat, she turned and walked towards the compound gate. One of the guards left with her; it seemed as though he was walking her home. It was late.

'And you?' Bunty asked Drishti.

She shrugged.

A few bystanders still lingered, but it was past midnight, and they moved on when they realized the action was drawing to a close.

Finally, Bunty perched beside Drishti and Mona.

'You should get back too,' Drishti said to him.

'No need. Anything I can do?'

Drishti shook her head.

'Who can I call?'

'My parents are out town.'

'The father?' he asked softly.

Drishti said nothing.

'We should go to the police,' Bunty said gently.

'Yes, we need to do that, don't we?' she asked, her throat catching. She stood up. 'I should go. But someone has to wait here.'

'I'm here,' said Mona, giving Drishti's shoulders a quick squeeze. 'Upstairs in the flat.'

'These guys can stay down here and keep watch,' said Bunty, nodding towards her band mates.

She nodded. 'Call me on Bunty's cell phone if she comes back, ok?'

'Of course,' said Mona, wrapping her arms around Drishti in a hug she didn't return.

Bunty accompanied Drishti to the police station. He had called Deepak, from the hotel, to join them there. Deepak, a short, stocky man of indeterminate age, was a bit of a fixer, and had good contacts with the police. 'Don't worry, madam,' he said to Drishti when they arrived. 'Give me all the details and I will handle it. You just be there to sign,' he had assured her.

Drishti and Bunty sat on the hard, brown-painted wooden bench on the verandah that ran the length of the local thana.

Drishti switched between sitting with her head in her hands and watching the door anxiously for any signs of action.

In about ten minutes, Deepak came out.

'They want to see you,' he said to Drishti, not making eye contact.

'Did they take the complaint?' asked Bunty.

'Not yet.'

Bunty trailed Deepak and Drishti through the thana to the desk of the officer on duty.

'Sit,' he said. So she did.

'How old is your daughter?' he asked, looking through the letter Deepak had given him.

'Four.'

'Has she ever run away from home?'

'No.'

'Does she often stay alone at home?'

'She never stays alone. Our maid was with her tonight. Usually my mother or a friend is also there.'

'Why not today?'

'My mother is out of town, no one else was free.'

'The child's father?'

'I am a single mother.'

'Divorced?'

'No. Not married.'

His eyes narrowed ever so slightly.

'Where were you at the time of the disappearance?' he asked, looking at her now.

'At work.'

'In the middle of the night?'

'I am a singer, I had a show.'

'Where?'

'The Victoria Hotel.'

He looked from Drishti to Bunty and back again.

'Have you searched the area?' he asked.

'As much as we could. Guards at the gate said no one left the building,' said Bunty.

'Children often wander off. They come back also.'

'She is only four!' said Drishti. 'She was asleep, safely in her room, when I left her.'

'What was the maid doing?'

'I don't know! I wasn't home!'

As the anger crept into her voice, Bunty squeezed her shoulder. He knew it would get them nowhere. The police station was not a place for sympathy.

'So you believe your child was abducted?'

'I don't know,' she sighed. 'I just know that she is missing and we need to find her,' she said, the crack in her voice returning.

He looked once more at Tara's photograph, which Deepak had submitted with the papers. Then he passed them a ledger. 'Write your details please. Someone will look into this in the morning.'

They left the thana. Deepak headed to his scooter and Drishti and Bunty turned back to the car.

'Shouldn't they come now to investigate?' asked Drishti, slumped against the passenger-side window. Bunty looked straight ahead at the road as he started the car and drove in silence.

When they reached home, Mona opened the door before they could ring the bell.

'Anything?' Drishti asked her.

She shook her head.

Bunty insisted that he sleep on the couch near the phone. 'Mona, you are staying here, right?' asked Drishti.

'Yes,' she said.
'No need for you to stay then, Bunty.'
He sighed. 'What about tomorrow?'
'We need to do something. I just don't know what.'
'Give me time till morning, Drishti. You are not alone.'
She hung her head and walked into the bedroom.

16 February 2001

So here's what Drishti remembered. Sore nipples, cracked and bleeding. A small mouth, too small even to smile. Feet so delicate that the light passed through them. Eyes unfocused and yet an entire life already lay in wait within them. Everything she'd ever be, she already was.

And then the wailing. Hunger, constant, instant, indefatigable – both of theirs. The zombieland between sleep and wakefulness that went on for months. The back-breaking pain of sitting up all night with a nursing child.

The fear, the awe, the immensity of the moment she had to leave the hospital for home. The awareness that once she walked through those swinging doors, it would be her and her alone – and despite her own throbbing pain, someone else would always come first, for the rest of her life.

The darkness that came in waves, crashing over the beauty of the moments and the memories.

What she didn't remember: the neighbours' gossip. Her parents' absence. Her bank-balance.

She had never wanted a father for her child. Even before she conceived, she had known that for her, men and childrearing would always be mutually exclusive. She was twenty-eight when she found out that she was pregnant, and she wanted to have nothing to do with marriage. So, if she was going to have a child at all, it was going to be alone. It had seemed so perfect, that she had never even thought to question it.

She soon realized that her enthusiasm was shared by no one: her parents threatened to cut off contact and they did for a while, her closest friends warned her that she would be walking uphill for the rest of her life and many more slipped out of her world without warning. The preservation of reputation was a pursuit so droll that Drishti had not spent any time worrying about it, but it seemed to be all that others cared about.

The options that friends and family had suggested for her had been hopelessly predictable:

1. Move city. Pretend she was divorced or widowed. Preferably widowed. Consider husband in armed forces.
2. Move abroad, where no one would care.
3. Go away temporarily and come back and then say she had adopted a child.
4. Have an abortion.
5. Give up the child for adoption.
6. Send the child away to be raised by distant relatives.

The views of others did not bother her at first, but when it came to doctors, she did not want to entrust her body to someone who did not share her enthusiasm for the life it was carrying. And while Drishti wasn't usually aware enough of her effect on others to process their judgement, when someone with their hand up your vagina tells you they *know* you've had sex very recently, and that you should get married immediately with a lifestyle like *that*, it is hard not to notice.

From the time Drishti could recall, there was nothing in this world that excited her more than gut-wrenching, family-wrecking, unattainable love. And the awareness that for love to survive, it must fail. Not only that: to really stand the test of time, it must have failed before it had even properly begun, but not so early that it hadn't yet been tasted. Less than half-a-dozen kisses would do the job. If sex had been had, it must not have been too much, to avoid the risk of the thing running its course entirely. Preferably more than once, because that first time was so often too tentative and anxious to be satisfying, but too much more and you might exhaust your entire repertoire of moves, leaving very little to the imagination.

For Drishti, the key to love was wanting more.

And so she had done her best to stay in love with the same man all her life. It was a different matter that they weren't together. Never really had been. They had first kissed in the shadow of a tree more years ago than she cared to remember. She could no longer recall the specifics: his tongue or the way his hand had cupped her breast. But she could feel, even today, her breath catch and the blood flow to her lips, electric to the touch and open ever so slightly. Moist as a blade of dew-soaked grass.

Did he remember it that way? When he lay next to his wife, did he think of her?

My nostalgia is better than yours, she wanted to whisper into his ear. Because otherwise he would be out of that bed so fast and into hers.

But she didn't want him. She didn't want anyone. It was easy for her, this absence. For in its arms the desire that fuelled her – her music, her energy – thrived.

Tara sat at her feet, playing in the sand, slowly funnelling handful after handful into a yellow plastic pail. Drishti looked at her watch. Where had the morning gone?

It was in moments like these that Drishti was able to admit what she hadn't known before: that family had its practical uses. If there was one reason to have a father in her child's life, it was purely for the purpose of logistical ease. At a terribly boring, practical level, some backup would have been good. Children needed the care of adults in a way that childless Drishti simply had not been able to fathom.

She had begun to wonder, unbidden, if what she had to give was enough. Enough for Tara, with a bit left over for Drishti herself. Though Tara had not yet begun to feel the absence of a father, Drishti feared it would come one day. And soon, too. Tara would never have what her peers, without exception, considered mundane.

Though, fortunately, Drishti's parents had come around. She had always trusted they would. She did want Tara to know her grandparents, and if that meant she would have to ignore the occasional sidelong glance and sideways remark, then that was a reasonable price to pay.

'Mama!' cried Tara, at her feet. She made the word sound like a song. It was sweeter than anything Drishti could ever write. 'Look at the cake I made for you!'

'Ooh – that looks so delicious!'

'It's valilla!'

'My favourite.'

'I'm going to feed you,' she said, standing up with a sandy spoon in her hand. 'Open!'

Drishti made her best, much-practiced pretend eating face.

'No, no Mama! Real eat it!'

She shook her head and held her daughter's uncoordinated arm at bay as it became clear she was not about to take no for an answer. And then the tears started – screaming, angry tears.

'It'll make me sick, sweetheart. Would you like Mama to have a tummy ache?'

Tara, who understood every nuance in her mother's tone,

realized that defeat was inevitable. The crying slowed down to a watchful, trembling whimper, fat drops still at the ready in the event a chink in her opponent's armour became evident. 'But it is a real cake, Mama! I made it in my oven!'

Drishti smiled. At that moment, a butterfly went by. 'Look Tara! Look at that butterfly!'

Tara dropped the spoon and spun around and chased the butterfly. 'Come, come,' she urged, holding out her hand so it would perch on her fingers. She did this every time she saw a butterfly, with no luck. But at least on this occasion, the butterfly decided to pause on a flower just inches away. Tara was transfixed. And then she lunged forward, scaring it into flight again. She laughed, eyes dancing with joy, mouth open wide, her whole being filled with the magic of the moment.

Day 1

The Morning After

Ahana always tried to be the first in office. It wasn't hard. Newsrooms are creatures of the night. She'd swing open the doors at about 11 am, turn on the seven horrid tube lights above her small corner cubicle. She'd set down her bag and then head down the hall to the canteen, switch on the coffee machine and wait till the milky, instant concoction bubbled out into the cheap paper cup.

She drew comfort from her solitary routine, before the phones started shrieking and the deadlines started hurtling. It gave her time to scan the papers and get on top of the day before being sent off for some photoshoot or store opening or party.

But that Friday was different. Some days just were. News would break in the morning, dragging reporters and the bosses out of their homes, too close on the heels of the previous night's paper being put to bed, or the trip to the Press Club.

When she came back to her desk, she saw that the news editor and his deputy – Ahana's boss – and three city reporters, as well as a couple of photographers, were already there. They were huddled in the news editor's office, the only enclosure on the floor, as the TV blared in the corner.

Ahana's ears tuned into the hysterical screeching of the news report they were watching. She recognized the voice of Ranadeep Mukherjee, the anchor of the most popular evening news show, Ajke Shohore. This was unusual enough, as he was only pulled out for the big stories, and never first thing in the morning.

'The complex has been searched, with efforts ongoing. We have also learned that the police have accepted a missing person's report but have not yet visited the singer's house.'

The more she heard, the more she gravitated towards the cubicle, positioning herself so she could see the TV through the glass wall.

The news editor saw her lurking. He turned his attention back to the TV, but before she could slip away, he waved her in.

'Don't you know her?' asked Atanu Biswas, the news editor and the ranking man on the floor.

She nodded as she continued to stare at the TV. 'Drishti Sengupta's daughter is missing?'

'She's a singer, right?'

'Yes. Also my parents' neighbour.' In the complex in which she had lived since she was born, all the way up to a year ago.

'Really?'

'There was a big ruckus about her a while back,' said Manash, her boss, the city news editor.

'That's right! That's why I remember her,' said Atanu, who usually gave entertainment news a wide berth. 'The nonsense about pulling her music off the air.'

They turned back to the TV. 'Have the police come as yet?' Ranadeep was asking a woman.

'No, it is the friends of the family, neighbours and all the staff of the complex who have been searching almost nonstop,' she said. Ahana had never seen her before, but it appeared as though she was a resident of the complex.

'How well do you know her?' asked Manash.

'Through work, mainly. But we are friendly.'

'Can you reach out to her?'

'I can try.'

Atanu looked at her, eyes narrowed. 'We might need you. Don't go anywhere.'

Half an hour later, Manash walked over to Ahana's corner.

'They aren't letting any reporters enter the complex,' he said. Probal Dey, who covered crime, had been outside for the past hour, but the security wasn't letting anyone through. 'Your parents still live there?' he asked.

So he did remember. 'Yes,' she said.

'Then they will at least let you in. Don't take a photographer, but carry a camera with you.'

She nodded. 'What about the police?'

'The beat reporters will catch that. But if the child went missing last night, I want to know what happened between then and now from Drishti, from friends, family, witnesses, anyone.'

It was a forty-minute drive from work to the complex on Ballygunge Circular Road. By the time she reached, there was a crowd of white ambassadors and Indicas, and several large OB vans parked outside the main gate. Everyone had seen the news report. On the ground were photographers with their SLRs and the fancy ones with their DSLRs, camera crews with their video cameras, journalists with their notebooks, all waiting – at least twenty-five people in all. The driver honked his way through and Ahana rolled down the window so the guard could see her face. He opened the gate to let her in, without his customary smile, before he and his colleague stepped in front of the mob in their wake, screaming at them to stand back, pushing the gate back in place. It was a press car, and the rest had noted this and were not pleased by the selective admission into the location of what was undoubtedly going to be the lead story of the day.

Ahana had not been entirely forthright at office: it was true that she had mainly known Drishti through work. But they had also both been long enough on the Calcutta nightclub scene to ensure they were more than passing acquaintances. They hung out at the same bars, the same parties; they inhabited the same circle and had many friends in common. Drishti was older, which was probably the only reason they didn't find themselves thrown together with greater frequency.

Then, after Ahana started working for the paper, their relationship had developed a more formal note. Though Drishti had dropped out of most social engagements since having Tara, she was still performing around now and again.

And when she had to provide celebrity quotes and the like for some report in office, Ahana was always guaranteed to get something sensible out of Drishti, so she was one of the first people she'd usually call.

Ahana had also bumped into Drishti around the complex. On several occasions, plans to meet and hang out had been made and not kept. Though neither were an active part of the community, there was the annual Durga Puja that brought everyone downstairs for at least one meal, and when theirs coincided they sat together.

And then, there was another incident; one that was giving Ahana a disturbing sense of déjà vu that Friday morning.

Once inside the complex, Ahana didn't quite know what to do. She couldn't just knock on Drishti's door, or at least, she didn't want to. So Ahana began by approaching the guards, some of whom she had known for years.

'Nimai-da,' she began, when she saw the elderly man at the main gate, 'What is going on here today?'

'Aar bolben na, Didi,' he said sadly. 'How a little girl can vanish like this, no one knows.' He gave her a rundown of last night's frantic search. 'I stayed back, even though my duty was over. Such a beautiful little girl. Just like a flower,' he said, with a slow shake of the head.

'And this morning?'

'She was out again even before my duty started.'

'Who?'

'Didi. Drishti didi. Some friends were with her.'

'And the police?'

'They came here, finally, at about 10.30 am.'

Ahana looked at her watch. It was 12.45 am. 'Are they upstairs now?'

'No, they left.'

'When?'

He shrugged. 'About an hour ago.'

Ahana thanked him and walked towards the playground. She pulled her Nokia out of her bag and called her editor.

'The police have been here,' she said. 'They are gone, but they spent over an hour with Drishti.'

'Okay,' he replied. 'Let me check with the bureau.'

She then considered her options. She could try to speak with Drishti; she could try to call her.

Ahana scrolled through her phone book, and found Drishti's number. It was a landline; if Drishti had a cellphone, Ahana didn't know about it.

She hit the green button, and put her ear to the phone, holding her breath. When it rang out, she was relieved.

Her other options: knocking on the neighbours' doors; or go home.

And that is what she did first. Her mother answered the door, khunti in hand.

'Eki, tui! What are you doing here?' she said. She left the door open and rushed back to the kitchen. Drishti smelled fish as she took off her shoes.

She followed her mother to the kitchen, but hung back at the doorway. With that kind of crackling happening over at the stove, there was guaranteed splattering involved. 'Do you want tea?'

'Na. Not now. I am here for work actually.'

Her mother shot her a look. 'About that missing girl?'

'So you've heard?'

'It's all anyone is talking about,' she said, matter of fact as always. 'My maid says that it was the nanny.'

'Why?'

'She was at home. Who else would it be? Anyway, apparently the police agree, because they went from here straight to the nanny's house.'

'She wasn't at work today?'

'Don't know all that. So what are you doing about it? Writing?'

Ahana shrugged. 'Maybe.'

'You should stay here. You'll get all the information you need.'

Her mother had always had unfailing faith in the grapevine. 'Let's see,' said Ahana. 'It's not my usual thing, so the bosses might pull me off it.'

Ahana pulled out her phone again. 'Why don't you use the landline and save yourself some money?'

'It's okay, Ma.' She wandered out of the kitchen.

'I am making tea for myself,' her mother shouted after her.

'Fine, then I'll have some.'

She called her boss again. 'The reporters are still trying to find out,' he said.

'Apparently the police have gone in search of the maid.'

'Really?'

'It's what I heard. Can't be sure.'

'Ok, good.'

'Should I come back and start making calls?'

'Have you tried to reach Drishti?'

'I called. It rang out.'

'Is she at home?'

'I don't know.' Her blood was pounding.

'You have to try to meet her.'

'But she won't talk to the press now!'

'How do you know?'

'Her child is missing!'

'That is not the point,' Manash said, pointed in his patience. 'Your job is to try. That is why you are there.'

She hung up and went to the kitchen. 'Ma, I need to go for now. But I will be back.'

'What about your tea?'

'No time.'

'Eat lunch here.'

It hadn't been a question so much as a statement, and Ahana just nodded her head.

She made the journey from the sixteenth floor of A Block to the third floor of B Block. She felt sick to her stomach as she smoothened out her hair and stood in front of flat B302. There was a brass nameplate on the door. 'Senguptas,' it read, in simple, black italics.

She rang the bell. For a long while, it remained shut, and Ahana had no expectation of that changing. She imagined Drishti curled up in bed, her head under the sheets. On the phone, speaking with the police. The house full of people rallying around her.

And yet, within there was silence. Unmoving, inscrutable silence.

Searchlight

Ahana went home again, for lunch, as decreed by her mother. And it was delicious, as always. Also, any homemade food that she didn't have to cook herself was ambrosial to her, now that she had to fend for herself in her tiny apartment kitchen.

Her father had also arrived for lunch, as he always did. He was an engineer with a large firm that had its offices down the road from their home. He would ride his scooter back every day at 1.35 pm and leave again by 2.05 pm, so he could be back at his desk by 2.15 pm. When she was in school, on summer vacation, she'd look forward to his arrival, and he would tell her about his day as they ate. By the time she was a teenager and their conversation had dried to non-existent, she had begun to wonder: her friends' fathers did not come home for lunch, so did that mean her father had no work at all?

Her mother would have food on the table for him, though she wouldn't eat at the same time. She would have a cup of tea at noon with three Marie biscuits and not eat lunch till 2.30 pm.

So it was just Ahana and her father that day, and it was not a combination that had felt comfortable in some time, which was perhaps why Ahana's mother took a seat at the table beside her.

'Ahana is writing about the child that has gone missing,' said her mother, as they ate chochori or stir-fry of greens with pumpkin.

'That's a change from the usual parties,' he said, without looking up from his food.

Ahana held her tongue: she had had enough of that

particular argument. It was why she had left the house and moved into her own place, pressured morning after morning to quit her job and do something with herself befitting her MBA degree. But there was a price to be paid for such liberation: it was why she felt she had to accept the 'boy' her father had chosen for her – the only one, from a reputed family, she was told, that would marry her despite her choice of profession.

'Babu called yesterday,' her mother said.

'Is he coming?'

Her brother – older by almost eight years – for the engagement. Her wedding, a scant three months away.

'He has put in his leave application,' said her mother.

'Naturally, if he can't get leave, he can't come,' said her father, for whom work and 'duty' were always of the highest possible priority – except when it came to Ahana.

Ahana sped through her vegetables and got started on the fish curry. She hated the smell of fish on her hands when she was at work, but she was in too much of a rush to use a fork, and it was too delicious to forego.

'We are meeting his parents this weekend at your jyetha's house,' said her mother. The 'he' in question was her future groom, Ashish. It was her father's elder brother through whom the proposal had come. He had gone to IIT with Ashish's father. The family lived in Delhi and Ahana had even met him a few times over the years at social functions. 'The boy' had been nice enough, but they had never really spent much time together.

After the proposal was accepted, they had been in touch on and off. They were trying to get to know each other better, despite the distance and their clashing work schedules. He had not seemed to share her parents' opinion of her choices, but Ahana also did not know him well enough to gauge if he was being sincere.

Also complicating matters was the fact that she hadn't announced her status at work yet, unable to face the prospect of leaving. But she couldn't put it off forever, especially if she wanted a transfer to the Delhi bureau.

'There are only three weeks left to the engagement. We have to go shopping,' said her mother.

'I am not sure when I will have time now, Ma.'

'Then what will we do? You need a sari. It is an engagement after all. We'll need at least a week to get the blouse made. Ten days would be better.'

'I'll try. If I can't make it, just go ahead and buy something. Anyway, you have my blouse sample.'

'And jewellery?'

'I told you not to buy anything.'

'Don't be absurd,' said her father. 'How would that look?'

Ahana finished and took her plate to the kitchen over her mother's protests to leave it where it was. She dashed to the bathroom and washed her hands with soap three times, to no avail. She found one of her old toothbrushes and tried to rid her mouth of the odour.

'Thanks, Ma,' she said, on her way out the door.

Her mother didn't crack a smile. 'Thanks abar ki.'

The police had sent Sumita, Drishti's maid, back home by that afternoon. Soon, all the other domestics in the complex, many of whom lived in the same slum as she did, came back with chatter.

It was the best chance for Ahana to glean some information as she waited for something to happen. She found Ratna, her neighbour's maid who at one time used to work in her parents' house, walking along the winding path around the buildings. With the compound's parking in the basement and fringes, the ground-floor flats had balconies and windows that opened out onto the common areas. Most of them had enclosed their balconies – in a futile shot at privacy – and usually they all had their curtains drawn. That day, however, quite a few people were peering out.

'Didi, you are here?' Ratna exclaimed. 'Have you heard what happened?'

'Yes,' she said. 'That is why – the paper sent me.'

'Tai? What can I say, Sumita is my neighbour. She lives in the same bustee, just in the next line of jhupris. How many times did I tell boudi what kind of a girl she is. Chhee chhee.'

Ahana knew that while her mother's stated reason for firing Ratna was for skipping work too frequently, the incessant chatter also had something to do with it. 'In what way?' she asked.

Ratna looked embarrassed, averting her eyes to a point somewhere behind Ahana's ear. 'What more can I tell you? She isn't a girl of good character, Didi.'

Ahana cringed in the depth of her being, but wasn't this why she had struck up the conversation in the first place? 'Why do you say that?'

'You know. With men, different men, all the time.'

'Have you heard anything about what happened that night?'

'Hain Didi!' Ratna needed little encouragement to move away from the awkward direction the conversation had taken to launch into a blow-by-blow-account as she had heard it. 'They came for her in the morning, one lady police and one gents. She was crying and screaming like she was being thrown in jail that moment itself, stupid girl. When she came back also, she was still wailing, though I didn't see even one drop of water in her eyes. She was going on about how she loved Tara like her own daughter, more than the child's own mother, that she would never harm her and had done nothing wrong. She said she was being unfairly targeted by the police.'

'She *was* in the flat, though, when the child was taken?'

'That she was.'

'She must know something. Did she tell you what actually happened?'

'Drishti didi had left that evening around eight at night. There was no one to help with Tara and Sumita was worried. Tara had gone to bed early, and Sumita had sat down to watch some TV. And it is true, what else would she be doing so late in the evening, with Tara asleep, but watch TV? She is also afraid of ghosts and all that, you know? Especially after old Banerjee Babu died on the eighth floor. Witches too. So the TV was on loud. I know that is something she did when she was home alone, because you can hear it all the way down the hall. She went to the bathroom before sitting down to eat food and swore up and down that when she came out, the bedroom door was open and when she went in, Tara was gone, just gone!'

'And then what did she do?'

'She ran out into the hallway, took the lift down and checked around the building, and then called Drishti didi at the hotel.'

Ahana asked a question she regretted even as it came out of her mouth. 'And tell me more about why you said she wasn't a girl of good character.'

'Aar ki bolbo, Didi,' she said, her coy look making a return.

'In our bustee she doesn't have a good reputation. Even her own sister has thrown her out of the house.'

'Why?'

'She wasn't happy with the relationship Sumita had with her husband. Her own brother-in-law, imagine! The family was trying to get her married off, but she wouldn't have that either.'

'And now?'

'What else? She is still carrying on with that man, but does that stop her from having relations with other boys as well?'

Ahana nodded in what she hoped was a sympathetic manner. 'Thank you, Ratna di.'

She smiled abruptly. 'Abar esho Didi, we don't see you very much anymore.'

Ahana went back towards the gate. The media throng had thinned somewhat since morning, but it was still there. She called the guard away out of their line of sight and asked if he knew of any developments. Nimai was clearly on the defensive now, having fielded the same questions over and over again. There were no records to double-check: the security protocol involved keeping note of only visitors' names and vehicle numbers. Not of resident movement. The service staff register had no entries either during the window in question. It had been late.

She was about to thank him and move away, but then he looked around and it seemed as though there was more he wished to say. Ahana waited.

'One more thing, Didi,' the old man said at last. 'There were one or two cars of residents coming in. While there is nothing on paper, a few guards made a list of what they remembered.'

She was impressed by their initiative. 'Can you share that with me?'

He rattled off the flat numbers as she jotted them down – there were only three. 'The police have already spoken to them, Didi. I took them myself to those homes.'

'What about people going out?'

'There was no one, Didi.'

'Any other searches made?'

'No, Didi.'

'Would it be possible to show me the visitors' book for the day?'

The guard went to the booth and brought it back for her. 'Quickly, Didi.'

Ahana did not know what she was looking for. There were only a handful of entries that evening, and the car numbers had been noted and the flats they were visiting too. She copied them into her little notebook.

Ahana left the building and started the wait for a cab. Five minutes in, her frustration beginning to mount, she noticed some men further down the road pasting something on a lamppost. Dusk had rapidly descended, but she could just about make out the outline of a familiar form.

'Bunty!' she called out.

The man turned around. She had been correct. 'Hi,' he said.

'What are you doing here?' she asked, approaching him.

'We've just got started with these,' he said, handing her an A4 sheet of paper. On it was a picture of Tara, in colour.

Ahana felt her stomach twist as she took it in. Tara was looking straight at the camera with eyes wide, with that unflinching look only children have.

Children and Drishti, thought Ahana.

Her long hair was tied up in a ponytail, her skin what

would be called 'wheatish'. Her eyes looked older than her four years, and her small, plump mouth was so very serious. She wore a red dress with black pin stripes.

Tara Sengupta, missing since 13 June 2002. Four years old, 105 cm tall. Speaks English and Bengali.

There was a number to call in case anyone knew or had seen anything.

'You made these?' she asked.

He nodded. 'Took a while for the colour prints to come. But thankfully there are a lot of people who want to help.'

Ahana looked over at the other two men who had moved on. They looked familiar as well.

'All from the bar,' Bunty said with a smile.

'A lot of her friends have come forward?'

He nodded. 'She does not want a lot of visitors now and her parents have arrived. They were out of town last night, flew in by the first flight today. And one or two very close friends are staying at hand. But the rest of us are doing what we can, running it by her first.'

'The police have anything to say about how we can help?'

'Police seem more bothered with ensuring the media sees them act than actually helping,' he said with a frown.

Ahana's eyes widened.

'Don't quote me, please,' he said quickly.

'I won't.'

He told her of the search the night before, the visit they had made to the thana and the helplessness he felt.

Ahana heard him out, not wishing to break the flow of words by taking out her notepad.

'Thankfully she wasn't alone,' she said when he had finished.

'Oh, she was alone. You can't share that sort of pain.'

Ahana felt the hair on the back of her neck rise.

'Can I take one of these?' she asked, holding up a flyer.

He nodded. 'Print it please, if you think it will help.'

'Thanks, Bunty. I'll call you tomorrow.'

Not Humble Enough

Back in the office, Ahana was summoned straight into a meeting. When she walked into the conference room, Atanu looked at her with the trace of a smile, and then at Manash.

It was encouraging, but with just the hint of condescension that always had her rattled.

'There were no police there when you arrived?' asked Manash, after she had given them a rundown of the day.

'No, they had left already,' she said. 'There doesn't seem to be any physical effort to find her.'

Manash and Atanu exchanged another glance. It was as though Ahana could never quite catch their frequency.

'We are going to go big with this story,' Manash said to her. 'You will be the Surya Apartments reporter until this is over.'

'Okay,' she said.

'There will be a lot of pushback from the bureau,' he added.

'Why?'

He shrugged. 'Usual territorial spats. But this story is lifestyle as much as it is crime.'

'Why?'

'Because of who she is.'

She looked from one man to the other, acutely aware of her own discomfort, trying to hide it as best she could.

'Will she manage?' the news editor asked her boss.

Ahana looked down at the table in front of her; pretending to not be in the room while 'seniors' discussed you was a craft she had already mastered. She assumed Manash indicated she could.

'Should we call him in?' Atanu said.

'Probal?'

A brief nod. Manash made the summons via intercom.

Probal Dey didn't walk; he strutted. With his brick-like Nokia Communicator strapped to his belt. The week Ahana had joined work, he had done his best to befriend her, cloyingly sweet and attentive whenever their paths crossed in the hallways. She had been quickly warned against him, but she found that his obviousness defanged him, unlike several others on the floor that had come to check out, and chat up, the new 'glam' recruit. When Ahana had shown no interest, Probal had backed off pretty quickly. Why waste time when he could find another target who was less standoffish? And he did so with speed. Thereafter he took great care to look through Ahana, as though her unspoken rejection had rendered her transparent to him forever.

Now, about two years into her time at the *Tribune*, for the first time she was at the same desk with Probal. Six days a week, they sat in adjacent departments, but their responsibilities could not be more different. Ahana's task was to find and cover lifestyle stories – food, fashion, parties – while Probal's was to work the crime beat.

'They brought the maid in,' announced Probal. 'They have been questioning her all day. She is sticking to her story that she had locked the door, and had been in the bathroom. She later admitted that she also had the TV on throughout, which may have made it hard to hear anything. She had also made a call after Drishti left the house. The phone records show that it was made to a local number, and the police grilled her about that. She said it was to her boyfriend, but he has still not been located.'

'Is he a suspect?' asked Atanu.

'They are looking for him now.'

'So what are they doing to find the girl?'

'I spoke to DCDD II Vinayak Agarwal and he said they are following up possible links, because they seem convinced that the only way for the girl to have disappeared without detection is for the maid to have let the kidnapper in. Particularly since there is no sign of forced entry.'

'But how will that help find her now?' Atanu said.

'Identifying the culprit could lead them to the child.'

'Fair enough, but how much time might that take?'

'They haven't said anything to that effect.'

'My question is simple,' said Atanu, leaning back in his chair. 'Finding the guilty party might help, but it might also hurt. Shouldn't they be doing more to search?'

'They did, last night.'

'Did they, or was that the girl's family?' asked Manash.

'Both, I think.'

'Not from what I heard,' said Ahana.

Probal didn't look at her. He only shrugged, smile fixed firmly on his face.

'Why did they release the maid?' asked Atanu.

'I don't know, but I suppose they must have had no grounds to hold her.'

'And they are certain it is a kidnapping?' asked Ahana.

'Yes.'

'What about CCTV camera footage?' asked Manash, looking from Probal to Ahana.

'The building security system is very outdated. They did not have anything,' said Probal.

Ahana nodded.

'But there are guards, isn't it?' said Atanu. 'Do they have any idea how the kidnapper could have left the building without anyone noticing?'

'There is a guard shift change at 9.45 pm. The police believe that while the duty staff was rotating, they simply could have walked out. There is a gate for cars, which is always locked, but there is also a smaller gate for pedestrians which is kept open.'

'Ahana, you know the building better than the police. Does that make sense?' asked Atanu.

'It is possible. The security guards are pretty efficient, but I have also been stuck outside in a car waiting for them to open the gate during shift change. It also fits in with when Tara apparently went missing.'

'Sounds like they knew the building well, then,' said Manash.

'Another factor pointing to the maid,' Probal agreed. 'There is also no record of the cars that left the building. The guards say there were none during that time, but there is nothing to back that up.'

'I do have the numbers to a couple of cars that came in at that time, and the flat numbers they were visiting,' said Ahana. 'But the police have apparently checked those out already.'

'Any other exits? How easy would it be to climb the wall?' asked Manash.

'Only one gate, and the wall is pretty high, with barbed wire and broken glass at the top. And at that time of night, the chances of being spotted would be quite high. Lot of people moving around.'

Atanu paused for a beat. 'No demand for ransom has been made?' he asked Probal.

'No. Not yet.'

'Or none that the police know about,' he said, stroking his chin.

'Any other possibilities?' asked Ahana.

'Nothing official, but one of the officers told me on condition of anonymity that there have been reports of several crimes in the area involving a local gang. They started with car thefts and petty crimes, but recently a man walking in the vicinity had his arm slashed and his bag stolen. Members of this gang were seen in the area last night also.'

Atanu kept his gaze fixed on Probal, as if he was weighing this piece of information.

'What about the threats Drishti had received?'

'They don't see a connection. It has been a year, and the outfit that had instigated it has been pretty quiet of late.'

'Isn't it a little early to decide that?' asked Manash.

Atanu turned to his computer and did a search. 'Here it is.' He turned the screen towards them. 'We had printed the letter in toto.'

Date: 21.08.01
Subject: Removal of all songs by Drishti Sengupta

Respected Sir,
I write to you on behalf of the Preserve Calcutta Heritage Committee, an organization to promote culture in Calcutta. It is our humble opinion that the song *Run for your Life* by Drishti Sengupta is offensive and should be taken down for indecency.

The artiste is known for her debauched lifestyle which is not in keeping with the moral values of Calcutta, the land of Rabi Thakur. Also the style of the artiste, to dance and sing at the same time, is objectionable. We ask your channel to ban this song, and any others by this artiste. It will affect the youth of Calcutta and Bengal and such influence is to be shunned by all god-fearing men and women.

Sincerely yours,
Prabir Kr Das,
Secretary, PCHC

'That's rather obnoxious,' said Atanu. 'It's worth checking out.'

'I will follow up with them again,' said Probal, 'but as far as I know, the organization does not exist anymore.'

'Really?'

'They were always rather small. They had received support from the local chapter of a right-wing group, the RCS. They've petered out now.'

'I remember. But they brought the city to a halt over this nonsense, so they must have had some clout,' said Atanu.

'It was the RCS that had clout. The PCHC simply were in the right place at the right time,' said Manash.

'Did any of the music channels act on it?'

'No.'

But it had been blown out of proportion by the media. And it had egged Prabir Kr Das on, in all his outrage, straight to PIL stage. The judge had quickly thrown the case out, calling it a nuisance suit, and the publicity had done Drishti more good than harm as an artist. And to the world, it seemed as though none of it got to her. She hadn't commented on it, or reacted in any way.

Atanu switched on the TV and flipped the channels till he found the 7 pm news broadcast. The regional channels were covering little else. With a day's time to work on it, they were using graphic re-enactments of what now appeared to be the official account, of the maid allowing a person in to carry away the child, and then feign innocence through a nightlong hunt. These were interspersed with clips and images of Drishti performing publicly, the ad campaign featuring her song *Nick of Time*, that had launched her into national stardom, the film song that followed, and then of course, the irresistible question: who was Tara Sengupta's father?

Drishti's status as a single, never-married mother was discussed, with outrage from some observers and faux sympathy from others.

'Who is to say what kind of conditions that child was kept in,' said the spokesperson for the leading opposition party. 'A child needs a family, a stable home with responsible caregivers.'

'The challenge of every working mother is tragically laid bare by this incident,' declared a campaigner for women's rights. 'Drishti was a singer, a job that required her to keep late hours. Where is the social security that could have prevented this?'

Ahana felt her editor's attention shift. 'Any clue who the father might be?' Atanu asked.

'No,' she said. And she didn't have to lie. Both in the party scene and from her parents' building grapevine, she had heard plenty of speculation, but none of it had any basis in reality. Drishti had neither confirmed nor denied any of it.

'And she isn't saying anything even now?' asked Manash.

'I don't know, perhaps to the police?' suggested Ahana.

'No,' said Probal with a shake of the head.

'What about her friends?' Manash asked her.

Ahana stared at him somewhat blankly, a feeling of dread rising up in her chest. Would she be asked to write a piece on who the father might be, according to popular opinion?

'As far as I know, no one has a clue. There was a lot of gossip, but she's never said anything. What I do know is that she wasn't in a long-term relationship around the time of her daughter's birth.'

He nodded. 'Ok. Get to work. Probal, cover the official aspects. Ahana, I want colour copy from you. What you heard, the mood at the building, the guards, the maids and anyone else you talked to.'

Atanu, Manash and Probal left the room and walked towards the lift. She knew they were going down for a smoke, and though they knew she smoked too, they'd never ask her to join them.

But she didn't mind. As she went back to her desk, she appreciated just how narrow her escape had been. How long it would last she was not sure – sooner or later, the muckraking would start, and Ahana would be expected to deliver.

Drishti's fame did not register with the police the first night she went to the thana to report her daughter missing. The officer in question did not recognize her, had not ever heard of her.

And the policy for missing children did not involve the kind of manhunt and instant action that Drishti had expected. There were seldom investigations into the disappearance of children – the thana recorded the details in the general diary, the information would probably go out to the media, and be shared with other child protection agencies.

But while a missing child is not the matter of a police investigation, a kidnapped child is.

Something had changed between Drishti's visit to the police station the night Tara had gone missing and the police visit to her home the following morning, and it occurred in the space of an eight-minute news bulletin. When Ranadeep Mukherjee showed up at Surya Apartments for a 9 am report on the matter, it brought with it the realization that Drishti was a person of clout. Apart from the attention the Calcutta Police knew would be coming their way, it also raised the very real spectre of kidnap for ransom.

Drishti did her best to explain to them that she had nothing to give, no fortune, no wealthy connections. But this made little difference. 'The reality of her situation never mattered as much as the perception that she had achieved a great deal of wealth and fame,' said Dr Debosmita Panda, professor of social justice and gender at West Bengal Institute of Social Work. 'Tara could be a very valuable pawn in a very dangerous game.'

For whatever reason, the police decided to act before a ransom demand had been made. And then the most cursory investigation revealed an obvious, sitting duck of a perpetrator: the maid. Not only did she have everything she needed to kidnap Tara – the opportunity, the information and the motive – the fact that she raised an alarm instead of running away seemed to be an act calculated to dispel suspicion.

'We zeroed in on the maid. The culprits have not made contact yet, but we believe they will once the situation cools down a bit,' declared the commissioner of police before the day was through.

By all accounts, the theory seemed a logical one. But as Day 2 turned to Day 3, there was no sign of that ransom call, and no sign of Tara.

Drishti wasn't the kind of famous that would cause people to stop and stare at her in the street, and she was happy to keep it that way. She was famous enough to be vaguely familiar when you met her, like someone you might have met at a party long ago.

She had this oddly disarming appeal. 'She was anything but your girl next door, but something about the openness of her manner and the warmth of her smile made you believe she was, or at least wish she was,' said Karṇa Das, one of her band mates. 'It was odd, because so many of us in the music scene were in it because we were misfits. We sort of formed our own tribe because of that. Drishti, for all her differences, fit in with us too.'

Part of her aura of public accessibility stemmed from the mass appeal of her song, *Nick of Time*, used for a mobile phone's campaign. The ad had told an irresistible story of lovers trying to meet, missing each other due to a series of unfortunate circumstances, finally coming together after they both got cellphones. (It was a gadget Drishti herself refused to buy. 'It was crazy that she didn't have one,' said her friend Mona. 'She would never say why.')

Then it was two songs in a film, unexpectedly turning one of her oldest originals into a smash hit as theme song to an edgy romance produced by a friend. *Run for your Life* was used as the soulful soundtrack to a beautiful, young, vulnerable girl, walking slowly down a Bandra street, a striking long take set against this haunting melody, soaring vocals animating perfectly a very particular brand of heartbreak. It was unabashedly, unapologetically sexy. Just like Drishti herself. Suddenly, the song became the anthem for every college fest across the country and Drishti had achieved the kind of fame a slightly quirky English-language singer in the year 2000 could barely even dream of in India.

In the clutter of Bombay, she may have disappeared, but in Calcutta, it was enough to make Drishti a bona fide celebrity. Her rise coincided with the boom in lifestyle journalism in the city, and the country as a whole. It didn't hurt that she was easy on the eye – lithe, leggy, sultry. She was invited for every store opening, society party, food festival and photo shoot. She skipped most of it, except the photo shoots. She was savvy enough to know she had to make the most of her moment in the sun. She had been long enough in the shadows to know how anonymity felt, and though the quietness suited her quite nicely, it was not a good way to get her music heard. She was also aware that her very English sensibility had its novelty value, but she didn't count on the moment lasting.

'Drishti's voice has the soul of Dido with the sex appeal of Shakira,' said Prasad Bhatia, who reviewed the film in which

Run for your Life had featured. 'It not only made singer Drishti Sengupta a national sensation, it is what made Neha Mehta this year's breakout star. She's beautiful, yes; a very promising actor, of course; but without *Run for your Life* setting the mood, it might have been a while till we noticed.'

The song was unlike anything to hit the charts in that era of music. Before the explosion of multiplexes in India and the new kind of cinema they brought with them, the urban sensibility was far away from the mainstream. Add to the foreign sound, the lyrics were in English too. And yet it clicked, with its simplicity and stirring message of love, loss and acceptance. Not only was it a national phenomenon, it made it all the way to the *New York Times* in a piece heralding the arrival of a new sound in the Hindi film industry.

While her song was going places, Drishti was content to stay where she was. 'When I started out, it seemed like Calcutta was a good place to be for live music. And by the time the rest of the country noticed, there was Tara, and moving base did not seem smart.'

At the end of the day, Drishti's motivation had never been fame. 'She has a remarkable ability to tune out the world. Actually, it is even more fundamental than that: to tune it out, you'd have to have heard it in the first place. She just doesn't care how others view her,' said Anurag Sethi, a former lover who has remained a lifelong friend.

Not caring brings freedom, but sometimes it also brings with it a certain kind of obliviousness.

Day 2

Not the Police

It had rained through the night. Ahana had been woken in the early hours by the sound of thunder, and she got up to close the windows of her small flat. She had a hard time falling back asleep. The room was muggy despite the dropping temperatures. And then she couldn't get Tara out of her mind. With the storm raging outside, it was hard not to wonder where the child was right then.

She must have drifted off, for when her eyes opened again, it was past 8 am. And Tara was still missing.

Ahana opened the main door to grab the newspaper.

Tara's face was all over the front page. She saw the stories, the pieces of them that she had cobbled together. Her reporting and Probal's had been fused on the desk. She recognized Atanu's style – lyrical and poignant without muddying the facts, without sentimentality.

She put the paper down, and wondered if there was any chance that Tara had come home after the paper had been put to bed. Ahana turned on the TV but, seeing nothing new there, made tea and pulled a couple of biscuits from the tin. When she was done, she lit her first cigarette of the day, and then called Bunty.

Every nightclub thrived on publicity, and she and Bunty had always shared a good working relationship. 'How is Drishti doing?' she asked him.

'I don't know,' he said. 'She's not talking much. I know she started out relatively calm. Devastated, but calm. When I dropped in yesterday, she seemed more and more despondent.'

'In what way?'

'She is concerned that the police is not doing anything. She'd expected more. Her parents have come back, so I think they will be calling a doctor if she gets more agitated.'

'That sounds bad.'

'It is. It's pathetic.'

'That first night must have been awful, too.'

'Yes, but she was too busy trying to find Tara to let the panic set it.'

'I can only imagine how difficult that must have been.'

'I haven't been able to sleep since. But how did you get involved in this?' he asked. 'Not your usual beat, right?'

'I know Drishti, I guess that's why. And my parents actually live in the same building.'

'Oh, is it?'

'So I was able to get in, speak to the guards, some of the neighbours.'

'The guards were very good that night. Very kind and caring.'

But what if they had let a kidnapper through?

'And the neighbours?' she asked.

She could hear him exhale smoke. 'Usual jokers. Standing around waiting for drama.'

'What about Tara's father?' asked Ahana, her fingers tightening around the phone. She couldn't believe the question had come out of her mouth.

But Bunty wasn't put out. 'He is not in the picture.'

'At all?'

'As far as I know.'

'Did she speak to the police about him?'

'No.'

'Have they been back after yesterday morning?'

'Not that I know of. If the maid had done it, you'd think they'd have found her by now, don't you? And yet, that is all they are focusing on.'

'Hmmm. Thank you, Bunty.'

'No problem, Ahana. Just don't quote me on any of this. I am speaking to you because I would rather you know the truth than print the kind of crap other channels are doing. Drishti gets the *Tribune*, though I don't think she is doing much reading right now.'

'I appreciate it.'

Ahana then turned her TV back on. It had been purchased just the month before, as soon as she could afford it. Her only other appliance was a second-hand fridge. Setting up house on a journalist's salary was not easy.

She found *Aajker Bangla*. There was Ranadeep, the star of

the investigative news programme. He seemed to have woken even earlier that morning for a truly nauseating reason: he and the cameras were outside a Montessori school – Tara's school. Her little friends – three, four, five, six years old – were seen entering the gate, their parents craning their necks to check out the director of the school as she talked to the crew.

'Since we heard about the news yesterday, we have little else on our minds. Tara is a precious child, just a beautiful, happy, bright and outgoing girl, and we cannot imagine who would want to cause her any harm. We are praying that we have her back soon,' said the director. She was an older woman, hair more salt than pepper, starched handloom sari – the very essence of Bengali elegance.

'Have any of the children been asking about their friend?' asked Ranadeep, pushing the bridge of his blue-framed glasses.

'Thankfully, no. But we have also sent a note to parents urging them not to share gossip and rumours with their wards. When we have more information, a decision can be taken on how to deal with it. But for now, it is too early to engage in speculation with such small children.'

'Are you providing any counselling?'

'No, but if the need arises, we will.'

'We have heard that several schools would not take Tara because she is the child of a single mother.'

'If that is true, it is a disgrace. We do not discriminate against any child on the basis of their family situation. All children are equal for us at this school.'

And then Ranadeep said his thank yous, and turned directly to the camera, walking slowly away from the woman and down the pavement. 'As the city waits with baited breath for the return of this precious child, her young friends too have been touched by tragedy. The entire city woke up yesterday to this event, and as we enter the second day of the hunt, we will bring you regular updates in a special section which we will be calling *Tarar Khonje*.'

Ahana could not take the sight of his smug face any longer, switching the channel to see what the others were reporting. She watched the parade of musicians, friends, neighbours on the two 24-hour Bengali news channels, and even a few national ones. There were snippets of a statement from the police the night before, saying little more than that the investigation was on. There was everyone possible, connected or unconnected to the case, except Drishti and her family. There were no appeals or interviews, no glimpses of her leaving or entering her apartment. There were plenty of stock pictures from her concerts, photoshoots and footage from her videos, but it was as though she hadn't surfaced at all.

Ahana already had her instructions to go straight to Surya Apartments that morning. The media crowding outside the complex was an even bigger throng than the day before. Ahana found her photographer Amit, who said that the police were currently inside and would address the press. So, seeing no sign of Probal, she decided to hang back.

She was out of her element with the other beat reporters, all of whom seemed to know each other. She quickly scanned the faces in search of anyone familiar. There seemed to be more national channels present, and even the regional BBC correspondent. The huddle, which had been restricted to just the front of the building the day before, had spread to the other side of the road as well. The result was a snarl of traffic and people: the building was on one of the narrower stretches of Ballygunge Circular Road, and there was a fair bit of traffic too at that time of the morning, made infinitely worse by the rubbernecking.

Opposite the building was a construction site where a beautiful ruin of a house used to stand, a two-storeyed building so eaten by the elements that it had become an unfettered breeding ground for weeds and rodents. It had finally been torn down two years ago, while Ahana had still lived at Surya Apartments. Now it was a gaping hole in the ground, since the construction company was facing some legal hurdles that had stalled the project indefinitely.

It was in front of the site that she saw Soma, the correspondent from one of the country's prominent English weekly news magazines, *India Now*. Being a small office, all the staff did duty across beats, and she had met Soma at the more prominent society events from time to time.

'Madness, isn't it?' said Soma.

'Yeah. Really sad.'

'I hear Drishti is a mess.'

'In what way?'

'Just, barely keeping it together at this point.'

'Can you blame her?'

Then she saw the telltale khaki hat approaching from over the gate, and the crowd squeezed in on the gate.

DCDD II Vinayak Agarwal himself came out of the building. Ahana had heard enough about him to know that he was the rising star of the Calcutta Police, having solved several high-profile cases in the past couple of years. That he was present at the scene himself was telling. He was short but very fit, with none of the swagger she had seen in other officers of rank. But he was not a friend of the press in general, Manash had warned her, not known to leak, and showing zero-tolerance for his juniors doing the same. Whoever was giving Probal his information, it was likely not this man.

He stood before the crowd. 'I will answer a few queries now, but we ask that, in the interests of law and order, you do not crowd here in future. We will be briefing the media about the investigation *when* we have information to share, at Lalbazar or some other appropriate place. The residents of the area are complaining, and it is also leading to traffic troubles. Questions please.'

The din was instant. Out of the chaos, emerged a voice. 'What is being done to find Tara?'

Agarwal didn't bother to identify the speaker. 'Investigations are on. We are exploring all leads.'

'Has the maid been arrested?' asked another.

'We will make an announcement regarding arrests if any are made. At the moment, we are questioning several persons of interest.'

'Has the area been searched?'

'What area? There is no indication that the child is in the vicinity. We appeal to anyone with knowledge of the case to reach out through the police helpline.'

'Is there any sign that the girl has been hurt?' shouted Ahana, struggling to make herself heard.

Agarwal's eyes found her, as she elbowed her way out between taller reporters in the front. 'There is no evidence at the scene indicating she has been hurt. Forensic teams are working to find out more.'

'Why the delay in collecting evidence?' she called out again.

'That will be all for now. Thank you, and please clear the area,' he said, moving towards his jeep.

'Why has there been no ransom call?'

'Who are the suspects at the moment?'

'Is it connected with recent gang activity?'

Many more questions were hurled at him by the crowd, but no more answers were forthcoming.

Ahana waited for a few minutes before attempting to discreetly get through the gate. Thanks to the announcement from Agarwal, the throng did begin to thin. She crossed the street, about to enter, when she realized Soma was by her side.

'Where are you going?' she asked.

'Uh, my parents live in the building,' she said, avoiding eye contact.

'Cool, can I come in with you?'

'Actually I am just going home for a little bit. To use the bathroom.'

'If you get me in –'

'Sorry, I've got to go,' said Ahana.

As she made for the walkway and the guard let her through, she heard some of the remaining voices behind her start up.

'Aiy, ki hochhe, dada! How come she is going in!'

Ahana saw Soma standing where she had left her, but others tried to tailgate and the guard stepped out himself, closing the gate behind her. 'She is a resident,' he said simply but firmly.

There was a collective clucking. The reporters recognized defeat but tried their best anyway. 'My boudi lives here too!' shouted one man. 'Will you let me in now?' There was a chorus of laughter, and some jokes of increasing lewdness.

The guard opened the gate and walked back inside. There was no pushing, no shoving; the congregation grudgingly accepted the discrimination.

'All okay?' Ahana asked him.

He smiled a broad smile. 'Don't worry, Didi. You go and do your work.'

Despite being the scene of so much misery and chaos, the Surya Apartments complex was surprisingly serene on the face of it. There was the usual activity of maids coming and going, security guards at their booth. At close to 11 am, it was past the morning rush of office goers, and there were no cars moving around either.

Ahana called the office to check in, and was told that Probal had had some more luck with other police sources, learning that the maid's house had indeed been searched, and investigators were speaking to local residents. The maid's boyfriend, Manoj, had also been located and taken in for questioning.

Ahana chatted with the guards, and was told that the police had been to visit Drishti that morning, and had stayed with her for over an hour. They had all been questioned in greater detail about what they had seen, and what they had covered during the first night's search, if they thought they may have missed anything.

Ahana was hovering around the ground floor, in the zone between her parents' building and Drishti's, wondering what to do next. She hadn't realized how rundown the building had begun to look of late. The exterior had patches of black mildew everywhere, even though it had been painted just a couple of years ago. There were loose tiles in the parking area, and one of the drain covers was submerged in water from the recent rains.

And then she saw a familiar face emerge from Drishti's building. It took a moment for Ahana to put a name to the face she was looking at suddenly, so out of context. It was Drishti's friend Malini, who Ahana was more used to seeing in the shadows of the bars and nightclubs that they had in common.

'Hi Malini,' said Ahana.

She gave her a sad wave. 'You've come to visit Drishti?'

'Actually, I am here for the paper.'

'Ah,' she said. 'You haven't seen Drishti yet?'

'Not yet.' Ahana looked at the ground. 'How is she doing?'

'As can be expected. She is now blaming herself for not sacking the maid before.'

'Oh – because of the police investigation?'

'At the very least, she has been extremely negligent. Drishti feels she is to blame for keeping her hanging around so long.'

'How could she have known she'd be so bad?'

'Well, she knew,' Malini said simply.

'Can you tell me why?'

'I guess,' she shrugged. 'The police will be all over this by now. About eight months ago, the maid's entire khandan landed up at Drishti's flat and demanded that she fire Sumita, because she was allegedly carrying on an affair with her brother-in-law, who she was living with at the time.'

Which matched what Ratna had told her. 'But what did it have to do with Drishti?'

'It seems the maid was living with Drishti for a few weeks after being kicked out by her own relatives, but the affair was still continuing. The maid denied the entire episode, said her relatives were causing trouble because they wanted to get her married off, and Drishti took the matter to the Women's Commission, determined to kick up a ruckus. That's when she called me – since the NGO I work for helps women in conflict with the law.'

'What happened then?'

'Her other maid, the cleaning lady, told her that the allegations were correct, but by that time, Drishti had already made the complaint. She was very upset.'

'She stood by Sumita still?'

Malini nodded. 'Classic Drishti. But she told Sumita that she would need to find her own accommodation fast, and made her promise that the family of this man wouldn't come to her house again.'

'And did she?'

'Yes, but now Drishti is questioning everything.'

'You are a lawyer, right?'

'Yes.'

'Shouldn't the police be doing more?'

She shook her head. 'Till it is proven that a crime has been committed, the police don't investigate missing children. Actually, they are doing more here than they usually do in such cases.'

'How else would a four-year-old disappear from her own house? That's just crazy.'

'Yes, it is. But this is India. Life is cheap.'

Ahana went in search of Ratna again. She rang the doorbell of the house in which she lived. An auntie answered the door – Ahana did not know her name, though she had been seeing her for years. She looked puzzled to see Ahana standing there.

'Oh, hello,' she said.

'Good morning Auntie. Actually I have come to meet Ratna di.'

She went away and sent Ratna to the door. She didn't seem surprised to see Ahana there.

'Hain, Didi.'

'I need you to take me to where you live.'

Her eyes lit up. 'You want to meet Sumita?' she said with a nod.

‘I am not sure. If possible, yes. I’d also like to meet Manoj’s family.’

Ratna didn’t question her. ‘I’ll finish work in twenty minutes. I’ll take you then?’

The twenty minutes stretched to forty-five as Ahana waited outside the building. But finally, Ratna emerged. They walked the ten minutes to the slum, which was in the bylanes, off Broad Street. Once off the main road, they walked through the narrow walkway between the shanties. First they went to Sumita’s home. It was a low, uneven structure of rough brick. The narrow double door was painted a peeling green, and a metal chain hung from either side, with a big, metal lock hanging in the middle.

Ratna went over to the next hut. ‘Do you know where Sumita went?’

‘I think the police sent for her again,’ said the elderly lady sitting at the threshold, on her haunches, preparing a thin, supari-filled paan.

‘Why?’

‘What do I know?’

Ratna looked at Ahana. ‘What else would you like to do? Seems Sumita isn’t here.’

‘What about her boyfriend’s home?’

‘That is a little further in.’

‘Could you take me there?’

‘Of course.’

They continued down the narrow lane and took a few turns that Ahana was sure she wouldn’t recall on the way out. The section they entered seemed more squalid – the pathway was narrower and dirtier, some of the homes had broken roofs that had been covered with blue plastic sheets.

‘Here it is,’ said Ratna, stopping in front of a blue structure with a tin roof. The door was open and a portly woman in a well-worn cotton sari sat on the floor inside.

Ratna entered the hut, with Ahana behind her. The woman sat before a little kerosene stove, with a dekchi of dal on the go. There was a high twin bed pushed against the wall of the small room, taking up most of the space. Under it were stacks of clothes and dishes. At its foot a small table was wedged in with a small but new-looking TV on it. A worn and blackened curtain hung between the room and another. Ahana could see past it to another space a little larger than a cupboard, which had a trunk against one wall and rolled up mats against the other.

'Mashima,' shouted Ratna, 'my didi has come to see you. From the newspaper!'

The woman looked up at Ahana, and turned back to the little bowl of potatoes and some sort of greens, which she was chopping with a bothi. She seemed to accept Ahana's presence in her house as a run-of-the-mill event.

'Mashima, I had a few questions for you about your son.'

'What else can I say? I knew that woman would ruin him. She knows black magic, she does.'

'What do you mean?'

'Why else would my son leave his own family to be with her?'

It took a second to register. 'Manoj *lives* with Sumita? When did this happen?'

'Ei, about six months ago.'

'Where is he now?'

'Still at the thana. His father is there now as well.'

'Does he have any children?'

'Three. Two girls, one boy.'

'Any news of when they will release him? He isn't under arrest, is he?'

'No. When do they ever tell people like us that? He could be there for weeks.' She finished chopping and pushed the bowl away.

'Isn't Sumita your daughter-in-law's sister?'

'Cousin. Just imagine.'

'And you went to Drishti when you found out what was happening between her and your son.'

'Yes. Stupid of us. I told them as much at the time. What would she have done anyway?'

'Do you believe Sumita had anything to do with Tara's disappearance?'

She shrugged. 'Who knows? The only thing that daughter of a whore wanted was my son.'

'Where is your daughter-in-law now?'

'She has gone to her father's house for a few days. Took the kids with her. My grandson. And left me alone. Can you believe that? This is what women are like nowadays. At the first sniff of trouble, they are off!'

'Have the police been here?'

'Here? No. Why would they come here?'

'They said they had come to look for Tara.'

'They may have come here when I wasn't home. I thought I would be relaxing in my old age, but that isn't to be. To make ends meet, I am working in three homes again. All because that woman stole my son away.'

'So you haven't spoken to the police at all?'

'No. What would they want with me anyway? It's his own mess, he will have to get out of it. Told his father that too. But he insisted on going to the thana anyway, and now they are both stuck there.'

When Ahana walked into the conference room for the second

night running, she was buzzing with the excitement of what she had to share, and yet she couldn't beat down the anxiety that was rumbling in the pit of her stomach.

'For now, the TV news channels are running the same old re-enactments and updates. We need something fresh,' said Atanu.

'The maid's boyfriend Manoj is still in lock-up. He's being questioned,' said Probal.

'Do they have anything to link him to Tara?' asked Atanu.

'No physical evidence that they have disclosed as yet.'

'No forensics?'

'They have only just sent the forensic team today.'

'So late?' asked Manash.

'Apparently the lead technician was busy,' said Probal.

'Right. What do they have on him then?'

'He was in the building at the time. He works as a part-time driver and was released from duty earlier that evening.'

'And of course there is no record of any of this,' said Atanu, shaking his head.

'They believe he went to Drishti's apartment for a tryst with his girlfriend.'

'But they were living together. Why not just meet at home?' asked Ahana.

All eyes turned to her and she felt her pulse spike.

'Manoj was working as a driver in a flat in A Block. The lady of the house said she released him at 8 pm. He was in the complex at the time. Both of their homes – the maid's and the driver's – have been raided,' said Probal, as though he hadn't heard Ahana.

But Atanu and Manash had. 'They live together?'

'I met the boyfriend's mother,' she said, her heart racing. She knew this was not what was expected of her, and she couldn't help but revel in their surprise.

'And?' asked Atanu.

'He left his family six months ago. The mom hates Sumita with a passion, and was adamant that the police had never been to their house for a search.'

'Not possible,' said Probal.

'What reason would she have to lie about that when her son was already in jail anyway?' asked Ahana.

'Not in jail yet,' pointed out Manash.

'Anyway, there was no child there, obviously, but the cops have hardly done their due diligence,' she said. 'He lives with Sumita in her rented room, but his own home is where his mother and wife are living, with his three children. Sumita is his wife's cousin, and she moved in with them when she came to the city for work. That is when the relationship started.'

'Then the theory that Drishti's house is where they conducted the affair makes no sense,' said Manash.

'They may have in the past, but not now,' added Ahana, explaining the pressure they had tried to exert on Sumita through Drishti, and how it had all backfired.

'But isn't it even more damaging then?' said Probal. 'If they were meeting there, it must have been to prepare for the kidnapping, or a robbery.'

She looked from Probal to Manash. Were they buying this?

'Does the boyfriend have a record?' asked Atanu.

'He has been linked to some petty crimes, stealing car parts and small items when he was younger,' said Probal.

'Is he a druggy?'

'Not known for it.'

'Could it have been a robbery gone wrong?' asked Manash.

'It's possible.'

'It seems like it is simply a question of opportunity,' mused Atanu. 'A small child is at home with a nanny. The child disappears out of her own bed and the nanny pleads ignorance. Not very convincing, is it?'

'I get that,' said Ahana. 'But Drishti seldom, if ever, left the maid alone at home with the child. There were always other adults present. This was most likely a last-minute arrangement, and kidnapping a child is hardly something you do in the spur of the moment.'

'They can easily argue that this was a rare event exploited by the maid – she knew there wouldn't be many more chances,' said Probal.

'What is the motive?' asked Ahana.

'Police expect a ransom demand any time now,' said Probal.

'What are you thinking, Ahana?' asked Manash.

She shook her head. 'Why would the maid wait around and raise an alarm if she had anything to do with this? Why not just leave and go into hiding if they were going to ask for ransom?'

Manash and Atanu looked at each other. 'I want both copies,' said Manash. 'Including everything you got from Manoj's mother,' he said to her.

'Good work, Ahana,' said Atanu. 'And Probal, please find out why it took so damn long for the forensic team to visit the home, and what guarantee they have that the evidence wasn't damaged, or worse, tampered with!'

Back at her seat, Ahana started drumming out her story. Somehow, in that office, on those desktops with their crusty old keyboards, default mode was pounding down on the keys as though she was a fake piano player. The words poured out; she would refine them later.

Her rhythm was interrupted when Priyanka, her colleague and sometimes party buddy, came and sat on the black swivel chair beside her desk.

'Working too too hard, gal!' she said.

Ahana smiled. 'Sometimes even wasting time gets boring.'

'You are still on the Tara case?'

Word had gotten around, of course. Yesterday's work was without byline, but the newsroom was by definition not a place for secrets. 'Yes,' she replied.

'They still haven't found her, have they?'

'No.'

'Ki pathetic,' she said.

Ahana nodded.

'Me and Tanu are going to Mocambo after this. Want to join?'

'I'll have to stick around till this goes.'

'So, 9 pm?' That was the deadline for the city supplement.

'Not sure. This is probably for the main paper. Don't know.'

'Too hot!' said Priyanka, with a laugh.

As she walked away, Ahana struggled to find pace again.

Long after her friends left, Ahana finally sent the file to her boss. She knew the unwritten protocol for big stories – she needed to wait around in case there were questions. She had ordered a plate of chicken chowmein from the dive bar across the street, which had been waiting patiently for her as she finished writing, slowly congealing into a solid mass, like lava. She attacked it, at last, and had just about inhaled half of it when her extension sprang to life. It was Manash, calling her to his desk. She quickly wiped her mouth and crossed the room, which was bustling with activity as the early edition was being sent out.

She slumped into the chair across from her boss.

'Your copy today was good.'

She smiled. 'Thanks.'

'Your first page-1 byline?'

'Page 1? Yes.'

'The news the beat reporters are bringing in is stale. The news channels have repeated every nugget of official information so many times through the day and night that our readers don't need it from us anymore. Of course, we have to carry it still, but we need to value-add. It is from your building eco-system that we need more material. Servants, guards, locals on one hand. But on the other, we also need inputs from her social circle.'

'Like?'

'Her friends. Her bandmates. Her lovers.'

Her stomach, with its stodgy contents, hollowed out. 'Ok.'

'Tomorrow track them down. Drishti is a mystery. We need to get to the bottom of it.'

'And the investigation?'

'Probal will continue on it. You get what you can.'

'Isn't there something more we can do?'

'Like?'

'I don't know – look at other possibilities apart from the maid?'

'Ahana, we aren't the police.'

'I know, but they are so fixated on this one theory that they aren't even considering anything else. What about a fan or something? Or the political party that threatened her?'

'To look into anything else, we need access to Drishti. If you can establish that connection, we'd have something to go on.'

Tara's disappearance had quickly become fodder for the nation's news machinery.

It was discussed in panel discussions with news anchors, by reporters outside Lalbazar police headquarters, in the news pages and magazines.

It was a city divided. In the cloying Calcutta of 2002, the moral outrage associated with single motherhood was strong, even within the cozy urban bubble where things appeared to be 'modern'. It was before social media had created a place for outliers to band together, for iconoclasts and rebels to make common cause, and if Drishti had a tribe locally, she was disconnected from it. It was hard to find people to defend Drishti's choices, and her marital status was growing to assume outsized importance in the treatment of the case.

'Single mothers come under a huge amount of scrutiny from all quarters. Much of this is negative attention,' said a leading female filmmaker, known for exploring feminist themes, on a news programme. 'When you make a decision to have a child, you have to put the child's wellbeing above your own. In choosing a path that brings with it so much notoriety, what is the mother's responsibility in what has occurred?' No one pointed out the inherent hypocrisy of this position.

None of the national channels could come close to matching the lurid tone of the Bengali cable news programmes. Fictional re-enactments of the child's abduction, graphical recreations of the scene, concert footage of Drishti on loop, residents of Calcutta with a need to be heard on a subject they knew nothing about. The soundtrack was heavy on cymbals.

Certain outlets seemed to take up the case with more zeal than others. *Aajker Bangla* was leading from the front with its special reports titled *Tarar Khonje*. The *Tribune* was also committed to keeping the case in the public eye – with its focus on the city and lifestyle, it fit the brief precisely. The child was taken from an upmarket neighbourhood, in a well-known building, and she was the child of a well-known singer. The greatest tragedy was that it could have happened to anyone. Anyone like us.

In all of this, what was being done to find Tara?

There had been no demand for ransom. No note. No contact at all by the perpetrators. No sign that she had come to any harm.

Fairly early on, it was clear that the investigation was being badly handled. By the time the police had come around, the morning after Tara's disappearance, several people had come and gone from the flat, touched the doorknob which might have had fingerprints, checked every inch of her bedroom and the rest of the home too. Forensics came by still later, half-heartedly taking fingerprints and collecting samples, very much aware of the futility of the exercise.

The police were focussed on the maid and the possibility of collusion with her boyfriend. The boyfriend was a driver by day and a petty thief by night. He specialized in headlights, manhole covers, music systems.

And yet, there was no sign of the girl at either of their homes, or any indication they had committed such a serious crime. His neighbours said they knew nothing.

If the priority was finding Tara alive, this was a very strange way to go about it.

Police requisitioned the telephone records for Drishti's landline, and confirmed that someone – the maid presumably, as the only adult at home – had been on the phone for a good hour, around the time Tara would have gone missing. Though this confirmed her negligence, it also corroborated her story. She had not been on the phone to her boyfriend, however; she had been calling home. The police initially believed it was a ruse, and that the boyfriend was actually in the flat, and had left with the child during this time.

How would he have done so undetected? One possibility was that he had got into the lift and had gone straight to the basement parking, leaving with Tara in a car. The problem was that no resident's car had been reported missing and they had not established how a visitor car would have slipped past the guards without being noted. The strongest possibility was one the police did not check: that Manoj took the car belonging to the family for whom he drove, in which he could have presumably driven out without drawing undue attention, with a child concealed. He could have then brought it back at a later time without arousing suspicion: all cars permitted to park in the basement had stickers, and would not have been checked or stopped on their way in or out.

And then there was the matter of the several eyewitnesses that placed the boyfriend at a nearby park, where he and his friends would go to drink, at around the time of the disappearance.

Police were tight-lipped about the other leads they were pursuing. But it later emerged that they were pursuing very little.

When it became clear that Tara was not with the maid or her boyfriend, the investigation shifted to a local gang of carjackers. Drishti had recently been involved in a road accident, and members of the gang had tried to extort her at the scene.

Drishti had mentioned this incident in one of her early interviews, when she had been pressed to mention anyone who might bear a grudge against her. There was also an eyewitness who saw a man identified as a member of this group in the vicinity, walking down the road at approximately 9 pm.

When it was discovered that Manoj also had a passing involvement with them, they speculated that it was he who had passed on the information that Tara was alone, and out of fear of reprisals, the maid had opened the door for them when they came to take her.

That led to a wider search of the slum in the days that followed. The police came up empty once again.

Confounding the police further, there still was no ransom note or call.

These developments should have forced investigators to consider other possibilities. And yet they were still stuck on the same tune, moving onto another opportunity to prove the maid was complicit. The new theory was that she was engaged in a scheme with one of the building's security guards, Tanmoy Das.

There were two ways in which Tanmoy could have entered the house: the maid had simply let him in (the same way in which she was believed to have let in Manoj, and it was implied, for the same reasons); or that they were not in it together, and that the guard had still come in through the main door or the balcony doors.

The stairwell of the building was open on all sides, and it would have been possible to use the window parapets to access the balcony of the flat. With Drishti's apartment being on the third floor, it would be a risky operation, but no more so than the daily feats performed by sundry workers for plumbing or electrical projects. This was the era before the hard-hat, the harness or even the tall ladder.

The guard could have entered the landing and manoeuvred his way onto the living room balcony of Drishti's unit, waited for the right opportunity to enter through a door that had been left open, intentionally or not. He could have picked the lock or had a copy of the key made at some point, then entered Tara's bedroom, taken the child and strolled out through the front door. However, this would only be possible if the main door had not been bolted from inside, contrary to what the maid had sworn up and down. A statement that had rapidly decreasing weight in the investigation.

Why was this particular guard chosen as a suspect? Tanmoy was seen leaving with Sumita after the search the night of Tara's disappearance. Sumita also admitted that when she used to take Tara downstairs to play at the park, the guard would often come by.

'I would see them together. He would touch Tara's hair, pull her cheeks. I thought he was trying to flirt with Sumita,' said Rashida Khanum, one of the domestic helps at Surya Apartments.

There were similar reports with other children. He would play cricket or football with the older kids, he'd help them when they fell off their cycles, and would generally be chatty. Not friendly, but over-friendly. Not smart, but over-smart. While there were no reports of actual impropriety, there was the suggestion of it, and this could be far more damaging, and far more difficult to shake off.

Tanmoy's supervisor had a different take on the man initially. 'He is one of our most diligent workers, and he has an impeccable record. We had expected him to rise to a supervisory role soon,' said Dilip Dutt.

However, over the following days, he seemed to change his position. In police records, he stated: 'Tanmoy was good at his work, it is true, but on more than one occasion, he was seen with various girls, maids, who worked in the houses. The maid who worked in Drishti madam's house was one of them as well. Also, he was asked not to get too friendly with any of the children or other residents, but he didn't heed any of the warnings.'

There was also the matter of an unoccupied flat that had been broken into the previous year. When the owners arrived from out of town, it had been clear that bathrooms and the kitchen had been used in their absence. The flat was furnished, and it was hard to gauge what precisely it was being used for. But there were rumours aplenty of a 'flesh racket' in the building.

Despite the outcry amongst the residents, they never gotten to the bottom of it. Many residents, including the owner of the flat in question, had demanded that CCTV cameras be installed in the complex. Several owners lived abroad and had championed the use of a technology that was still relatively uncommon in residential set-ups in Calcutta of the time. The managing body had moved to make the upgrades, but after only about half of the residents paid up the per-flat contribution of Rs 2,000, the project was abandoned.

The electronic eye aside, what about human surveillance? If a man had been slinking across the face of the building at 9 pm, wouldn't one of the other guards noticed? What of other residents? The brazenness of such an act stretched beyond the physical daredevilry involved – it would require a degree of confidence in going undetected. The police seemed to have considered this when they questioned neighbours, but finally, in the absence of good answers, they decided to forget about this line of inquiry. Whether Tanmoy Das was Calcutta's own Spider-Man or not, by some means, the police had decided that the guard was their man.

And then the next day, the story changed again.

Day 3

Private/Public

Drishti stood at the podium.

Free of makeup, hair combed neatly down. No jewellery.

No tears.

To the side of the platform stood several friends, relatives and fellow musicians. Their girth across the stage made her seem somehow smaller.

But she showed no fear. In fact, perplexing to those who watched, she didn't show much of anything.

The room fell silent as she began to speak.

That morning, Ahana awoke to a message from Bunty: 'Drishti Sengupta to hold press conference at 11 am, KGR House. Request your attendance.'

She leapt out of bed, got her tea on and called Manash to deliver the news.

'Ok, this is big,' he said. 'But it's going to go out on the channels through the day, so we need every little detail from you. Try to find an angle.'

'Have you heard from Probal on this? Does he have anything from the police?' she asked.

'No. There was no hint of this. Go there straight,' he suggested. 'I'll send a photographer. Coordinate with him on the way.'

She drained her cup and shoved toast into her face while she texted Bunty back to ask if it would be possible to get a one-on-one with Drishti.

He didn't respond till she was out of the house, on her way there, with an hour to spare.

'Not today. Only press con,' he replied.

It was too late to turn back, so Ahana arrived at the venue early, so early she was not allowed to get past the reception of the high-rise office block. She was told to wait in the lobby. KGR House was headquarters of a large company with several business interests, from steel to education. One of its owners was Udit Dalmia, and Ahana knew him a little as he was a regular on the party scene when he was in town, and a fixture in the society pages. He was also Drishti's love interest from a couple of years ago. Ahana would not have gone on rumours alone, but she had also seen them together at Blue Banyan, and it had been clear they were more than just friends. Drishti had already had Tara by then, so she wasn't partying much in those days, but apparently Drishti was never short on friends, or lovers.

Ahana wondered about the wisdom of the choice of venue for the press conference: it was bound to spark off speculation on whether or not Udit was Tara's father. There were plenty of people who could attest to the affair – they had not tried to hide it, and it did not seem as though his wife was overly aggrieved. But he was married with two teenaged children. Was it tacit confirmation of Tara's parentage? Or was it just another example of Drishti's disregard for appearances?

After a while, Ahana saw Bunty walking into the building, and she chased him down.

'Come up,' he said to her, pressing the lift button twice more than necessary. He was dressed in the same grey suit she always saw him in, but without the hotel-issued nametag. He was here on his own time.

'Is she here yet?' Ahana asked.

'I'm not sure,' Bunty said. 'I am just in charge of getting the press in.'

'Whose idea was this?'

'Drishti's, I think.'

'Why now?'

He shrugged. 'Desperation? Because doing something is better than doing nothing?'

'Are the police involved?'

'No, as far as I know.'

The lift door opened and they were on the top, the seventeenth floor, of the building, in a terrace that had been converted into a covered hall. The air-conditioners were blasting, but it was still hot under the corrugated sheets.

The room was empty, save for a technician getting the sound system running, and now Bunty who disappeared into an enclosure at the back.

There was a stage at the front of the room, with a podium left of centre. It seemed a makeshift affair that had been put up some time ago.

Ahana walked over to the window, looking down at the street below them. It was a perspective of Park Street she had never had before. The spaces that usually occupied her evenings and nights – the nightclubs and restaurants – were hidden away, and all she saw was a silent river of cars and humans trying to get where they needed to go.

She heard the doors swing open as a few other journalists started trickling in, so she decided to grab a good seat before it filled up. She sat down in the front row.

Soon, it was standing room only. The camera crews vied for the best vantage point, and she watched as the *Tribune*'s photographer Amit Das wisecracked his way to the front of the line. He was older than most, had done favours for most, and seemed to get away with anything.

And then, without warning, the doors behind the stage opened, and Drishti walked out. She stared straight ahead, making eye contact with no one.

She stepped onto the stage in a blue cotton sari. She took her place at the podium, her people filtering in behind her to stand awkwardly to the side, like back-up vocals in a high school annual show. The room went silent, the only sound the clicking of cameras and the closing of shutters, the odd shout to a photographer to get out of the way.

After a minute or so, that noise too fell away. Drishti cleared her throat and it was as though the entire room held its breath.

She unfolded a piece of paper that she held in her hand and then began to read from it.

'As you all know, my daughter, Tara Sengupta, aged four, disappeared from our home on the night of 13 June. We believe she has been abducted from the safety of her own bed while she was asleep.'

She paused, and then started again in the same, flat tone.

'We did our best to search the complex where we live, and the surrounding area and, not being able to find her, reported the matter to the police that night itself. Despite concerted efforts to locate her, we have not found her or any evidence that might lead us to discover where she is.

'It has been three days and she is still missing. Though the police has been doing its best, and continues to investigate, we ask anyone with any knowledge of the events of that night, or Tara's whereabouts right now, to come forward.

'Information can be passed on to the police, and also, our friends have come together to create a 24-hour anonymous hotline to support the search for Tara. The number and other details are in a press release you can collect at the door as you exit.

'Please call with any information you may have, and we will tirelessly pursue any leads you have for us. We have full faith that Tara will be with us shortly, and we ask you to make this possible by coming forward with what you know. Thank you.'

She looked up, panned the room for a moment, as questions went up from every seat. Ahana felt the bleakness of that moment radiating from Drishti's empty gaze, and knew the cameras, clicking without pause, could never capture it. And yet it sat in the room, and inside Ahana.

And then she turned and walked off stage and the room erupted in shouts.

Bunty took Drishti's place. 'Thank you friends for coming for this announcement. We have press releases at the exit, please do stop to collect them.'

'Questions please! Ask her to come back and answer some questions!'

'I am sorry but today she only had this statement.'

'E ki, dada. What was the point of calling us all here for this?'

'Please, Bunty, just for a few minutes.'

'Thank you,' said Bunty, turning off the microphone and following Drishti off the dais.

Ahana met Amit at the entrance to the building and they climbed into the back seat of the office Ambassador. The heat off the road was like a blast from a hair dryer on her face.

'Chinta koro, what state that woman is in,' said Amit.

Ahana said nothing. She couldn't bring herself to speak.

'Some of these people, what can I say. I am amazed at how stupid they can be.'

She cleared her throat. 'Why?'

'They think to call a press conference, she should have been ready to answer at least a few questions. They don't understand what she is going through.'

'Such nonsense.'

'They think she is cold, that she should have been crying.'

'That would have been better for them. Better pictures.'

'Cigarette?' he asked.

'Please.'

She pulled a cigarette out of the packet he held out to her. Then he handed her the lighter.

And finally. 'They do have a point, though. It is a little

strange how composed she was,' he said, pulling deep on the cigarette, and blowing it out through his teeth.

'She is used to performing, I suppose.'

'But still, she is a mother after all.' He took a deep, loud drag. 'You know, the police are not at all happy about today's press conference either.'

'Really? How do you know?'

'I heard. They had asked her to stay quiet.'

'Why?'

'Who knows? Just what I heard from one of the reporters.'

Ahana was back in office, and it seemed as though half the floor had huddled in front of the TV in the small conference room. All the channels had been playing footage from the press conference on loop. The pundits were each having a go, and while anchors delivered a blow-by-blow of the event, they also picked it apart – why was she doing this? Was it just about announcing a new hotline? Was it a hidden appeal to Tara's captors? And shouldn't there have been tears?

The opinions in the room also came thick and fast.

'Just look at her. Very sad. I just can't imagine.'

'Why did it take her so long to say something?'

'I heard that her husband left her before Tara was born.'

Ahana turned on her heel and left before anyone noticed her. She found Manash, and gave him a rundown of what had happened.

That was when Probal came in. Ahana had sent Manash a text with Amit's take on the police being unhappy with Drishti's press conference, but his sources refuted it outright.

'Check, check some more,' said Manash. Probal shrugged.

'The maid is back at Lalbazar today,' he said.

'Any idea why?'

'No, not yet. But I should find out by evening,' he said, leaving them alone again.

'So what is your take?' Manash asked her.

'I think she is unhappy with the police,' said Ahana.

Manash nodded. 'That's for sure.'

'They are still stuck on the maid–driver–security guard angle, and have not really looked beyond that.'

'As far as we know.'

'Why, have you heard something?'

'You know what it's like.'

'Actually, no I don't.'

'There are just too many mysteries around Drishti. There is talk...'

'About?'

'Who Tara's father is. Who are the people in Drishti's life.'

'Where are you getting this from?'

'Probal. We are carrying a piece today. We have been holding it from day one, but it has to be said now.'

'But she is the victim here!'

'No, Ahana. Tara is the victim. Don't forget that.'

She slumped in her seat, rubbing her temples.

'What about the press conference?' he asked more gently.

Ahana shrugged. 'It is tough to read, but that is Drishti for you.'

'What do you mean?' he asked.

'She's one of these people who are hard to pin down.'

'Explain.'

'If I could, it wouldn't be hard, right?'

'Give me an example.'

'Most rebels reject societal norms, but they validate themselves in some other way. She's a musician, and they have their own code. But she had this ability to be one of them, without really *being* one of them. She'd go to their parties, she'd enjoy herself, but it is almost as though she holds back. But at the same time, everyone loves her.'

He frowned. 'Do they?'

'Well no, maybe not everyone.'

'Maybe the guys love her more than the girls?'

'Maybe,' she admitted softly. 'Maybe some of the women have something to be mad about, too.'

'Like what?'

'She doesn't always discriminate between men who are taken and men who are not.'

'So she lives by her own rules.'

'Yes, but it is more than that. It is complicated.'

Ahana didn't want to bring up the affair with Udit Dalmia, it felt too much like gossip. But she knew she couldn't keep it from Manash indefinitely – Drishti had brought him into the story by holding the press conference in his office. But then Manash was called into a meeting with the editor-in-chief, and she was spared once again.

19 April 1993

He could count on one hand the number of times he had met Drishti. But he had always known who she was. Even at twenty-four, she couldn't hide it. And she had never tried.

The first time, she had been standing on the stage, mid-song, when he entered the hall, walking through the swinging doors at the back of the room. He simply had to stop and listen.

It was *Summertime*, and she brought a rasp to it which rendered it especially sultry. Her voice washed over him in caressing waves, over the entire congregation.

And then the spell was broken. Though he was behind several rows of students standing in the packed auditorium, he had been spotted and a couple of second-year groupies rushed at him, offering to escort him to his reserved seat. He put a hand out to shush them.

He had seen few people with the skill to hold the attention of 2,000 restless engineering students. It was as though everyone had recognized that they were in the presence of a rare talent.

And then, at the end, after the raucous applause that followed, it was as if the moment had never existed. It was back to Guns N' Roses and Def Leppard, sung with more exuberance than thought. He made his way to his seat.

It was a music competition organized by the Arts Council of France, an effort to commemorate the obscure collaboration between an old French jazz pianist no one had heard of with an even older Indian guitarist a few of them had heard of. As the only staff member with any exposure to western music, he was named professor coordinator of the two-day event, even though he was only visiting faculty. It's what happens when you jam with students and look the other way when they drink on campus.

So it had fallen upon him to host the award ceremony after the team from Delhi beat the host band to first place. He made the announcements, and he found himself watching the lead singer with more than the usual interest. She seemed almost offhand in her confidence as she and her bandmates came up on stage to receive their medals. They were excited though: they had won a trip to Paris to immerse themselves in jazz at a music school for eight weeks.

As they posed with the judges for pictures at the end of it, he was called over to join them. He stood at the end of the line. He and Drishti were separated by a judge who barely came up to his chin. He turned to look at her, almost as tall as he was. He had not been able to really see her from the rear of the auditorium, but he was unsurprised to find that she was beautiful. She gave him a quick glance, eyes luminous, but he knew she had not seen him. Not really.

And then there was the after party. He was invited, not as the staff coordinator for the event, but as a friend of the student body. He decided he'd go, have a beer and leave in half an hour.

He had only just arrived when Drishti walked in with her band. There was a dip in the volume of the room, or perhaps it seemed that way to him.

She fluttered on the fringes of the crowd. He was surrounded by the managing committee guys, and their friends from other institutes. She didn't attempt to make her way into the throng of the party, though one of her bandmates seemed to know one of the MC guys.

He couldn't stop his eyes from drifting over to her every now and then. She was chatting with her friends, and a couple of other quieter ones from other colleges. She had an Old Monk and Coke in hand.

And then their eyes met. It must have been clear to her – and he thought, to everyone else – that he had been watching her. So he smiled, and she smiled back. A minute or two later, he broke away. The thirty minutes he had intended to spend had already become sixty and the one drink had become two. It was time to leave, but on the way out, he stopped by Drishti's group.

'You guys were great,' he said, aware of how silly he sounded. 'Refreshing to hear something so different amidst all the hairband faithfuls.'

'Yeah,' laughed the drummer. 'Though we do that too.'

Drishti smiled again, but said nothing.

'Your voice is special. You should stick with music,' he said, unable to walk away.

'I hope to, though my parents aren't happy about it,' she said.

'What are you studying?'

'Botany.'

'Then that's not much of a plan B.'

She laughed and it was a throaty punch to the gut.

'Unless that was the plan all along,' he managed to say.

He shook hands with them all once again and left. He would not be that guy.

It turned out, he should have stayed. Because the next morning, there he was, sitting in the office of the dean. With Drishti across from them, telling the dean all about the attempted assault on Sanju, one of her band members, who was sitting there in silent discomfort. By the convenor of the fest, a burly final-year computer science student. Sanju had been cornered at an after-after party, and when he had refused the convenor's advances, had been beaten up to within an inch of serious damage.

They had come to see the dean straight from the local hospital. The dean could not meet Drishti's gaze, but it didn't seem to faze her. She paused to check in with Sanju every now and again, reaching out to take his hand, as she spoke.

'It is simply not possible,' said the dean, who would have liked to throw them out altogether, except for the fact that the boy's face, and the medical reports, told their own story.

'Why?' asked Drishti.

'He is a fine boy, academically brilliant and a leader of the student body.'

'I witnessed the assault, as did others,' said Drishti.

'The nature of this accusation does not sit well with me, young lady,' he said.

'It is what happened. We could take the complaint to the police.'

Sanju flinched, already stretched beyond what he could endure.

'We have physical evidence and at least one other witness from a third college,' Drishti pressed on.

That was when he had indicated to the dean that they needed to speak in private. Drishti and her friend were asked to leave, told that they would be informed of the next course of action shortly.

He considered the best approach. He knew that evangelising would get him nowhere with his boss. 'I was there at the beginning of the party,' he said.

'Is it?' replied the dean.

'I left very early. But I should take responsibility as the staff in-charge of the event.'

'Responsibility for what? These things must be lies. I cannot believe it.'

'We have an obligation to treat it like any other case of abuse, and investigate it. But do consider that it takes a great deal to bring up an incident like this, and if it is true, the boy from Delhi has much to lose as well.'

The dean closed his eyes.

'Also, the Delhi team won the competition. The international community is involved with this event, and our reputation would take a serious blow if it came out that we did not handle the complaint with due diligence.'

The dean finally accepted this position, but he insisted that it would cause too much of a scandal to launch an investigation. If there were eyewitnesses, it would be much easier to simply expel their own student, and to ask the guests to provide a written report and then leave.

So they called in the accused. He denied the incident, but when confronted with the boy's injuries and hospital reports, under threat of investigation, he admitted to the beating but to nothing else. He was told to remove himself from the college grounds with immediate effect; that he would be allowed to return to campus after the event to collect his personal effects as long as he did so quietly.

It fell to him to break the news to the visitors.

Sanju and Drishti would have to submit an account of the events in writing, along with the medical records, stating also that they understood that the institute was taking the harshest possible measures in its power.

He wasn't at all sure they would accept the terms. But

Sanju seemed satisfied, and Drishti seemed to be following his lead.

Sanju hadn't wanted to stay on campus and face the crowds, so he took them both to the only hotel nearby that was any good. After they checked in, Sanju said he just wanted to sleep, so Drishti and he were left together.

'Thank you,' she said as they stood on the porch.

'It's the least I could do,' he shrugged.

'No, it's not,' she said simply.

He could feel himself blush. 'Do you like walking?' he asked her, more to say something than anything else.

'Sure?' she said, confused.

'There is a trail a little up the hill. If you continue, you have the best views of the valley.'

'What are you doing now?' she said.

'Nothing,' he said with a shrug. 'I'll probably head back to campus.'

'Why don't you walk with me instead?'

The request surprised him, but he was powerless to say no. They wandered those meandering paths for the better part of three hours. She told him about how she wanted to pursue her music, despite her parents' resistance. He told her about the company he started and sold, and his mother's cancer, which had brought him back to the country to be closer to her. They stopped to watch birds, which it turned out she was impossible at spotting.

Then, hungry and tired, they finally returned to campus. She also had to find her friends, to tell them not to worry and that she and Sanju would meet them at the station in time for their train the following morning.

For some reason, he stayed by her side. He could have left, he probably should have left. He was doing himself no favours.

But then, at first, they couldn't find her friends. Someone sent them to the performance area – it was late, but one of the students had taken over the controls. It seemed as though the entire student body was drunk, or high. The music was loud and fast, and somehow they were dancing. Drishti had her back to him, and as her hips swayed, she pressed into him. He couldn't breathe, he thought it must have been a mistake, but then she turned to look at him, putting a hand on his chest and he stopped thinking.

At the end of the song, he walked out there as fast as he could.

But even then, he didn't have it in him to walk away – back to his room where she couldn't find him. He stood at the periphery of the shamiana, where he knew she'd be able to see him. At first, he didn't think she was coming, and he was flooded with relief and disappointment.

But then she did.

'I'm sorry if that made you uncomfortable,' she said.

'Shouldn't it be I who apologizes?'

'Why?'

'I'm a professor.'

'So what? I'm not *your* student.'

'You are *a* student.'

'In the final year of my master's. An adult.'

'If someone sees us, I could lose my job.'

'Is that why you left?'

'No.'

'Then?'

'Tell me how this is any different from what happened to your friend last night.'

'You are being ridiculous. How is it similar in any way?'

'It is an abuse of power.'

'How is it abuse when it is welcome? When *I* am initiating it?'

'This is not a level playing field. I have authority here.'

'Not over me.'

She was always so bloody clear that it hurt.

'I can't,' he said simply. 'It's wrong and you know it.'

'You are a prude.'

'No, just a coward.'

They were standing in the shade of a tree, and there was just enough light to see her eyes. He realized he was afraid of her judgement, but he found none there.

'You know what? Fuck it.' His arms wound back around her waist. They came together and her lips on his were as intoxicating as the song she had sung the night before. It was almost enough to make him forget. But when he felt her callused, guitar-playing fingers on the skin of his back, he pulled away, trapping her hands in his.

He rested his forehead against hers and caught his breath.

'You leave tomorrow?'

'Morning. 6.30 am.'

'It's time to walk you to the hotel.'

'If that is what you want.'

'It is what I need to do.'

She didn't protest. If she had, he wasn't sure he'd be able to hold back.

He was seen, of course, by several students that night, but none of them reported the incident.

After the fest, the student who attacked Sanju left the institute. It became generally known around campus that he had been falsely accused by 'that bitch from Delhi' and had been thrown out without a fair hearing. Though there were whispers of another story, it never gained much traction.

It was a few weeks later that he learned that the student had not, in fact, been expelled. He had been asked to leave, but had been issued a transfer certificate. With that, he had gone on to study at a lesser known university in Australia.

If he had planned on reaching out to Drishti before, after he learned what the dean had done, he couldn't stand the thought of it. Three months later, his mother's cancer officially was in remission and he returned to the States.

And that, he had thought, would be the end of it.

Day 4

Public/Private

Ahana had the next day off. She finally succumbed to her mother's demands that she come shopping with her, going over the night before to at least get a free meal out of it.

It poured for half the night, but Ahana slept right through it all. She woke up to the ginger tea she so missed but was always too lazy to make for herself. And Marie biscuit. She passed on the offer of luchi for breakfast because they had to go out. The engagement sari could be put off no longer.

'Where are we going?' asked Ahana.

'College Street, I thought.'

'But I don't want a boring sari, Ma.'

'What kind of sari do you want?'

'Something I will wear later. Anyway, if I want a Benarasi, I can always borrow from you.'

'You won't be here, remember? You will be in Delhi.'

She scowled at the reminder.

'Fine,' her mother said. 'This is just the engagement anyway. Let's get something lighter.'

'Light is good. Anyway, heavy saris look so frumpy on me.'

'Why do you say that?'

'Because I am so short.'

'Don't talk nonsense.'

But she knew she had won. 'A nice crepe would be lovely. Park Street?' Ahana suggested.

'So expensive!'

'I can pay. Or we can buy fewer of them.'

'Thik ache, let's go. But no more nonsense about you paying.'

The shopping went surprisingly fast – to her, the whole thing felt a bit like fancy dress, the idea that the engagement party was her own still hadn't penetrated.

'I like that one,' Ahana said, pointing to a dark blue and pink crepe silk.

'Isn't it a little too simple?'

'Ma, it is beautiful. Just feel it!'

She asked the price and looked at Ahana with wide eyes.

'Is that too much?' Ahana asked. She had scrupulously avoided all wedding finance-related conversations at home. One more way to pretend.

'No, but it should be more *gorgeous* if it costs so much.'

'Uff, ma. That is not how it works. It is about the material.'

'It is about the address of the store. At this price I could get the best possible Benarasi at College Street.'

'I am sure you could. And if this wedding happens, you can.'

'What do you mean, "if"!'

'Whatever. It's a slip of the tongue.'

'It's bad luck!'

'Uff.'

'Don't take me for a fool. What do you mean by this, Bonnie?'

'I don't know what I meant. Sorry. Ignore it.'

Her mother paid for the sari, taking out a bundle of notes and peeling them off gingerly. It seemed to take forever.

'Where should we go for lunch?' asked Ahana, as they waited for their package. 'This one is my treat.'

'You say. I don't know these fancy places.'

'Uff Ma, hardly fancy. Let's go to Mocambo.'

'How was your meeting with Ashish's family that day?' asked Ahana over the Pepper Devilled Crab they were sharing.

'It was ok.'

'You don't sound happy.'

'All these modern things – I am not sure if there is a point to it.'

'What modern things?'

'It is awkward meeting your future in-laws in this way.'

'I don't know how modern it is. Weren't arranged marriages often between families who knew each other quite well?'

'It wasn't like that in my time. I met your father once before marriage, and my parents and his parents may have met once or twice more, or more likely, someone from the family was sent to sort out the details.'

'So what did you discuss?'

'Not much. Luckily your uncle did not stop talking, as usual.'

'So no changes to the plan?'

'Changes? Why would there be changes?'

'Just asking.'

'Not just this, what you said in the shop as well – why are you saying these strange, strange things?'

'Ma, it's my wedding. To a man who is practically a stranger. Can you expect me to be swooning in anticipation?'

'Stranger? How can you say that? You have known him since you were born.'

'Hardly. I met him at weddings and other events. We barely spoke.'

'How is he a stranger any more than a man you might meet at one of the nightclubs you are always at? You wouldn't know anything except what he wanted you to see.'

And there it was again. Her mother never mentioned the Ex-Boyfriend by name, but he was never far below the surface of interactions with her parents. Disapproved of in every way, the subject of so many lies for so many years. She had moved out after it was all over, which had probably been about a year too late. The thing had quite simply run its course, but there was no burying it for her parents. Not when they somehow blamed him for her drastic shift in career from management track to city reporter.

They fell into silence as they waited for their sizzlers, and then Ahana got a call on her cell. 'It's my boss,' she lied, standing up. 'I'll be right back.'

Ahana stepped out of the restaurant. It was her friend Tanya, and she had been given prior warning as to the possible contents of this call.

'Listen,' Tanya began, 'it's on. Can we please come to your place after?'

Tanya had a big date with the new guy in her life, and had called Ahana the night before to ask if they could go to her flat for some alone time. Tanya and her guy both lived with their parents, making privacy impossible. Ahana had been uncomfortable with the request, and had been so swamped at work that she had managed to get out of making the decision then. Later, she had thought about why it bothered her, and she could think of no good reason that didn't sound exactly like something her father would say.

'Why does it matter what people will say?' Ahana had asked her father during one of their fights about her job.

'One day you will understand that reputation is all you have!' he had shouted.

'It makes no sense to never do what you want to because of the fear of gossip.'

'That which causes others to gossip about you cannot be good for you in the first place,' he had replied.

How despicable she had found that logic. And yet, here she was, unable to break free even now that she was mistress of her own space. 'Yes,' Ahana said, before she could change her mind again. 'Come over before your date, I'll give you the key.'

'Thank you, thank you! Where will you be?'

'I'll go out. I do have other friends you know. Just message when you are done. You can stay over, he can't.'

'Obviously. You are the bestest friend in all the world, Nana.'

'Don't thank me. Use protection. And change the bedsheets when you are done.'

She returned to the table. 'How is your work going?' asked her mother.

'I am still working on the Tara case.'

'I saw her parents yesterday morning.'

'Where?'

'They were downstairs, talking to Mrs Banerjee.'

'Did you speak to them?'

She shook her head. 'What is there to say?'

Ahana grimaced. How well she knew that feeling.

After lunch, they went straight to the tailor. Then, her mother went home and Ahana was at a loose end. Not having regular weekends off meant her off-day was usually a mix of errands and hanging out with friends in the evening. Tanya met her for coffee, and more importantly, to take the house keys off her. Then Ahana managed to lure Priyanka out of office early for a film in the evening. When they were done, it was only 9 pm. So they grabbed chicken rolls and headed for the Blue Banyan.

'Are you secretly working tonight?' Priyanka asked.

'No, but if we are going to be out anyway, we might as well go there,' Ahana said.

Bunty wasn't there when they arrived, but they grabbed the last table in the corner, farthest from the stage. There was a cover band trying their best to do Nirvana, to chilling effect.

'So how is the wedding stuff going?' asked Priyanka. She was the only one in office who knew.

'We bought the engagement sari today.'

'Are you feeling any better about it?'

'I don't know. It's not like I feel badly. It's more that I don't feel. It is not registering as my own wedding.'

'Why?'

She shrugged. 'I guess I never saw myself here, having an arranged marriage.'

'So why are you going through with it?'

'I don't know, honestly.'

'Why are they so on your case?'

'They think it is time. I am twenty-six. Sell-by date is fast approaching in their books. Plus, some fortune-teller told them I'd be married by twenty-six.'

Priyanka scowled. 'That's such bullshit. But you are on your own, independent. You don't have to do what they say. You don't even live with them anymore.'

Ahana felt a stab of irritation. 'Priyanka, your parents are cool. Mine are not. There is just so much pressure. And I messed up, didn't I? So maybe they are right after all.'

'Oh Ahana, you don't still have feelings for him, do you?'

'No. We were over, and it had nothing to do with family.'

'Are you sure? Their constant disapproval couldn't have helped.'

'This is a conversation that should be happening after drinks, not before.' Ahana looked around. No waiter was coming their direction, so she got up abruptly and walked over to the bar. As she waited, she felt a tap on her shoulder. She turned around, thinking it was Priyanka. But it was one of the bartenders.

'Ahana?' he said tentatively.

'Yes? Oh, hi,' she said, remembering him from a photoshoot they had done a few months ago. He had made chocolate martinis.

'Can I talk to you for a minute?'

'Sure.'

'I mean, alone.' His voice was low and he kept his eyes on the ground. 'It is about Drishti.'

She held her breath. 'Ok.'

'Not here. Can you meet me outside in fifteen minutes, at the cigarette shop at the crossing?'

She looked at her watch. 'Ok.'

'It will only take five minutes.'

She collected the drinks and returned to the table.

'What was that about?' asked Priyanka.

'I am not sure,' she said. 'He wants to meet me alone. He was being pretty shady about it.'

'Don't go.'

'I've met him before – he works here. He said it was about Drishti.'

'Still. I can come with you.'

'No. It might scare him off.'

'What if he is a psycho?'

'Relax, we're meeting on the road, right here. What could he possibly do? Plus, he knows I am a journalist.'

'How does that help? Journalists get hurt all the time.'

Ahana took a sip. She asked Priyanka about her boyfriend, happy to be the one listening for a change.

When the time came, Ahana went to the appointed place. The bartender was not there yet, and after waiting a couple of minutes, she began to think of going back in. But then he arrived, changed out of his uniform and into a cream shirt and brown trousers. She almost didn't recognize him. He was carrying a helmet, and he put it on the cigarette shop shelf.

'Do you mind?' he said, taking out a packet of cigarettes from his pocket.

'No.'

He lit up, and took a drag.

She waited till he took his second. 'You wanted to tell me something about Drishti?'

He nodded, breathing out a cloud of smoke.

'You have been covering the story? I saw your name in the paper on the front page today.'

'Yes.'

'The people are all saying that Drishti came here by 9 pm, but that isn't true. She wasn't here till 9.30 pm.'

'She was in the bar by 9.30 pm. They said she was getting ready before that.'

'It's not true.'

'How can you be so sure?'

'Because I was late that day for duty and she pulled in right ahead of me and went straight to the bar, not to the bathroom.'

'Ok, so they are mistaken.'

'Maybe. Or they are lying.'

'Why?'

'I don't know about the others. But Drishti – if she wasn't on the premises and she wasn't at home, where was she?'

Good question. 'What do you think is going on?' asked Ahana.

'I don't know. This is just something I happened to see. At the end of the day, I thought someone should know the truth in case it made a difference.'

'Have the police been here to speak to any of you?'

'No.'

'Thanks. This could be valuable.'

He nodded, and turned to the shop owner to buy another pack.

'Did you notice anything different about her that night?' Ahana asked.

'She's usually so cheerful. That day she just seemed hassled.'

'And anything else, from her friends, other musicians, that you may have heard?'

He tapped the new pack of cigarettes on the side of the stall. 'A few weeks ago – I can't be sure exactly when – a man came in to the bar looking for Drishti. He said they were old friends. Someone gave him her phone number. He already had her address anyway. A few days later, when she found out, she was furious.'

'Why?'

'I don't know. She didn't say. But all I know is that Drishti has been singing at the Blue Banyan for longer than I have worked there, and no one has ever seen her angry before.'

'What did she do?'

'She yelled at the guy who gave the number. Said he shouldn't be handing out her details to anyone. He had tried to tell her that the man had her old number already, so he didn't see any harm in passing on the new one. But she didn't care.'

'Any idea who this man was?'

'No, but I saw him.'

'Could you describe him to me?'

'He had a head full of white hair.'

'Was he old?'

'No. That is why it was surprising. He'd have been in his forties or something.'

'White, or salt and pepper?'

'Salt and pepper. Close cropped,' he said. 'It looked very good. He had dark skin, very sharp features. I remember thinking there is no reason to colour your hair when grey can look so good.'

'Anything else?'

'Not really. He wasn't very tall.'

'Skinny, fat?'

'Very fit.'

'And you are sure you couldn't place him?'

'No. We see so many faces at the pub, but he is pretty striking so I think I'd have remembered if I'd seen him before.'

'Ok, thanks. If you think of anything else, can you please reach out?'

She didn't have her card, so she got a scrap of paper and pen from the paan shop owner. She scribbled her phone number for him and then headed back inside.

Day 5

Found

Ahana was in a taxi on her way to office the next morning when she received a call from her boss. 'There's been a sighting,' said Manash, his voice heavy with sleep and yet still urgent. 'Where are you?'

'Park Street. What sighting?'

'Of Tara. They think.'

Her fists clenched, heart racing.

'At Sealdah station – the call came in about twenty minutes ago, to the police from Phone a Friend and now they are on the scene. Probal is too far away to get there in time. You go there, right away. Get everything you can. I'm sending you a car as well; they are likely to move out from the station with the girl.'

She hung up and asked the taxi to turn around.

'I won't go to Sealdah station,' said the driver, pulling over.

'It is an emergency,' she pleaded. She couldn't afford to lose her ride in that moment. 'Police case.'

He glared at her for a moment, apparently deciding whether he should believe her.

'I am a reporter,' she added, increasingly frantic. She knew it would take forever to get another cab at that time of day. 'They may have found the little girl, Tara.'

He gave her a long glare before he finally started the car again.

The traffic crawled. She only had a vague idea of what Phone a Friend was – it was a helpline, she knew, for children in distress. She had an even vaguer idea of what police procedure could be in a situation like this.

Ahana was equally lost when they finally reached the station. It seemed like the usual, bustling day, with long queues of taxis and cars piled up in the approach, people rushing in and out of the station and vendors crowding the pavements.

She paid the driver, got out and surveyed her options. There was no sign of the police outside. There was a group of children on the pavement. Some asleep, others sitting and chatting.

'Can you tell me where the Phone a Friend booth is?' Ahana asked.

'One right there,' said a boy of about eight.

'Thank you,' she said, rushing away in the direction he had pointed. But even before she got there, she could see that it was empty. She knew she didn't have time to waste, running instead to the entrance of the station and approaching the uniformed guard there.

'Dada, have the police come today?'

'They come every day,' he said, looking bored.

'From the detective department, to find a child?'

'What are you, a reporter?' he asked, looking at the notepad and pen clutched in her hand, at the ready.

'Yes.'

'From?'

The sharp pang of irritation spiked as he continued his casual perusal of her. 'The *Tribune*,' she said.

'Police are inside near platform no. 3.'

She ran as fast as she could through the throng of morning commuters, long-distance passengers with their luggage, hawkers and coolies with their loads on the heads. She was about a third of the way down the platform when she saw them, and knew at once that she was too late: a girl was being carried away in the arms of a female officer. As they were getting into the jeep, Ahana strained to catch a glimpse of the child's face, but the crush of bodies got in the way. And then they drove off.

The assembled crowd was at least 50-strong. Ahana pushed her way through to the centre of the huddle where two employees of Phone a Friend stood.

'Excuse me,' she said, quickly introducing herself. 'Do you know where they are taking her?'

The woman turned to her. 'Park Street PS. The mother will come there.'

'Why Park Street?'

'We have a partner shelter home in the vicinity where she will be taken in case she turns out not to be Tara.'

'Do you know how the child came to be here?'

'A passenger came and told us that there was a child here who matched the description of the missing girl in the news. We came and found her and called the police.'

'What do you think – is it her?'

'It looks like her, for sure.'

'Did she say anything?'

There was the beginning of a response, but Ahana never heard it, as they both got swept up in the crowd. She saw the woman move towards a car – some sort of emergency vehicle that was allowed in the service road inside the station. Ahana could have stuck on to speak to the people at the platform. But there was no time; she had to get to the police station as fast as possible.

There was no crowd outside the thana, and certainly no media crew – yet. So Ahana was able to just stroll inside, hoping the information she had was correct. She had never been on official work to the thana before. Crime was not her beat.

In fact, the only time Ahana had even been inside a police station was to report her stolen wallet once when she was home from college one Christmas. She'd been told off by the officer for saying she wanted to file an FIR. 'Not an FIR,' he said. 'The public should know these things. It is a general diary.'

That experience did nothing to help her. There was no sign of the child, nor anyone from the railway platform.

She kept her notepad and her pen in her bag, and sat on the bench, waiting. When there was no action for five minutes, she approached one of the officers sitting at her desk inside.

'Has Tara Sengupta been brought here?' She tried to sound casual.

'Who are you?' the woman asked.

'I've come for some other work. Just thought I heard something about it.'

'Go sit down in the visitor area. No one is allowed back here,' she said, not bothering to give her a second glance.

Ahana did as she was told.

And then, about ten minutes later, the crowds arrived. Two officers stood at the main door to keep the mob of media personnel out, her photographer Amit among them. Ahana sat tight and held her peace.

Soon after, Drishti arrived through a side entrance. Her face was drawn; her eyes glazed. By her side was a police escort and an elegant older man who Ahana had also seen at the press conference the day before. He must be her father; the resemblance was striking. They were both tall, he would be close to six feet, and she might be four or five inches shorter. They both had large eyes set wide in their faces, now hooded and heavy with distress.

Drishti had none of the trappings of the celebrity that day, not even a pair of sunglasses to shield her tired eyes from the gaze of bystanders and cameras. She seemed oblivious to the chaos in her wake – the cries of the reporters had doubled in volume since they had spotted her inside the premises. They pressed forward, straining against the thick nylon cordon till the police decided it was time to close the heavy wooden doors against them.

Drishti and her father were led straight to the back. They didn't see Ahana sitting there. As soon as they passed her, she was up off the bench and, like a minnow, she followed in their wake.

She didn't get far, though, stopped by a gate that blocked off the rear of the thana from the visitor section, and as

Drishti and her father went through, it was closed firmly behind them.

Ahana didn't object; to do so would be to risk being identified as a member of the media. Or perhaps it was Drishti's attention she wanted to avoid.

From the outside, she could see a loose circle of officers huddled around a desk. A wooden chair was in their midst, and on it sat the girl, her back to Ahana. As Drishti rushed forward, Ahana thought she saw her shoulder's drop. The police parted to let her through, and Drishti sat down on the chair opposite, and took the girl's hands in her own. The tears were now flowing down her face.

After a moment, she looked up at Vinayak Agarwal, and gave a little shake of her head. And then, reluctantly, she got up to leave. She squared her shoulders but in her eyes there was a spark: of rage, anguish, energy.

The girl may not have been Tara, but she was someone's little girl and she had been found alive and safe. And Tara would be too.

Ahana shrank back in to a corner. When Drishti tried to walk out the way she had come in, she saw that the throng of cameramen and reporters had expanded to cover the side entrance as well. She stood there with her father, wondering what to do. Finally Agarwal found them there.

'There is no point,' he said, surveying the situation outside. 'These animals won't show any respect. Come with me, I'll drive you out.'

They disappeared through the back again. Soon, Ahana heard the sound of the engine starting up.

At the same time, there was a roar of a different kind at the gate. Through the barred window she could see, a fight had broken out between reporters and photographers. While several people had rushed towards the driveway when they saw the police vehicle emerging, there were others still pushing and shoving near the entrance. It seemed incredible that all this was at the very door of the police station, and yet nothing was being done to stop it. Two men seemed to be at the centre of the skirmish, locked into each other with an inextinguishable rage, being held back by their colleagues.

It wasn't till lathi-bearing officers descended on them that they were pulled apart for good. While their voices continued to grow in volume, the fists stayed in place by their sides.

Ahana couldn't leave even if she wanted to. So she retreated back to the bench and waited there till she saw one of the Phone a Friend staff she had met earlier emerging from the inner chamber of the police station.

She was possibly in her early thirties, dressed in a neatly-pleated cotton sari, with a big red bindi. The woman didn't seem to remember Ahana, so she introduced herself again.

'It's not Tara,' she said. She seemed disappointed.

'Any idea who she might be?'

'No, she hasn't said much yet. It has been a very busy day, and it is not the right way to try and question a child,' she said with a shake of her head. 'But hopefully we will be able to find out more soon.'

'So what happens to her now?'

'We'll take her to a children's shelter home and continue to work with her to get some information on her origins, and then we will try to match her against missing children who fit her description.'

'And what about Tara?'

She sighed. 'If it is a kidnapping, it is a police matter. But we will always have our eyes peeled for that poor child.'

'You thought it was her?' asked Ahana.

'She matches height, weight and probably age too, though we can't be sure of that till she starts speaking to us. Her skin colour, hair length, were all good fits. It is hard to identify a child from a picture alone.'

'What about the police? What do they do now with this child?'

'For the moment, she is our responsibility. This girl could have come from anywhere. She could be from the city, or she could have come in on any one of the local or long-distance trains. We will try to find out all that first.'

Ahana gave the woman her card and took down her phone number. 'In case anything else comes up, please do give me a call.'

She nodded her head, but Ahana doubted she would ever hear from her again.

Ahana and Manash went through the photographs Amit had come back with of the chaos outside the thana, and together with her copy, Tara would take up most of the front page again.

'What was the fight about, Amit da?' she asked.

'Arre, do these things ever have a reason? One of them wouldn't move. Someone asked if he was doing a photo feature on the closed door of the Park Street PS. And that was that.'

Ahana told Manash what she had learnt about the other missing girl – the one who was not Tara.

'It's part of the story.'

'Should I follow up with Phone a Friend later?'

'Of course. You must. Once they figure out her identity, we can carry a follow up.'

'That's it?'

'Yes.'

She frowned.

'What's wrong?' he asked.

'I don't know – why is she so different from Tara?'

He shrugged. 'It's not PLU. If you find out more, we will take a call then.'

PLU. People Like Us. Tara was, but the girl who was mistaken for her might not be. It didn't matter that she was a child too, just like Tara, separated from her family. She was just another body on the railway platform, not of any real interest to readers of the *Tribune*.

Day 6

Who is the Victim?

It had been one phone call after another.

Each beginning with the same gambit, delivered with her head in her hand, legs twisted together like a cheese straw.

Hi, you might remember me from (insert name of party here).

Yes, great to speak with you too.

Actually today I am calling because we are working on the Tara case, and we are looking to hear from any friends who might have a different perspective to share or any information.

No? Yes, I can imagine. Sorry to intrude and thank you for your time.

There were a few variations.

Oh, yes, it is so tragic. So happy to hear she has friends who are helping out at a time like this. Of course, we'd like to hear about the search party/postering you were part of.

And, surprisingly only once:

I apologize for the inconvenience. There was no offence meant.

By and large, all the refusals were more polite than Ahana had anticipated.

But she was now ever more sure that the strategy was not a winning one. She had enough to cobble together a piece on how Drishti's friends had rallied around her in trying times, but there was nothing sufficiently new to say.

And yet this is what Manash had expressly asked for the night before, after she had filed her copy. 'Anything we can get on her, and her state of mind. The tide is turning. Probal is coming back every day with some story or the other of Drishti, and how she is not cooperating with the police.'

Ahana hadn't told him yet about her chat with the bartender. She knew she should, but what did she really have that could be put in print?

'Ahana di!' whisper-shouted Shalmoli, the intern from her desk nearby.

Her head snapped towards the girl, whose diffident nerviness always managed to annoy her.

'What?'

'Atanu da is calling for you!'

She looked mutely towards the extension on her desk, which sat there in stony silence. It was only then that she registered her name was being bellowed out from across the room.

As she rushed across the floor to Atanu's glass cabin, several sets of eyes followed her. There was curiosity, but also irritation that it was sheer dumb luck that had put Ahana in this position of daily interaction with the news editor, whom she had spoken to barely half a dozen times in her two years at the office prior to the disappearance of Tara.

The TV was blaring as usual, as Ranadeep was doing a piece-to-camera from the gate of Drishti's building for the latest *Tarar Khonje* segment. 'What's the matter?' Ahana asked.

'This man is going on about some other time Tara went missing.'

Ahana didn't say anything as she watched, and Atanu's gaze was fixed on her face.

She had to make sure she knew exactly what they were talking about. Could it be?

'Do you know something about this?' he asked.

Her mouth went dry. 'I was there when it happened.' The anchor had stopped now, and there were three experts holding forth on how the police must look at the case one more time in the light of these revelations.

His eyebrows shot up. 'Explain.'

'It was about a year ago. Tara was playing in the park, with her mother on the bench. Drishti must have dozed off, and Tara wandered off. She was found soon enough by one of the domestic helps who worked in the building.'

'And what were you doing there?'

'I still lived there at the time, and I was leaving for work. Drishti was so distressed that I joined the search.'

Atanu took off his glasses and pinched the bridge of his nose.

'And you didn't think of mentioning this earlier?' he asked, slipping his frames back on again.

'It didn't seem relevant to a kidnapping. She was missing for five minutes. It could have happened to anyone!'

'If Drishti has a history of neglect, of course it is important! Everything is important at this point! And who knows that this is even a kidnapping! For all we know, it could be a murder case.'

Ahana opened her mouth to object, but the words wouldn't come out. She looked down at her hands instead.

'It was bad enough when I thought we missed this. But we didn't miss – you were actually the only reporter there!'

She felt the injustice of the accusation. She had been a bystander to a woman's moment of anguish, that was all. She had not been there as a journalist or even as a friend, and she was being hauled up for not thinking it was relevant and appropriate to mud-rake. But as loud as the protests were, they stayed inside her head.

'Everything about this woman is necessary to know. Every relationship she has had. Every man she has had in her home. Everyone she is in touch with now. We need to know. You are treating her as a victim here. But it is Tara who is the victim, and don't you forget that we don't know anything about what happened that night.'

Hadn't Manash said exactly the same words as well? Tara. This was all about Tara. How could she deny that?

'Drum out a first-person account of what happened that day. We'll carry it tomorrow. Quickly. 500 words. Page 1 anchor.' He pulled the dummy in front of him and crossed something out with a decisive stroke.

'There is something else,' Ahana said.

'Yes?'

Ahana told him about what the bartender said about Drishti coming in late on the fateful night. She held back on the salt-and-pepper haired man – she wanted to find out first how he fit.

'Amazing that the police have not questioned any of them at all,' said Atanu.

Ahana shrugged. 'They aren't investigating. Not really. Else they would have gone there.'

'And yet, they seem to be closing in on Drishti.' He sighed. 'Your piece need not be unkind. Tell the truth. That's all we are asking.'

She nodded and rushed out. It was time for the gloves to come off. She had seen Probal's article for the night. The leader of the opposition had called for a CBI enquiry into Tara's disappearance, claiming the local police force were inept and corrupt and had endangered the life of an innocent child. The stakes in the disappearance of Tara Sengupta had just gone up several notches.

It was early in the evening for a trip to the Blue Banyan. Ahana had expected no customers there, which was fine, as she was only in search of Bunty. And there he was, overseeing the prep while the band for the evening did their soundcheck.

'Ahana!' he said with a smile. 'Here for happy hour?'

'No, Bunty, not today. I need your help, actually. I need to track down one of your regulars.'

'Who?'

'Sagar Deb.'

'He hasn't been here for a while,' he said, moving glasses from one spot to another on the bar top. If he had heard about their history, he didn't let it show.

'Really? How long do you think it has been?'

'Five-six months. Maybe more.'

So her avoidance had been in vain. 'Any way to contact him? It's important.'

'I can give you his number.'

'The landline?'

He checked his phone. 'Looks like it,' he said, showing her.

'I tried that already. He isn't answering, and a friend of a friend who knows him told me he no longer lives at his old address.'

'I had heard that he was planning to move somewhere very far, now that you mention it. He had been building a house for a long time, and I think it was finally finished.'

'Any idea where?'

'No. But I know some people who might. I'll make a few calls. Are you sure I can't get you a drink? It might take a few minutes.'

'Actually, what the hell. I am done with work for the day anyway.'

He brought her a vodka-tonic with a twist of lime, and disappeared into his office.

Ahana was almost done with her drink by the time Bunty came back. 'Sorry, couldn't get a number. He has never had a cell, and apparently he doesn't have a new landline yet, and doesn't get out much either. But here is an address.'

Ahana glanced at the piece of paper Bunty handed her. It was clear across town, somewhere between Behala and the end of civilization. She'd have to make the trek, and it would have to be tomorrow morning. She didn't want to risk finding him drunk.

She drained her glass.

'Another?'

She was sorely tempted. She was feeling ragged, and the first drink had taken the edge off. But it had also made her crave hard for her bed.

'Not today,' she said.

And if she had to meet Sagar in the morning, she'd rather not be hungover. It would be awkward enough.

27 September 2001

Drishti opened her eyes. There was Tara, fast asleep. Her hands were joined together as though in prayer, tucked under her cheek. She had never imagined that flesh-and-blood children actually slept like that, but Tara did. Her skin was a little flushed, and Drishti knew that she was still running a temperature. She did not dare move for fear that she'd wake Tara, who seemed to have an infallible radar for when her mother was up in the morning.

Drishti looked at her watch: 7.44 am. After a night of little sleep. She needed her coffee desperately, but it would have to wait.

She drifted off. When she opened her eyes again, it was 8.30 am. Drishti moved ever so slowly out from under the sheet, and was so focused on not disrupting Tara that she half fell, half rolled off the bed. She tiptoed out of the room and into the bathroom. By the time her pyjamas were down, she heard the crying.

The fever was coming down, but there would be no Montessori for Tara that day, and probably the next. As Tara picked up her glass of milk, Drishti walked over to the phone and dialled her mother.

'How is Tara today?' she asked.

'Better, but her fever is still there. Not so high though. Will you be able to come over?'

'Not till evening. The carpenters will be home all day.'

'That's fine. If you could stay the night, it would be great, Ma.'

'Ok. Your father won't be happy.'

'Uff, Ma, seriously, why doesn't he just come too?'

'Aar bolo na. He might come over, but he would never stay and leave Koko behind.'

'You have a house full of help to look after the dog. Or just bring her here. Tara would be thrilled.'

'Why don't you come over instead?'

'Ma, my student is coming tonight. I can't miss another class.'

'I thought you were going to quit all that.'

'I have, mostly. Sanjana is special.'

'Ok. I will deal with Baba, don't worry.

'He's a bigger baby than Tara.'

'Men always are. But I'll be there. I can stay tomorrow too.'

'Thanks, Ma. I haven't slept in days.'

'Yes, I know. I'll bring food, so don't bother to cook.'

Drishti went back to the dining room to tell Tara that Dida would be coming later. There was milk all over the table, the stainless-steel tumbler on its side. Tara was busy drawing a self-erasing design in the white puddle with her finger.

Washed up and changed, Drishti and Tara headed to the playground.

'Come Tara.' She had on her socks and shoes and looked terribly grown up in her little white cotton dress. She was dawdling with her doll.

'If we don't go down now, it will get too hot.'

'Okay, Mama,' she said, walking towards the door with her doll in her hand.

'We need to leave Piu here.'

'Why?'

'She'll get dirty.'

'Why?'

Tara was definitely feeling better, if the endless whys had made a comeback. Drishti prised the doll out of her hands. Tara looked at her, as though she was contemplating protest.

'Come, take your sandpit toys,' said Drishti.

She seemed to forget the urge to fuss, and picked up the pail and took off out the door.

But then she turned back. 'Cycle too!'

'Are you sure you are feeling well enough?' asked Drishti.

'Yes, Mama! I am fine!'

There was little point fighting it, and Tara's little hands had already grabbed the handlebars, pushing with all her strength. As it swerved away from the door, Drishti leaned down and guided the wheels over the threshold.

Downstairs, they headed to the small paved area that doubled as a cricket pitch and basketball court. 'I want to do it myself,' Tara declared.

Drishti considered the request, trying not to succumb to the kneejerk 'no' she was inclined towards. 'Are you sure you don't want a hand?'

'Yes, I can do it, Mama.'

Drishti recognized this as part of a plot to impress Sasha, her older neighbour who zoomed around the building at lightning speeds. Tara thought there was no one better.

'Okay,' she said, as Tara walked around the green net that contained the court, and sat on the bench just outside. She watched, the filthy mesh a screen between her and Tara.

This wasn't her first time riding without training wheels, but it was her first time trying to get started alone. Tara had just turned four, which was fairly young to start riding solo, but she was tall, strong and fearless. There had already been two months with uneven training wheels, a week without training wheels at all, with Drishti running behind her and letting her go. Then a brief pause for a fever that had lost its hold. Tara seemed ready to take a stab at independence, to venture out into the world in full command of her own vehicle, and Drishti would not be the one to stop her.

Tara got on the bike. The first effort was a stumble, but then she wiggled her way to balance, before losing it again. Her feet went down to break the fall. The third time, the wiggle was repeated, but she stayed upright and then she was off! She concentrated fully as she pedalled furiously for more than a minute, going in circles around the space. Then she looked up and saw her mother. The glee on her face was instantaneous. 'Mama, look at me! I'm doing it, Mama!' But the self-consciousness killed her flow. Her handlebars began the tell-tale dance again, and from that moment to being sprawled across the concrete was the work of seconds.

Drishti got up and walked quickly across the court, but she tried not to run, not wanting to make the spill seem more significant than necessary. Tara was up before she got far, and was busy inspecting her elbow. It wasn't till she saw her mother that the crying started.

'You did so well!' said Drishti, as Tara's cries turned into rivulets of tears.

'Mama! I need a Band-Aid!'

'It's a scrape, it's not bleeding.'

'It hurts!'

As if out of nowhere, a man, mid-fifties or so, appeared.

'You should be holding her, na?'

'Excuse me?'

'Such a small girl. So thin. How will she ride on her own? She will break a bone!'

'Tara? She is very good at cycling, Uncle.'

'She's so small. So skinny. Does she eat properly?'

'Yes, Uncle.'

'Fruit, fish,' he said, addressing Tara directly. 'That will make you strong enough.'

And then he was on his way.

Drishti looked down at Tara, whose tears had dried up by then, gazing after the man, nonplussed. 'Who is he, Mama?'

'I have no idea, Tara. Ready for another round?'

She nodded her head. 'But stay here, Mama.'

'Are you going to let that fall scare you?'

Tara stared after the stranger's retreating back.

'Will you eat your fruit and fish too?'

Tara was off again. The worst part about the judgement of strangers was that only the bad stuff stuck.

They were alone in the park that day. All the other children were at school. It was already uncomfortably humid and hot, though not quite 10 am. The park was in the shade at that hour, so they shifted from the basketball court to the playground. She sat on the bench as Tara played, making her cakes from wet sand.

About fifteen minutes later, their neighbour Palash who lived on the ground floor of the block facing the park, drew back the curtain and waved at them.

'Look Tara, it's Palash uncle,' Drishti said, waving back.

Tara gave him a little smile as she played.

'No school today for her?' he asked.

'She's running a temperature.'

'O ho.'

She looked at him. He looked pale, though it was no wonder. 'How is Uncle today?'

'Today, not so good.'

'Is that why you are home?'

'Yeah. Another round of chemo begins tomorrow.'

'How is your mother?' asked Drishti.

'Well, you know, she's handling it.'

'And the move?'

'We are doing it slowly. But Ma is busy getting all the work done in the new house.'

'Tell her to come by when she's free. We miss her.'

'I think she tried calling you a few days ago, at night. You didn't answer.'

'I must have been out.'

'Mama!' said Tara. 'An ant!'

Drishti looked down. 'Oh, it's a tiny black thing.'

'It will bite me!'

'Those ants don't bite.'

Tara threw sand at it.

'Don't throw sand,' Drishti said.

'Why?'

'Because you are sick and it could tickle your nose and make you sneeze more.'

'Tickle my nose! Silly Mama,' she said, delighted. The sand throwing continued undeterred, but she kept looking up at her mother. Drishti could either fight it, or ignore it. Ignoring it was simply the easier option.

She looked back at Palash's window. He was gone.

Drishti had a notepad and pen in hand, and the beginning of a song that had started rumbling in her brain before Tara got sick. She closed her eyes, hoping to get it back.

She felt a fly crawling on her face and her eyes opened with a start. Tara was gone.

It couldn't have been more than a second, but Tara was

nowhere to be seen. Drishti shot off the bench and looked around. Nothing.

She knew she must have fallen asleep, and realized with horror that she had no idea how long she had been out. She screamed out, 'Tara, Tara!' She was frozen by her frantic desire to run in every direction all at once. Finally, she began to move towards their block of flats, calling out the whole time.

Two or three guards arrived and she told them what had happened, and they quickly went in different directions to start the search. People had begun to peer out of their windows, and a few had also rushed down to help – maids mostly. Palash had come out, too.

'What happened?' he asked.

'I don't know – she just disappeared!'

'She was just here,' he said.

'How long ago did we speak?'

He was confused by the question. 'I don't know, five minutes ago?'

She cursed out loud. How could she have been asleep for five minutes?

Tara wasn't near the entrance to their building, she wasn't upstairs at the flat. She wasn't near the gate. The guards at the front had not seen her. At every turn, Drishti was sure she would find her, and at every turn, her despair mounted.

In fact, the dread that enveloped Drishti was like nothing she had ever felt before. It was as though every cell of her being was vibrating with intense heat. She tried to think through where Tara would logically go – under the slide, behind the bushes – but none of those turned up results.

Drishti almost ran into Ahana, on her way to work.

'What's wrong?' Ahana asked immediately.

'I can't find Tara,' Drishti squeezed out.

Ahana dropped her bag on the ground and fell into step beside her.

Finally, Tara was found by a neighbour's maid and a security guard. She had been wandering around in the basement, in the car park, terrified. The entire ordeal lasted all of twelve minutes.

By then, concerned neighbours had stopped in their tracks, murmuring amongst themselves as mother and daughter were reunited. Had Drishti been watching, she would have noticed a moment when their relief transformed into judgement. Such things turned on a dime.

The Loss of Tara

Drishti grew up in Assam. Her father Rajendra was a tea man by profession. She had a childhood she often described as magical – moving from garden to garden, playing with the local children of the tea pickers, living in grand old estates with liveried servants catering to their every whim. However charming the trappings of this throwback kind of life, Drishti was an early rebel against the strictures of that world, and from the age of eight or nine, she seemed engaged in a constant resistance against every effort at turning her into a lady.

Drishti's father was a man whose focus was on providing for the family. He and Drishti were always close, and he instilled in her a lifelong love of the outdoors. They would take long walks together and go for treks over the holidays. They would bird-watch and go fishing. He taught her how to climb trees. As she grew up, however, his expectations of her changed dramatically, and it was her father who first intervened when a twelve-year-old Drishti was spending all her time with the staff of the estate and their children. He made it clear to his wife Subhra that it was not suitable behaviour for the pre-pubescent daughter of the manager of the estate, and she agreed. Drishti, however, did not.

The battle continued for two years, with her mother managing to tone down her daughter enough to placate her husband, and to pacify her husband enough to spare her daughter. But finally, Drishti was sent away to boarding school.

While Drishti saw this as a betrayal in the early days, as an adult and as a mother, she had begun to take a more charitable view of their decision. There were real challenges inherent in tea garden life, in the form of constantly moving from one estate to another, an absence of good schools, and perhaps most pressingly, a growing threat of violence throughout the region. Her parents had been witness to no less than three of their friends' abductions, and had not seen any good reason to keep Drishti there and put her at risk.

She went to Welham's College, where she again refused to fall into the behaviour patterns expected of her, repeatedly getting hauled up for her boisterous ways. But then she found the music room.

Drishti hadn't always loved music. She had suffered through piano classes as a child, with an extremely strict British teacher, who had been the nanny of some of the little foreign children in Assam. She held a ruler over Drishti's knuckles to ensure her movements were controlled, and used it to deliver a tight rap in case they weren't. Drishti's complaints went unheeded, until eventually the nanny left for another job and she was off the hook.

Drishti sang, always. In school concerts and in the shower, and always in tune. Her mother had suggested coaching, but the ghost of nanny Beatrice had been too much for her and she said no. She knew that once she committed, her mother would not let her wriggle out of it, so she chose to avoid it altogether. But in boarding school, the music teacher Miss Diana was kind yet persistent when she recognized talent. And she pushed and pushed and pushed Drishti till she gave in.

After boarding school, Drishti went to Delhi for college, where she studied botany with no clear idea of what career may await her at the end of it. She also joined her first real band, being selected through a campus audition. It gave her a taste for the lifestyle, though it was more classic rock than Drishti liked.

'That is when Drishti realized that her place was on the stage. She had a magnetic presence,' said a bandmate of that era, Kushal Datt.

'Drishti loved the stage almost as much as the stage loved Drishti,' said Rohin Sharma, one of her college boyfriends.

After her bachelor's, she enrolled in a master's programme, again in botany. It was an excuse to delay entering the real world. She dreaded the act of finding a job that would have nothing to do with singing. Through that time, she played with two different bands, making enough to scrape by, with some help from her parents.

'She was barely attending classes in those days, but like everything else, she made passing her exams seem effortless. So she graduated, perhaps not at the top of her class, but with respectable enough grades. She even had all the profs eating out of her hand, convinced that she enjoyed botany!' said Rohin.

Finally the time came to leave the protection of the campus. Drishti continued playing for a few months after post-graduation, but soon realized it was not sustainable. So she went back home.

It was no secret to Drishti's parents that their daughter had decided her calling was music. They had fought it for the past few years with no impact. So it came as no surprise when, after a brief pitstop in Assam, Drishti decided to go to Calcutta to try to make a career in music. 'Her plan was to sing when she could and teach kids the guitar to support herself, while she wrote her own material. She had even started playing the piano again,' said mother Subhra.

Drishti got a job as music teacher in a school, more or less to mollify her parents. And since she was staying in their Surya Apartments flat rent-free, it was enough to see her through. She lived simply enough, and most of her money went into savings for a car of her own.

And then she started the hunt for musical kindred spirits. Not ever having lived in Calcutta, it was hard at first. She didn't have much of an existing circle of friends, and the music scene in the early '90s was not great. There were no real outlets for English music in Calcutta in those days. The golden years of Park Street seemed well and truly dead. The homegrown rock bands of Bengal were just starting out, even as the stages for live music were vanishing. Trinca's and Blue Fox, once amongst the hottest nightspots in the country, were not what they once were.

But then, the Victoria Hotel, in a beautiful old mansion on Little Russell Street, decided to convert one of its restaurants into a live music venue, with performances six nights a week. The owner, Ravi Kampani, a former drummer with a band that had its last hurrah in the late 1980s, was missing his music. He would play with his band once a week; the rest of the evenings would be dedicated to a mix of young blood and the few old hands that had hung about in Calcutta, despite the exodus of talent that plagued the city.

When Drishti went to meet Ravi on the recommendation of a fellow musician, he told her he would not be having any nights for crooners. Drishti had no idea what a crooner was, and was appalled when she found out. She was quick to explain her own brand of music, but he was less interested in singer-songwriters and more interested in bands that could play the hits. He suggested a couple of people she could meet, the remnants of bands that were once fixtures on the Calcutta scene, and were shopping around for new talent in the hope of a comeback.

Though she was already outgrowing rock, she would take what she could get in those days. Drishti knew the only way to become a singer was just by getting out there and singing. It also helped that she was bad at taking no for an answer. So she kept knocking on doors till she found four others who would work with her.

And that was how she became a part of Devasthal. The frontman at the time was Devraj Mukherjee. Drishti was happy to play backup to his lead singer. She wanted to learn the business, and Devasthal had been around for a couple of years in a number of other iterations, tasting moderate success with live shows.

But when they took the stage, that wasn't how it went at all. When Drishti began to sing, it was clear she could never be back-up to anyone. Devasthal quickly embraced this, and soon became the best thing about Blue Banyan.

Devraj was what many of Drishti's friends described as her one great love. Those who saw them perform together were mesmerized by their chemistry. They lit up the stage, and every room they were in together. They started dating about six months after they began working together. Everything was going smoothly at first: he was funny, warm, razor sharp and the perfect foil for Drishti's spark.

But about a year into the relationship, trouble raised its head. Though neither Drishti nor Devraj have spoken publicly about the reasons for the breakdown of the relationship, at the time or since then, friends speculate that it began when he proposed and she turned him down.

Drishti, according to friends, wanted a relationship but

didn't want marriage – she was happy the way things were, and didn't see any point in change. But Devraj, a few years older and desperately in love, was ready for a lasting commitment. He had a day job at Bharat Steel, and was known as one of the company's rising stars, and he felt that it was time to put down roots.

After Drishti's refusal, they stayed together at first. He accepted her rejection in the spirit in which it had been meant, but as another year rolled on, the rift grew, and it began to tear them apart. While they attempted to keep their musical collaboration intact, it became so acrimonious that eventually Drishti exited the group.

Friends say that the break-up left Drishti heartbroken as well. They were never sure why she had sworn off marriage – her parents were happy after more than twenty-five years together, and she seemed to truly love Devraj. But the experience, they said, seemed to leave her ever more convinced that marriage was not for her. She was alone for a while as she regained her bearings, and when she opened herself up again to romance, she gravitated towards men who she knew would not ask her for more – which often meant those who were already accounted for.

But that was only one side of the story. Devraj went from Drishti straight into a rebound relationship that resulted in a hasty marriage and an equally quick divorce. His friends insist he never got over her, and that Drishti had walked away unscathed, a cold, heartless manipulator who used him to succeed musically and discarded him when she had achieved her goals.

It was soon after that she landed a big professional break. And there is no more beloved Calcutta pastime than shooting down a star when it is in the ascendant.

Day 7

Forgetting

Sagar Deb was the real reason Ahana had stopped going to the Blue Banyan bar, except when her work demanded it. He was there, every night. After a point it was just awkward. Which was a pity, because despite its rough edges, it had always been Ahana's favourite bar in town, with its ramshackle stage and rotating cast of bands.

Ahana was not like Drishti. Though if you asked her, she'd have told you she wanted to be. Ahana's relationships, so far, had been long, committed. There had been two of them, to be precise. She tended not to keep in touch after they were over. What was the point?

No one at her office would believe this about her, because, despite being the ones to put her on the job, in their books, late-night-party-girl equalled slut, or at the very least, slacker. She wished she didn't care about it, but she did. Not enough to cave to her father's pressure to quit, but enough to ensure she worked harder than anyone else in her team.

It was the same vigilance that made the bar too awkward for casual visits after the Sagar Deb episode. Luckily, it had always been just enough of a dive to pass under the radar of the paper's regular nightlife coverage, so her job didn't demand it of her unless they had a special night of some sort. Which was conveniently the kind of night Sagar avoided.

The last time he was there, her eyes had gone straight to his spot – the last barstool right in front of the speaker. Between the number of decibels and whiskies he imbibed on a nightly basis, it seemed as though he was intent on stomping out every sensation he possessed. She had turned away without detection, but moments later, she had sensed his gaze on her. Like always, when they encountered each other, he had given her a two-finger salute. She had smiled in return, but inside, she had cringed. She had told herself it was the memory of the mouldy, dank stench of his flat that filled her with discomfort. Did he ever clean? Open a window? Not that she had seemed to care in the moment.

Ahana and Sagar had met rather improbably, when he accidentally knocked over her Cosmopolitan about a year ago, just before she had moved out of her parents' place, seconds after the bartender had pushed it towards her. He had apologized profusely, and insisted on buying her another, which Ranjit had nixed by bringing her a free refill. Such were the perks of being a lifestyle journalist. They ended up chatting between sets of the night's band, when the music was at a bearable volume. But she had been on the job that night, so eventually she had to leave to get to another assignment, another party.

The next time she was there, she was on her own time, with friends. He had given her that little salute then too, and she had taken the seat beside him.

They had chatted for a while. She still remembered that part of the evening. They talked about cricket, which Ahana had no interest in; a recent political scandal precipitated by a sting operation and a damning ride in a lift; and why long-stemmed glassware had no place in a modern bar. And also, her job.

'So what is it that you do really?' he had asked.

'I write about parties and hunt for lifestyle stories. Food and fashion, mainly.'

'And you like this?' he asked, his dark eyes reflecting his confusion.

'Shouldn't I?'

'You seem...'

'Smart?'

'Well, yes.' He seemed only moderately embarrassed, and it raised her hackles. If it hadn't been for her last Cosmo, she would have walked away. Surely.

'I had a corporate job for a couple of years and could not imagine a more mind-numbing world than that.'

'Fair enough,' he said with a shrug. 'But why choose between two evils?'

'I don't see journalism as evil. What I am doing now is a means to an end. Even if I only write about parties now, it doesn't mean I always will. What about you?'

'I am a psychiatrist. A failed psychiatrist.'

'Why failed?'

'Can't you tell?'

'Alcohol?'

'Not really, but also that.'

'Sounds like a problem that might be fixed.'

'Only if I want to.'

'Ah.'

'Point being, I am not judging you.'

'And I will return the favour.'

And then she had gone back to her friends. 'He's not your usual type, is he?' Tanya had said.

'What is my usual type?'

'Square. Boring. Clean cut and good looking.'

'You don't think he's good looking?'

'He is, in a scruffy sort of way.'

When her friends were leaving, she found Sagar's eyes on her again, their intensity reeling her in. 'I think I will hang out here for a while, girls,' she had said.

Followed by uncomfortably loud wolf whistles.

They didn't stay at the bar long after that. He took her home, where they had another drink, kissing on the hard wooden bench he called a couch. He tasted of cheap whisky and cigarettes, and she found him electrifying. He spoke in a raspy whisper, and for the life of her, she could not remember a word of what he had said later on. What she did recall with no trouble was that they were stumbling towards the bedroom, when she decided to take a detour to the bathroom. She hadn't dilly-dallied, and yet, by the time she had gotten back to him, jittery with desire, he had been lying diagonally across the bed, making noises that could only be described as snoring, though such an extreme manifestation surely warranted its own name.

She had left. And all she had got the next time she had seen him was that damn salute.

And now she had to seek him out.

Because if Ahana wasn't completely mistaken, Sagar Deb used to be Drishti's shrink.

Ahana woke up to messages of congratulations for the prominent page-1 byline. And yet she couldn't even bring herself to look at the paper. She made her tea, drank it far too fast, got ready and left the house.

Ahana got to the office and hopped into one of the white Ambassadors that were part of the paper's aging fleet. There was no air-conditioning to be had, despite the stifling June heat, made worse by rains early in the morning.

It took a full two hours to reach the address Bunty had given her. They finally found themselves on an empty road, surrounded by vacant plots, eventually pulling up outside a standalone house – a tiny one surrounded by a large garden that was not full of grass or decorative plants, but vegetables – greens, pumpkin, tomatoes, brinjal, chillies. The exposed brick façade had several creepers growing across it as well, as though it was trying to disappear amidst the green.

She walked through the garden and stood at the front door. She looked for the bell, but when she couldn't find one, knocked as hard as she could.

And then, suddenly, Sagar was standing before her, his surprise evident. His white kurta was thin but spotless, his jeans worn. He smelled like freshly dug earth.

'Ahana!'

'I tried calling, but I couldn't reach you.'

'New house. No cell. No landline yet either, actually.'

'So I discovered.'

'And yet you managed to find me,' he said.

'Were you trying to disappear, like your house here?'

Everything else may have changed, but his smile was still the same – small, lopsided, a light for his eyes. 'Not at all. Come in, come in!'

Ahana followed him into the small, clean, but sparsely furnished room. There was a mattress on the floor, as well as a few bamboo mats, and mora-stools, with a small wooden table on one side. The high ceiling made the room seem much more spacious than it was, with windows letting in light from all sides. It was surprisingly cool, lacking the mugginess of most Calcutta homes in the monsoon.

'When did you move here?' she asked.

'About four months ago.'

'And you are a farmer now?'

'No,' he said with a laugh. 'But I do grow my own food. Or as much of it as I can. I even have a couple of chickens in the back for eggs. Want to see?'

She laughed and stayed put. 'Not my favourite bird, I must admit. Unless it is on my plate.'

'I am vegetarian, but can I tell you how delicious a freshly-laid egg is?'

She wasn't sure the conversation could be any stranger than it was in that moment, and had no idea how to bring it around to where she wanted it to be. Luckily, he stopped talking about eggs.

'So tell me, what brings you out to the middle of nowhere?'

Ahana had rehearsed this many times over in the car ride. But everything about seeing him in his new state had confused her. She had been prepared for bluster, for scrappiness, but with this new pastoral version of Sagar, she had lost her footing. 'You have heard about Drishti's daughter?' she said, far more abruptly than she'd intended.

He went stiff, but he nodded his head.

'I'm a little cut off here but not that cut off either.'

'I know you were... close.'

'We still are.'

She lost her nerve again. 'I don't see you at the bar anymore,' she said.

'Not the kind of place the newly sober can be trusted.'

'I... I didn't know.'

'No reason you should have.'

'Congratulations.'

'Thanks. So how can I help you?'

'You know that I am a reporter, right?'

'Yes, Ahana. Some things I do remember.'

Ahana was almost overcome with embarrassment. What did he mean? 'We are trying to put together a more holistic view of Drishti's life.'

Regardless of how he felt, Sagar was gentle in his response. 'I am sorry to disappoint you, but you've come to the wrong person.'

It was as she had expected, but she couldn't give up so easily. 'There has been a shift in the tone of the investigation. I am afraid she is about to be massacred by the police and media alike. We want to get ahead of the story they are desperately trying to put out there.'

Now he looked annoyed. 'Does it look like I care what those clowns are doing? And more importantly, does it look like she cares?'

'Maybe not, but the force of this thing is on the verge of derailing the investigation.'

'How would it do that?'

'If the media focuses on her personal life, so will the

police. And there is a good chance the police are invested in smearing her as well.'

'You may be right, but do you think one honest report on her as she really is will change that?'

She shrugged. 'It's what I can do.'

'You are kidding yourself if you think you aren't doing exactly what they are doing.'

The scathing honesty of that remark was enough for her ego to get on the defensive. 'I didn't say I wasn't. But I want to do it better. With honesty.'

'Like your report this morning?'

She felt as though her face was on fire. 'I had no choice in the matter. It was out already anyway.'

'We all have a choice.'

'Do we? Would you be so quick to judge my desire to stay in my job if I were a man?'

His gaze gave away nothing.

'You know her well enough already,' he said at last. 'You don't need me to give you a character sketch. So why don't you come out and ask what you specifically want to know?'

It was a challenge more than a question. She had no choice but to meet it.

'Were you Drishti's therapist?'

'You should know better than to ask that.'

'I do. But I have to try anyway. Were you and she in a relationship five years ago?'

His lip curled up, and suddenly she saw the old Sagar. 'It's none of your damn business.'

'You are right, it's not. But it will soon be the police's business.'

'I'll talk to them if I have to. But I won't be adding to any headlines here.'

'It's not a headline if you say "no".'

He laughed, which wrong-footed her again. 'I appreciate that you are doing your job. I am sorry if I seemed condescending before. And if I could help you in any way that didn't involve causing more pain to a dear friend, I would.'

It seemed pointless to continue, so she stood up, and so did he.

'Sorry to have intruded,' she said. 'If I'd had your number...'

'I know. Have you tried asking Drishti any of this?'

'Me personally? No. But the police have and she has refused to divulge anything. I can't imagine it is a strategy that will pay off.'

'Let me tell you this: Drishti is no fool. She must have weighed the risks of secrecy at this point.'

'If her aim is to get her daughter back, she knows it is not the dad. Is that what you are saying?'

'A reasonable deduction.'

'But the police?'

'They aren't as clever as you, I'd wager. So trying to establish Tara's paternity will simply waste time – precious time they could actually use to try to find the child.'

'She might tell them what they need to know, just so they could get on with it.'

He shrugged. 'I can't say I know what she is thinking. You could try to talk to her, however. You are friends, right?'

'I don't know if I'd go as far as that. Acquaintances is more like it.'

'She was comfortable with you. She liked you.'

They had discussed her? She gazed out the window, eyes fixed on a papaya tree that was growing outside.

'I don't know... I tried to call. I knocked on her door once.

But I just can't bring myself to insert myself into her life right now.'

'Well, as you said, it's the job. And you seem to think it might help.'

He walked her out, and as he opened the door, she turned to face him. 'Thanks,' she said softly.

'No need to thank me,' he said, looking down at the red cement floor. 'But I should perhaps be the one apologizing to you.'

She almost missed it. 'Don't. I don't know what I expected coming here.'

'Not about this,' he said. 'I am sorry about that night.'

It sent a rush of blood to her face. So he did remember. Nothing to be sorry for, she was going to say. But then it occurred to her that he may have been talking about the entire evening – not just the part where he fell asleep.

'I wasn't myself then,' he continued. 'Part of recovery is taking stock of past mistakes and making amends. I hope I didn't offend or hurt you in any way. My memory of those days is blurry at best.'

'You can rest easy,' she said. 'Nothing really happened.'

He gave her a small smile. 'So we didn't spend the night together?'

After her intrusion, the least she could do was fill the gap in his memory. 'I thought we were going to, but then you fell asleep.'

'Oh, how embarrassing,' he said with a groan. 'Or maybe it is for the best. It would have been a shame to have forgotten.'

30 August 1996

It had been years since Drishti had last seen him. He had been transiting through Calcutta on work about a year after Drishti had moved there. He had called her and they had all gone out – some of his former students had been there too, and it had become a loud, boisterous reunion. His eyes had sought her out from across the long table that had separated them, as if to apologize, or to guage if she would want an apology, if she wanted to be alone as much as he did. At the time, she hadn't known the answer to that question.

After dinner, they had all gone to the sole disco the city had in those days. He and Drishti did not dance. Instead, while the others were away, they tried to talk above the music, holding hands under the table like teenagers. And then he had wrapped his arms around her when she was leaving, and she would have wished the others away if she could have, but his adoring ex-students didn't leave till it was time for him to head to the airport.

After that, he had tried very hard, to keep in touch even though he was so far away and always so very busy. Had asked her to visit him, too. But as much as she had been drawn to him, what would be the point?

It was almost two years later that a common acquaintance – one of his former students, now her friend too – said he'd be in town again for two days. She suggested that they all meet, but he didn't call her himself, and after she had resisted so hard she could hardly have expected it.

That's why when she had gotten on stage that evening and seen his face in the crowd, it was almost like a physical blow. She had been derailed by the sudden intimacy of that moment, amidst hundreds of people, of having his eyes locked on hers, watching him watch her.

She tore her gaze away, but she felt that same warmth every time her eyes found his in the crowd, the noise effervescing, her breath quickening, time stopping.

She fought against the image that played in her head, of him jumping on stage and sweeping her up in his arms, like some '80s music video.

Afterwards, he approached her with a small, almost shy smile.

'You are better than I remember.' Warmth came to him easy. 'Your sound has evolved into something I have never heard before. It is… sheer poetry.'

'Thank you. I didn't know you were coming tonight,' she said, feeling as gauche as a girl talking to her first crush.

'I met some of the guys – Ronnie, Kush. They were coming, so I decided to join. Buy you a drink?'

Drishti knew he had been drinking already. She could see that slight glaze over his eyes, the smile wider than usual. And could he have been this at ease if he had been sober?

They moved toward the bar. Two Old Monks with Coke. Lime. Not a drink she had had in years, but it was their drink, the sickly sweet and sharply chemical burn scenting her memory. She had caught it on his breath earlier, and together with his cologne, it rose up to fight against any effort at resolve she might have shown.

They wandered around the grounds of the club, as she asked him what he had been doing for the past couple of years, which was how long it had been since they had last spoken. She listened to him speak in an accent only slightly altered by his time abroad. They stopped under a tree on the fringe of the golf course. It was the wrong place to stop: they both knew that without the safety of people, they should not be trusted together. And they both knew that the other knew it, too. This shared knowledge was tacit consent for all that might follow.

They sat in the rough, and passed a few moments with small talk interrupted by increasingly heavy silence. She knew the conversation was slacking largely due to her brief answers, but found herself inexplicably annoyed with him.

'I meant to call,' he said, the final long pause forcing it out of him.

She nodded. 'How's Sandhya?'

He grimaced just a little, and tried to hide it in his drink. 'She's great. In Delhi with her parents now.'

'You'll be joining her?'

'In a week. I have some stuff to finish first.'

She stared back at the stage, lights and sound being dismantled, her bandmates sitting down for post-performance freebies. 'I should go,' she said. But instead of standing up, she stayed put.

'How have you been, Drishti?'

'Fighting, on all fronts.'

'Your parents are still not behind you with the music? Have they heard you?'

'Not just that. You have to fight the rest of the world to get the music heard, and then you have nothing to show for it. Sometimes you really wonder if it is all worth it.'

'You have talent to burn, Drishti. You should think of getting out of here.'

'And where would I go?'

He shrugged, knowing how it would sound if he suggested any place closer to him.

'I'll take my chances here. What will be different anywhere else?'

'A lot could be different. You could try Bombay. There is a lot of stuff happening there in the music scene.'

'And I'd be another no-name talent trying to make it in an industry not known for its kindness.'

'And that matters to you?'

'It has to for the sake of survival.'

'Are you seeing anyone?' he asked abruptly.

She took a sip before she shook her head. 'No one serious.'

He drained his glass.

'That's great. Why did you stop returning my calls? My letters?'

'What would I have said? Where would we have gone? We were – are – almost strangers.'

He looked down, and away. 'Is that how you feel?' he asked.

'It is how it was. We've had two evenings together, if you could even call it that.'

'Only because that is all you would give us.'

'As opposed to you? Who went half a planet away, but still wanted to be pen pals?'

'And you hold that against me.'

'No. But I do respond to what is in front of me.'

He looked at her as though he were seeing her for the first time.

'See?' she said. 'What do you know about me, anyway?'

'If things had been different…'

'You would not be with her? I don't think so.' She stood up.

'You don't think,' he said, volume rising, 'that if you had in some way indicated that I meant something to you, I would have done something about it?'

They were both standing now, and they locked in again, this time in anger. She could see the light of the party dancing on the water hazard behind him, but his face was in the shadows.

'What *did* it mean to you, Drishti?'

'Everything. In the moment.'

'And that wasn't enough?'

'For me, yes. It always is. But not so much for the people I am with.'

He shook his head. 'You had to know how crazy I was about you!'

'That is the problem! You were headed for marriage! How could I take all that away from you for the sake of that which was not real?'

'Not real?' His brow twisted. He turned away for a second, and when he faced her again, she could see the anguish. He stepped in towards her, hands on her shoulders, pulling her closer. 'This isn't real enough for you?' he said, lips a whisper away from hers. He bent down for the kiss she had been waiting on for years. Too quickly, he pulled away. This time, it was she who leaned in for another and another, till it wasn't enough. His hands snaked down, roaming her back. There was plenty of time to pull away, had she wanted to. Had he wanted to. But instead, his thumbs were grazing her nipples, and it was only then that she felt the shock through her body that forced her to put her hand on his chest and push him away.

'Can we get out of here?' she said, gasping for breath.

She looked him straight in the eye, clear of doubt, embarrassment or regret.

There was a moment – a flash. And then he pulled out his phone. 'My car is waiting outside.'

Day 8

Action

The cry rang out under the blazing midday sun: 'Bring Tara home! Bring Tara home!'

Ahana had been sent to cover a protest held by students of the Gender Studies department of Vivekananda City College. The only reason she had been assigned to the event was because the organizers had made the disappearance of Tara its headline grievance. Really, it had been a long-planned dharna to protest against the growing breakdown in law-and-order across the state, and the spate of crimes against women, in both urban and rural Bengal. But in those days, there was one route to a sure-shot headline, and the students' union was smart enough to know what it was.

Ahana had expected a crowd which would quickly melt away like an ice cube in the heat, but instead it only grew. As classes gave over, around 200 students from the campus itself joined ranks with the handful of placard-wielding protestors. And then a prominent women's rights NGO also showed up with a small but high-profile cohort of activists. And finally, the All India Mahila Sammelan, which was nominally a non-profit, but was actually a thinly veiled arm of the opposition party.

The speechmaking began. 'We demand a CBI enquiry into Tara's disappearance!' shouted the leader of the AIMS contingent. 'A child cannot disappear into thin air! Why did it take police so long to reach the scene! Why hasn't she been found yet?'

And so it continued till the now-political dharna – suddenly 500 strong – began its scheduled progress towards Lalbazar police headquarters.

Ahana could have marched with the crowd, but it was a long, sweaty walk. So, after getting comments for her piece, she decided to get ahead of it, taking the Metro to beat the traffic. When she arrived at Lalbazar, she grabbed a bite from a roadside stall, and then began the wait. Finally, about an hour later, the crowd arrived. Their numbers seemed to have swelled further, and largely-female protestors formed a chain of hands all along the crowded street, demanding that the Commissioner of Police come out to meet them and accept in person a petition to further the safety of women in the state.

As they waited, they produced images of Tara, others lit candles. They cycled through tuneless renditions of 'We Shall Overcome' and the Bengali translation, 'Amra Korbo Joy'.

The police came out soon enough, but it was someone far down the pecking order, to declare that the protestors had not been granted permission by the police for their protest against the police, and the entire city was gridlocked because of it. They must, he said, clear out, or face consequences.

The talks went nowhere. The students from the college were side-lined completely as the AIMS leader took over. No one seemed to be in a mood for compromise. Finally, they were ordered to disband. An order that was politely but firmly declined.

And then without warning, as it seemed to Ahana, the lathis descended. Officers, wearing helmets rushed forward, wielding their batons. Though many moved away quickly, those in the front were stuck, with the police already upon them.

Ahana had been standing to one side on the pavement, frantically taking down every detail she could, hands shaking as she saw a woman in khaki approaching, and she felt the push of the mob from behind. Some tried to flee even as others charged. Before she knew it, Ahana was pushed to the front of the pack. Her arms came up reflexively as the rods came down. There was a blur of limbs and hair, a large object – probably a bag on the shoulder of one of those around her – hit her in the ribs with the force of a battering ram, and she was winded. Just as she was catching her breath, a policewoman locked in with a protestor swung her baton and hit Ahana straight on the arm. She cried out in pain, but there was nobody to hear or to care. Clutching her shoulder, she knew she had to find a way to escape the throng. The crush of bodies seemed to intensify. Then, instead of trying to move ahead, Ahana turned around and pushed her way through to the back, her arm screaming in agony with every inch of progress.

Finally on the fringes of the skirmish, she filled her lungs with greedy gulps of air. After what felt like an age, dizzy and confused, she surveyed her options. She tried calling the photographer who she knew was on the scene, but couldn't get through to his phone. Trying to find him was out of the question. Even if she could hail a taxi, which was unlikely at that time of the evening, she knew she wouldn't get very far. The roads were jam-packed with buses and cars at rush hour, engines were switched off and drivers were out of their seats to watch what they could of the live drama unfolding.

Without the jostle, Ahana's arm didn't seem so bad. She could walk without pain, and so that is what she chose to do.

Back in office twenty-five minutes later, she found that TVs had exploded with images of young women being dragged away by their hair, another with blood trickling out of a police-baton inflicted wound, a bus full of protestors rounded up. Elsewhere, a state bus was burnt in protest of the action against the protestors.

'What happened to you? Where have you been?' asked Manash as she entered the room.

'I was there,' she said.

'I know that!' he asked, exasperated. 'We've been trying to call for the past thirty minutes!'

'I didn't get any missed calls,' she said.

'Check your phone.'

'My arm – it's hurt,' she said.

It was peak time in the newsroom, and there were no chairs available. Manash instantly got up and made her sit.

She was thoroughly chastised for walking back alone in her state, which, she supposed was his brand of concern.

She told him what happened. 'I thought I was okay,' she said. 'Didn't see much of a choice.'

Manash tried to reach the office doctor, but he had left for the day. But on hearing what happened, he advised an X-ray. Manash ordered Ahana, along with Priyanka as escort, to head for the nearby clinic.

'If it is a fracture, just go straight to Wood Street Medical,' he said, scribbling a name and number on a piece of paper. 'Meet this doctor. Let me know, and I'll call ahead.'

In the end, it was not a fracture, but there was severe bruising. The doctor at the clinic advised cold compresses and a sling to immobilize the arm.

'How will I write my story?'

'You can dictate it?' Priyanka suggested.

'No, I can't think aloud. I am a terrible public speaker!'

'What's the connection?'

'Uff. Whatever. It's my left arm. I will type it out with two fingers even if it takes all night.'

'You don't have all night,' Priyanka said. 'You have a deadline.'

'Thanks for the reminder.'

Back in office, after assuring the bosses that she was okay, Ahana got straight to work. Priyanka brought her a bag of ice from the dive bar next door for the cold compress and a strip of Combiflam. She handed her a packet of biscuits too. 'Eat. Then take the meds.'

'Thanks, Priyanka,' she said. She was hungry, and in pain, so she did as she was told.

The office had exploded with activity by then. There had been one trainwreck after another that day: aside from the police action at the protest, at another unrelated event, the chief of the Women's Commission had gone off script in a public forum, attacking Drishti when reporters questioned her about the lathicharge. 'Women can sometimes be their own worst enemies,' she said. 'By stepping so far beyond accepted norms, what was she hoping to achieve?'

There were not many reporters, since it was an art exhibition opening, but there were enough to latch on to the comments. Then she brought up the incident with the maid, on whose behalf Drishti had approached the Commission. 'Drishti said her domestic help was being harassed by family members over false accusations of an affair. But then she called to apologize for the inconvenience, because she came to learn that the allegation was true.'

It was as though this point was being used to bolster her larger argument, that Drishti's acting as an advocate for a woman who turned out to be having an illicit affair was somehow a sign of her bad character. 'She is a smart, confident girl, quite capable of taking care of herself. How could she allow her child to be left in the care of someone so clearly questionable?'

Reporters then asked her if she blamed Drishti for the child's disappearance. She dodged that obvious minefield, but didn't step too far away from it. 'Sometimes there is wisdom in our societal norms,' she said. 'Abandoning them is not without consequence. There is a difference between India and the West that we would be wise to respect as we move towards a more equal society.'

After the first edition went out, Atanu and Manash called Probal and Ahana for a meeting.

'It looks like the CBI is going to be coming in soon,' said Manash.

'Why?' asked Probal. 'He was resisting till now.'

'After today's violence, the chief minister implied he is

going to do it,' said Atanu.

He turned to Probal. 'What updates on the investigation – aside from all this hungama?'

'The police are pursuing new angles,' said Probal.

'Like what?'

'They aren't revealing them just yet.'

'Is this Agarwal playing games with us?'

'Might be. He doesn't say much. Everyone is fed up.'

'Who is everyone?'

'Everyone from the commissioner to his juniors. He doesn't have a lot of friends.'

'Except for the CM. Who is on the team?'

'They have set up a task force. Six to seven men who are reporting to the commissioner, under the lead of DCDD II.'

'They have stopped physically searching,' said Manash.

'So many days later, they don't expect to see results with that approach.'

'Their words or yours?'

'Very much theirs, sir. Hundred per cent,' he said with a cocky smile to cover the bristle at the challenge. 'Off the record they are saying that it is kidnapping by a known person. They expect a ransom demand soon.'

'Why? They've heard nothing so far. What about the helpline?'

'Apparently they have been getting a steady stream of calls and emails,' said Ahana. 'Many are just from people with too much time on their hands, wishing the family the best and what not. But the other stuff, the team of volunteers, is making a database and sharing it with the police as the information comes in.'

'That's probably why the police are so angry,' said Manash.

'Extra work,' scowled Atanu.

'Apparently they haven't found a single solid lead,' said Probal.

'Please – are you telling me they have investigated all of them?'

Probal shrugged. 'I am just reporting what they said.'

'Sometimes question what they say too, Probal,' said Atanu. 'She didn't vanish into thin air, did she? She couldn't have gone far – she is four years old!'

Ahana had never seen Atanu lose his temper. He had a daughter too, not much older than Tara.

'Do they have evidence that it could be anything aside from kidnapping?' asked Manash.

'They have been looking. But there was no blood at the scene, no sign of a struggle or forced entry. No one saw or heard anything,' said Probal.

Atanu shifted focus from Probal to Ahana. 'Any news on the father angle?'

'None yet. No one in her network seems to know. What you see in the other papers is just rumour.'

'We don't want to speculate, but if we have reliable information, we need to put it out,' said Atanu. His pointed look was meant to remind her of her earlier slip – another would not be tolerated.

She nodded.

'What about her daily routine?'

'She has been holed up, for the most part. Some friends and family are coming and going – her parents seem to have moved in with her.'

'Neighbours?'

'Have been kept out of it. But plenty of feathers ruffled. The society is having a security system put in place sometime soon. They will be putting in CCTV cameras through the complex.'

'Good,' said Manash. 'Let's put a piece together on that. Ahana, are you up for it?'

'She needs a day's rest, Manash,' said Atanu.

'No,' she said. 'I am fine. I can do it.'

'Stay at home – your parents' home. Can you file from there?' asked Manash.

'Yes.'

'Then I don't want to see you here,' said Atanu. 'Take care and don't strain yourself. Let us know if you need anything.'

Day 9

Why were you Protesting?

Ahana went to her parents' home from work. Her mother came to the door and ushered her in with a series of tongue clicks and o—hos. It was past midnight, and the Combiflam was just not cutting it. Ahana knew she would need assistance before long.

'What happened?' she asked.

'Just a minute.' Ahana was holding her bag in her good hand, which she now put down and went to the kitchen. There was no ice in the freezer, but there was a bag of peas that she grabbed.

'What are you doing?' yelled her mother as she collapsed on the sofa, removed the sling and gingerly held the bag of peas to her throbbing arm.

'There is no ice. I need a cold compress.'

'I have to throw those peas away now.'

'Why? They are in a sealed bag.'

'Please, Ahana.'

'Fine. Throw them away then.'

'But what happened?'

'I was hurt at a protest.'

'Why were you protesting?'

'I wasn't the one protesting, Ma! I was covering the protest. Please, Ma. I need to take my medicine. Is there any food for me?'

If there was one thing she could rely on, it was that there would always be food. Her mother quickly got dinner on the table, by which time her father had also emerged from the bedroom. She told them what happened over dinner and then quickly downed her pain pills. She took the peas out of the freezer again as they all sat in front of the TV to watch the protest unfold once again on the news.

Ahana was surprised afresh by how quickly it all had escalated.

'Your company is paying for your medical fees?' asked her father.

'Yes, Baba.'

'You are lucky you didn't break a bone.'

And then he got up and went to his room.

'Will that thing heal before the engagement?' asked her mother.

'We still have, what, two weeks?'

'Shouldn't you know that?'

'Yeah, it'll heal.'

Ahana woke early, her entire arm and shoulder engulfed in pain. Her mother quickly brought her toast with tea so she could take the analgesic again, and then set about making her father's breakfast.

Ahana ate a few bites, popped her pill, and then closed her eyes, resting her head against the sofa. She considered getting up to see if the paper had arrived, but before she could, she dozed off again.

She awoke when her father emerged from the room. He didn't drink tea, which had always seemed proof of her parents' ultimate incompatibility to her. But like in so many marriages, Ahana had grown up with the knowledge that compatibility was never an expectation, and so the absence of it was never perceived as a problem.

He sat at the table, and her mother brought out two rotis and some sort of mixed vegetable sabji.

'How are you feeling today?' he asked her.

She hid her surprise. 'Sore,' she said. She couldn't remember the last time he had asked her how she was feeling about anything.

'You have the day off?'

'I am home, but I need to file a story.'

'About?'

'The security in the building. They are apparently putting in some sort of new CCTV system.'

And then he surprised her again by seeming interested.

'Where did you hear that?'

'The security guards told me.'

He looked impressed. Also a first, at least in recent memory. 'You should talk to Balai Babu. He's the current secretary. Very proactive, too.'

'Do you think he will speak to me?'

'That I don't know. He is usually in the association office in the mornings.'

'Ok, I'll try to catch him there.'

'It really is inexcusable how outdated our security system is. It has come up for discussion several times in the past, over several years.'

'And?'

'Nothing has been done. Newer complexes all have CCTV and intercom, and so many other facilities. When our building was built in the '70s, there was nothing of the sort of course. But after there was a robbery at one of the flats a few years ago, there was a lot of discussion. Then, I think last year there was another theft, and the committee at the time wanted to install cameras. They asked all the members to contribute, but not everyone did.'

'Why?'

'Because they are stupid people.'

'Ok, Baba. I won't quote you on that.'

'Why not? Go ahead. I wouldn't have said it if it wasn't true.'

As her father had predicted, Balai Babu was in the owner's association room in the basement of the building.

She introduced herself, half expecting to be thrown out, given how strict the guards had been about letting media in through the gates. But instead, he seemed rather pleased she was there.

'You had sent someone here during the Puja for coverage,' he said with a smile. 'A photographer.'

Oddly enough, he didn't seem hesitant about sharing

details of the security upgrade planned for the building. The money, he said proudly, would come solely from the building's soaring corpus following the previous year's highly successful Puja event.

'The *Tribune*, in fact, was our lead sponsor,' he said, with a wag of his forefinger.

She remembered it well, having been on the Puja beat, part of the paper's plan to woo the People Like Us middle classes away from the aggressive competition. So many days and nights, so many hours stuck in traffic that she'd never get back, going from building to building, writing the same things about each venue and trying to make it sound remarkable, unique, historic. Pandals made of plastic bottles! Lights from China, not Chandernagore! A drawing competition for kids!

'They didn't give us any cash,' he said. 'Only write-ups. They featured our Puja very well though. And we won the award for the most environmentally-friendly Puja, which had a cash prize.'

'And the building made money by selling stalls?'

'Yes, so many food stalls. No one eats at home during the four days of Puja in our building. Fire-free days for the women of the house,' he said with a chuckle.

'So you don't need the flat owners' cooperation this time to put in the security system?'

'We held a meeting to discuss the fund use, but the decision was already approved under a previous committee, so it wasn't a problem. The resolution had already been passed, they just couldn't complete the job then. If they had, things would be different today.'

'Why couldn't they get it done?' she asked.

'People didn't make their monetary contributions.'

'And now, no one will complain?'

'Not when they don't have to pay for it.' He chuckled again.

'What were the plans for the money raised by the Puja before this incident occurred?'

'It hadn't been decided. Some people wanted to stop chanda collection and use the money for next year's Puja.'

'And now that won't be possible?'

'No.'

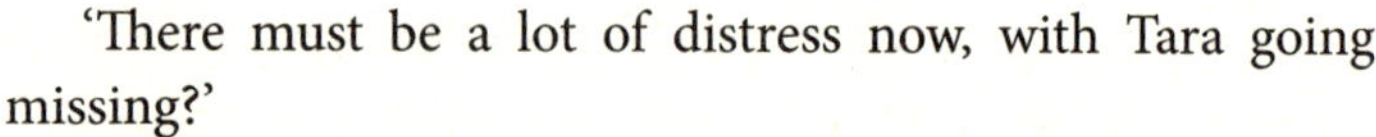

'There must be a lot of distress now, with Tara going missing?'

'Lots. Lots of people adding locks to their front doors, collapsible gates, putting grills all the way up to the ceiling on their balconies. People are shaken up.'

'Many people also coming forward to help.'

'Yes. Funny, how it is often the same people who complain that come forward.'

'Complain about what?'

The smile on his face was fixed. 'Noise, late hours, visitors at Drishti's house.'

'That sounds serious.'

'It was a few years ago. I remember because I was on the committee then as well.'

'Was anything done about it?'

'We had a few policies put in place after that, and people were happy with the outcome.'

Not to mention the fact that Drishti had become famous in the interim – but the increased tolerance must have merely been a coincidence.

'What were the policy changes about?'

'Rules regarding noise etc.'

'And that was enough to make the complaints stop?'

For the first time, he looked uncomfortable. 'A group of owners have been trying to ban single tenants.'

'Can they do that?'

He shrugged. 'Even if they could, many people in the building would not allow it. I am a father myself. My daughter lives in Bombay – if she couldn't find a place to rent as a single girl, where would she go? Though my daughter…,' he trailed off, with a shake of his head.

Would never have a child out of wedlock. It wasn't hard to guess how he'd have liked to finish that sentence. 'Drishti is a tenant?'

'No, an owner. There was nothing one could possibly do to evict her, and so they gave up.'

'And what about Drishti? Did she ever say anything?'

'No, she didn't. But you are a woman yourself. You know the importance of maintaining one's reputation. As sitting secretary, I shouldn't say anything more than this.'

'I believe there have been other break-ins, too.'

'One person's empty flat was being used by some domestic staff.'

'Anything else?'

'Oh, you know. Small incidents here and there. Someone's own son stole gold from the almirah, and tried to blame it on the maid. These things happen, you know. Despite all the security you put in, we will still have incidents like these. That's life. What can you do about it?'

'But four-year-olds just don't vanish into the night.'

'No, they don't. And that is why it is time to act.'

A man walked into the office just then, and Ahana waited as he and Balai Babu discussed some paperwork required for the sale of a flat. He shot her a look or two. She wondered how much he had heard of their conversation.

She had a few more questions after the interruption. When she finally climbed the stairs to the ground level ten minutes later, the man was still standing there, by the entrance of B Block. He seemed as though he was waiting for her, but he didn't come forward. So she approached him.

'You don't remember me?' he asked abruptly.

'No, I'm sorry, I don't.'

'We've met at the Puja many times.'

She should have felt embarrassed, but found herself irritated instead by his accusatory tone.

'We also met the day Tara went missing in the park.'

'Oh, I remember now!' she said, though she didn't at all remember seeing him that day, or any other.

'I couldn't help hearing you back there,' he said.

'I'm a journalist,' she explained. 'And I live here too.'

'Yes, I know, I read your articles on Tara.'

She felt contrite. 'Yes,' she said. 'This entire affair has everyone shaken up.'

He watched her, as though wondering whether he should speak.

She waited.

'He was lying,' he said at last.

'About?'

'The fact that there were no other untoward incidents.'

'Could you tell me more?'

'Drishti has always had some problem or the other. Once, someone threw a rock at her window and broke it – and all the broken glass landed in the child's room. Then someone drew disgusting drawings on her front door. Another time, she found a parcel on her doorstep filled with dog excrement.'

'Ugh. When was all of this?'

'About three years ago.'

'Maybe he didn't know about it, if he wasn't secretary that time?'

'That is possible. But everyone was talking about it.'

'Did they ever discover who did it?'

'No. And they didn't really bother to try and find out.'

'Can I ask how you know this?'

'Drishti is a friend. She told me.'

'Right.'

'My mother used to watch Tara sometimes before we moved away.'

'You've moved?'

'Yes, some time ago.'

'And now you are selling the flat?'

'We are in talks.'

'Would you know who was the secretary at the time of the earlier trouble with Drishti?'

'No.'

'Thanks anyway,' Ahana said. 'Could I get your name, please?'

'Palash. Palash Banerjee.'

'Would you mind if I quoted you?'

He shrugged. 'I don't live here anymore, anyway, so I guess it doesn't matter what they think of me. Go ahead.'

Back upstairs, Ahana called her father at work. He remembered the incidents Palash had mentioned and who the secretary was at the time with no trouble – it was just the kind of information he stayed on top of. The man she should meet now, he said, was another septuagenarian, by the name of Kamal Datta. Her father gave her his flat number, though he didn't have a phone number handy.

'But just go and visit. He's superannuated some years ago now. He'll be at home,' he said.

Her mother wandered into the room.

'Ma, do you know someone called Palash Banerjee?'

'Who?'

'He lives in Drishti's block.'

'Oh, Palash. Yes, Sulagna's son. I told you I saw Drishti's parents with her the other day.'

'He told me that Drishti's house had been vandalized – stones thrown, some obscene drawing.'

'Yes, now that you mention it, it sounds familiar. His mother knows Drishti quite well. Which is rather strange.'

'Why?'

'She isn't the sort of woman I thought would be Drishti's friend.'

'And what sort of woman is that?'

'She is a very serious sort of a woman. She doesn't really have very many friends in the building at all, and she spoke out against Drishti's lifestyle for years. And then, for some reason, after Tara came along, something happened and they all became friends.'

'Did she watch Tara sometimes?'

'I believe so. When Drishti's parents were busy.'

'Do you know where they live now?'

'Somewhere nearby, I think.'

'Why did they move?'

'His father has cancer. I think they needed the money. So they shifted to that flat, and they are selling off this one.'

'Does Drishti have other friends in the building?'

'I wouldn't know about the young people. But amongst the older residents, most prefer to stay away.'

Ahana's mother flipped through her tiny red address book and fished out Sulagna's new phone number. Ahana scribbled it down on her notepad.

Kamal Datta was, as predicted, at home. She received a warm smile of welcome, and she remembered seeing him around the complex on his evening walk.

'Of course, of course, Tarun babu's daughter!'

She entered. The apartment was identical to her parents' in design, but while theirs was spare and spotless to the point of being spartan, this was a jumble of bric-a-brac collected from world travels, with baby blue walls and dark green marble floors. She followed him into the sitting area and sat awkwardly on the divan, covered with maroon and gold upholstery. 'What can I do for you today?' he asked with a smile.

'You may know that I work for the *Tribune* newspaper now.'

'Yes, I had heard that. Very good, very good. Our community here has its share of brilliant people. It is wonderful!'

'Thank you,' she said. 'We are trying to look at all aspects of the case, and in the course of our reporting, we heard that there had been several residents who did not want Drishti to continue living here after Tara's birth.'

'Is it?' he said. 'But I am not secretary now, so I won't be able to tell you. The person to speak to would be Balai Babu.'

'I was told you were secretary in 1998, when some vandalism took place.'

He nodded. 'I *was* secretary then, but there is nothing I can tell you. It was so long ago.'

'Such disputes between members must not arise very often.'

He laughed. 'That is where you are mistaken. Every day brings a new dispute. Why do you think I am no longer involved with the committee?'

She smiled. 'Anything you can tell me will be useful.'

'From what I remember, there were a few complaints

because of the hours she kept. Sometimes there would be music rehearsals quite late at night as well.'

'And how was it resolved?'

'The committee had issued a formal letter to her about the music, and she complied with the demand to restrict her noisemaking to before 9 pm.'

'But there were other complaints, weren't there?'

'Not that I remember.'

'Tara would have been quite small then. Wasn't Drishti's music on hold in those days?'

'I couldn't tell you.'

'I heard that there was a meeting about three years ago, where residents expressed their discomfort with Drishti being a single mother.'

'Perhaps.'

'You were involved then?'

'I have a vague recollection of it. It was not an official meeting for sure, and no action was taken.'

'Why?'

'If I remember correctly, it is because she is an apartment owner.'

'And nothing could be done to get rid of her?'

He ran a hand over Brylcreemed hair. 'These are the opinions of a few concerned people. Nothing more than that. No one meant any harm. This is one of the best known apartment complexes in the city. It is a place for families, and if certain behaviour is not appreciated, what is the harm if they wanted to have some rules, some restrictions?'

'But it went beyond a lack of appreciation – there were threats as well, weren't there?'

'Threats!' he said, shaking his head vigorously from side to side. 'Impossible!'

'That is not what other residents have told me.'

'What have you heard?'

'Her window was stoned, and once she had obscene images drawn on her front door.'

'I know nothing about that. Did she file a formal complaint?'

'I believe so, and nothing was done.'

He brushed it away with wave of his hand. 'See, that could have been any childish prank.'

'Even if the threat included harm to Tara? The glass from the broken window entered her nursery.'

'So you think our residents had something to do with it?'

'It is possible. Or that someone might know something about it.'

'Look, I don't like the tone of your questions. If you choose to live in a society, you have to accept certain norms.'

'A child is missing, and people here did not all like her.'

'So what? We have a beautiful community here, and it is being made out to look like an unsafe building with no security. Don't you think that makes us even more vulnerable to miscreants? And now you want to make it look like we had wanted to hurt a child! Never!'

'That is not what I said.'

'I know you people in the media! Anything for a headline! Tarun babu is a dear friend, so I agreed to meet you, but it is best you leave now! All you young women nowadays – you don't know your place!'

She stood up. 'Like Drishti?'

'Obscene behaviour will not be tolerated in a respectable community like ours! Dirty things, dirty women!'

Ahana fled the flat and struggled to regain her composure.

She had swallowed all the insults she had wished to hurl back at that hateful man, and it was as if it was making her arm throb even more.

She headed to the garden, lush and green, the monsoons helping it along. She sat on the bench to take a minute, closing her eyes, breathing deeply to calm herself. She noted once again that the life of the building and its residents was ticking away as usual. All of the outrage against Drishti, all of the rushing around to find Tara the night she went missing, had dissolved away. The guards were going about their business, cars were coming and going, a school bus had dropped off children who were slowly walking towards their homes. Safe and sound. For today.

A few minutes later, Ahana found herself standing in front of Drishti's door once again. If she had felt like a thief the last time, coming to take what wasn't hers, this time she felt like an ally. She finally had questions that only Drishti could answer, and she was going to at least try to get her to respond to them.

Ahana rang the bell.

No one came to the door. She closed her eyes, gritted her teeth and rang again.

A minute later, just as she was getting ready to head back down, it opened, slowly, tentatively.

Ahana held her breath.

There stood Drishti.

'Ahana?' she asked. She seemed smaller, diminished somehow.

'I am so sorry to show up unannounced.'

'Your paper sent you?'

'Yes.'

Drishti seemed to consider this for a while before taking a step back. 'Come in.'

Why would Drishti open the door for a journalist that particular evening, when it had stayed firmly shut so far? And for the very same journalist who had reconstructed one of her most vulnerable moments as a mother – and possibly one of the most damning – for all the world to see?

If I had hoped earlier that she hadn't read or heard about the article I had written on Tara's first disappearance, the hope disappeared as I saw a stack of several days' newspapers on the coffee table. They had been read by someone.

Drishti's home was just like her: unexpected, warm and effortlessly stylish. The walls were dotted with art and photographs, the standard issue wooden sofa set covered in upholstery that combined texture and colour. And everywhere there was Tara: toys in a cubby in the living room, a small red cycle parked near the door, muddy shoes by the entrance. It felt like she was only in the other room, and would explode into the space at any moment.

But not only was Tara not there, it seemed that there was no one else in the house but Drishti. In all the times I had imagined Drishti's state, she had never been alone. I had thought she'd be surrounded by family and friends, providing support, helping out, tending to her every need. Even at the press conference, she had seemed to have many well-wishers ready to buoy her up whenever needed.

'You are alone today?' I asked.

Drishti shot a quick glance at me, and then away, towards the dining space, towards her foot, anywhere that wasn't my face.

'My parents went home to collect some more things. My father usually insists on sleeping in his own bed every night, but he has been here since...'

She trailed off and I quickly tried to fill the silence. 'I met Bunty outside a few days ago.'

'Yeah, he's really been amazing. The rest of the guys from the bar, too.'

'I saw him last at the press conference. How is the helpline going?'

'All day, the line connects to Udit Dalmia's operators. They are getting so many calls. At night, we have volunteers to ensure no call is missed. Most are random people asking for information, people wanting to speak with me. The few callers who provide information, all the details are recorded and passed on to the police.'

'And?'

'Nothing so far,' she said.

And then she closed her eyes. When she opened them, she looked at me at last, and seemed strangely focused.

'What happened to your arm?' she asked.

No one else that day had displayed any curiosity at my arm being in a sling. 'I was at the protest yesterday. Got on the wrong side of a police baton.'

Her hand went up to cover her mouth. It was as though she had decided that the injury was on her account.

She shook her head. 'I need your help,' she said.

I was taken aback by the sudden request. So much so that I made my first mistake.

'Anything,' I said, a beat too quickly. And yet, who was I to promise help?

'I will give you an interview. Everything on the table, everything on the record. But I need you to promise that whatever happens next, you and your paper will not give up on Tara.'

'What do you mean?'

'There are a lot of people in the media who want me to speak to them, but you are the only one I know. And more importantly, you know Tara. You... have been there for us before.'

I felt all the blood rush to my face. 'About that – '

'No need,' she said, with a quick shake of the head.

I was choking on all the explanations I wanted to give. But my guilt was to remain my own burden. 'Ok,' I said.

'That was just the beginning. They will make this entire thing about me soon enough.'

'Who?'

'First tell me – do we have a deal?'

'I don't know what the newspaper will do, but *I* can promise you that I won't give up on the story – on Tara.'

I took out my Dictaphone and held it up. She nodded, and I turned it on and put it on the table.

'This business about the first time Tara went missing, it is all part of the new story the police are trying to sell.'

'What makes you say that?'

'The questions have changed. The way they are looking at me has changed. Sumita – my maid, went to the police and told them a bunch of stuff, and now they think they know me, and they don't like it.'

'But what do they know?'

'Every detail about my life. Every dirty little detail.'

She paused and looked at me, her piercing gaze unapologetic. 'Believe me, it is unavoidable. They will come for me, and when they do, they will stop looking for her, and then there is no hope.'

'Wait, back up. Please – it is not that I don't believe you. I am just trying to connect the dots.'

Drishti leaned forward. 'It has been twenty-four hours since Sumita spoke to them again. Something has changed. I can tell by the questions they are asking me. They are focussing on my whereabouts now. And Tara's father.'

'Do they know who he is?'

'No.'

'You haven't told them.'

'No.'

'Can I ask why not?'

'Because he is not a part of Tara's story. Never has been. They've asked me about all my friends and boyfriends who have met Tara, and I've told them all they wanted to know about that. This isn't about being coy.'

'And they aren't accepting it?'

'No.'

'But from a police perspective, you understand why?'

She shook her head. 'No, I don't. It is just another distraction when I know he had nothing to do with it!'

Pushing her further would have been a mistake. So I changed track. 'Drishti,' I said. 'Have you received… a call?'

'You mean for ransom?'

I nodded – the word had stuck in my throat.

'No, nothing.'

Something caught my eye on the floor, under the sofa on which she sat. It was a small scrap of cloth with purple and blue stripes. A single, dirty sock.

'Do you have any idea what might have happened?'

She rubbed her eyes. She shook her head. 'No.'

'Anything you think needs attention, that they are missing in the investigation?'

'I don't know. The political goons who were after me, maybe.'

'What about any fans?'

'I've shared that stuff with the police already. Who knows what they are doing with it.'

'Would you be able to share it with me, too?'

She nodded. 'I have copies. I made sure I made copies of everything I handed over.'

'You don't trust them.'

'The police? I wanted to. I wanted to be wrong about them. But after a couple of days it became clear that they weren't going to look for her, that they weren't even going to try.' Her voice was raspy, as it so often was when she sang.

'Could I ask you some questions about what happened that night?'

'Go ahead.'

'The door wasn't forced open?'

'No.'

'Does anyone else have the key?'

'My parents, who weren't in town. My neighbour, who was not in that night. I've checked with her, too, as have the police.'

'Have you had any break-ins in the past?'

'No.'

'What about the maid? Despite everything, she really does seem the most likely suspect.'

'She has been working here for over two years now. She was more or less reliable, and Tara was fond of her. But the police have finished that line of enquiry, is what I am told. They haven't found anything to indicate she took Tara. So I have to assume it wasn't her.'

'Then why do you think she gave up all your secrets? You tried to help her out when her family was after her, right?'

She gave an exasperated little shake of the head. 'When did "being of help" ever help anyone in return? I don't know why she did it – to gain favour? Because she thinks I did something terrible? Because she was threatened? Your guess is as good as mine.'

'Any other people – carpenters, drivers?'

'Not anyone recently. And how would they have a key? And how hard is it to make a duplicate key anyway? People do it all the time when they get locked out.'

'Have you ever done it?'

'No. It is to avoid that that I always leave a key with a neighbour.'

'Which neighbour?'

'Next door. Used to be with a family downstairs, with whom we were quite friendly. But then they left the complex.'

'Is this Palash Banerjee?'

'Yes. Well, his mother.'

'And they don't have a copy anymore?'

'No,' she said. And then she changed the subject. My second mistake was to let her. 'But the shit is about to hit the fan. That horrible, horrible man from the TV channel has managed to get a story that is about to hijack everything.'

'What?'

She rubbed her face. 'I need a cup of tea.'

'Ok,' I said, picking up the recorder, about to stand up.

'Please, stay here. I'll be back.'

I turned it off and waited.

'I had terrible, terrible post-partum depression,' she said, back on the sofa, tea cup cradled in her hands. 'Now the police and that man are digging that up to imply that not only am I a bad mother, but also an unfit mother and possibly a dangerous mother.'

'You mean Ranadeep?'

'Yes.'

'So this story – the one of Tara's first disappearance – was a calculated leak. There is more?'

She nodded her head. She put her feet up on the sofa, tucking them under her. 'If I have ever made any mistake, it is in not keeping enough secrets.'

'Why is that?'

'After Tara was born, people knew I was struggling. I think I was the last one to realize it. I had a couple of rather public meltdowns before I got help.'

'When did it start?'

She ran a hand across her forehead. 'When I was like you, single, unattached, I thought I knew motherhood. I think we all do, just by virtue of having been children ourselves once. How ridiculous it is. But the truth is, you can't imagine it until you have a child of your own.'

'It was hard?'

'In ways I could never have foreseen.'

'You didn't want to be a mother?'

'Oh no. Not that. Tara was most dearly wanted.'

'Even under the circumstances?'

'I didn't care that the father wasn't in my life. Many people find it hard to understand this about me – I didn't, and don't, want a husband. But I have always wanted a child.'

'It must have been difficult, though.' I was thinking of gossip. But that isn't where she went.

'It is a hard job for one person to do. I was hit by a tonne of bricks. Part of it was real. It was harder than anything I had ever done before. The sleepless nights, the lack of help, the physical pain. Then I had to get a job, and things got even more insane. The rest, I think, was chemical. Can you imagine wanting to leave your own child? Leave your whole life behind and make a new one somewhere where nothing is expected of you?'

'But you didn't.'

'No. But I felt like I'd been an imposter. A fraud,' she said, her voice husky. 'Till that point, it felt like I had been wandering around all my life, looking for a familiar face. Friends, relationships… It was all fine, but it wasn't… home, you know? I was always looking for something deeper, a flash of welcome extending beyond the polite detachment that seemed to gild the surface of life like Teflon. And here came a human being, wanting only me. I should have been… Grateful? Instead I was, at times – if I am being fair to myself, it was only at the worst of times – resisting. Pushing back against the intensity of pure need.'

She looked at me. 'You must be wondering, *who says these things about their own child?* You wouldn't be the first.'

'No. I know it is hard.'

'I could not give all of myself, as she demanded of me, I needed to hold back for my own sanity. I needed to return to music. It was the only way I could be the mother I wanted to be.'

There were many things I could have said: that she did what was best for them both, that she wasn't the one who harmed her daughter, that she should show herself more kindness. But her look told me that all such thoughts had been considered and dismissed well before my arrival on the scene. She didn't seek my approval.

'It was all so long ago. But the weight of that fantasy is in the guilt I live with, for having the thought in the first place, and that is what they are pulling out now to hurt me.'

'Strange.'

'Why?'

'When I see you, I see someone with no time for that sort of censure.'

'I might disregard the demands put on me as a woman, but when it comes to motherhood, I am as conventional as they come. Marriage feels fake to me, but I expected caring for my child to be as natural as breathing.'

And then the flash of pain at the realization that what was previously unthinkable was now true: her daughter was all alone in the world, and possibly – most probably – in danger.

'How did you beat it?'

'In large part, the treatment of a very good doctor. And also thanks to the success of my music. It was rewarding, and financially freeing.'

'And Tara?'

'I hired a nanny. A very good one. She left two years ago to take care of her own grandkids. If she hadn't…' She shook her head as if to silence that train of thought. 'But by then, Tara wasn't so small, and I was able to care for her and still have time for myself. And my mother was helping a lot more. When I had a show at night, she would come to spend time with Tara.'

'But that night, your mother couldn't be here.'

'She and my father were on holiday in Bhutan. So I asked another friend to help – Palash's mother, Sulagna Banerjee. She had really been a great help to me on so many occasions when she used to live here. She doted on Tara. And even though she has moved out, she still comes by sometimes. But her husband passed away a few months ago, after a long battle with cancer, and she has lost some of her vitality. She said she was indisposed that night.'

'I met Palash Banerjee when he came to get some work done with their house sale.'

'Yeah. They are selling it to pay off their debts from the treatment.'

'He mentioned some problems you had in the building.'

She rolled her eyes. 'Yeah. Nosy neighbours. The usual, you know?'

'You don't see any serious threat in any of that?'

'Not really, no. They were all people with no life.'

'The broken windows? The obscene drawings?'

'Still a long way from… this, isn't it?'

'Okay – so you left Tara with Sumita that night.'

'I thought it would be okay,' she said softly. 'It was only one night, and Tara would be asleep through the whole thing.'

'I have read about it, but I still don't understand how Sumita could have not heard anything.'

'Neither did the police at first. But she was apparently in the other bedroom, watching TV, talking on the phone. Any sounds could have easily been drowned out. That much is true.'

'And she didn't hear or see anything at all?'

'No, but when she finally emerged and found Tara's bedroom door ajar, she went in and found her gone.'

'And then what did she do?'

'Called me in hysterics. I was in the middle of a performance.'

The memory of that moment took over, and Drishti picked up her cup again.

I marvelled at her resilience. I knew then that she was a fundamentally different breed of person, that what tethered her to the earth was not what attaches the rest of us to our lives and our promises. To view her through the lens of Surya Apartments was like expecting a tiger to behave like a housecat.

I put my recorder in my bag and stood up.

'I should get to work,' I said. The only words that could possibly help. 'Are you sure you want to be here alone?'

She nodded. Her mother was on the way. And she couldn't leave – not when there was a chance that Tara would return, that a call might come.

'Ahana, could I ask you to let me know if you hear anything significant?'

'Yes, but I have to confess, my sources are not the most connected. By the time I learn what the police are doing, it is all over the news anyway.'

'Call me with anything at all. Anything is better than this not knowing.'

'Okay,' I said. 'Thank you.' I was unable to make eye contact. As I let myself out, I caught a last glimpse through the gap in the closing door – head against her hand propped up by the armrest, that tiny striped sock by the leg of the chair.

As Drishti had predicted, the allegation that gained most traction in the days following the interview in the *Tribune* was that she was an unfit mother.

Tarar Khonje had found a psychiatrist – not Drishti's own doctor, but someone who said she had 'heard of the case' – who claimed that Drishti had suffered from postpartum depression of the most intense kind. 'She appeared to have the classic symptoms of postpartum psychosis, with thoughts of self-harm and harm to her child.'

In an era before the mommy blog, there was very little public awareness about mental health issues faced by new mothers. The public and journalists were equally ill-equipped to sort fact from fiction. Even if the statements from the psychiatrist had been true, the fact that four years had elapsed since Tara's birth and Drishti had apparently overcome her issues were not touched upon. Not to mention the egregious violation of professional standards and ethics in divulging such details – or fabricating them.

As Drishti had predicted, the tide had indeed turned, and a section of the media were happy toeing the police line, which was focussing more and more on the glamorous mother as being a possible part of it all.

And how could they not? It was a narrative brimming with drama, tragedy, sex. There was a celebrity at the centre of it, who was beautiful, single and in no position to defend herself. It gave news persons the license to treat rumour as fact, and therefore, as currency. There were petty people to be quoted and splashed about at will. It was nothing short of a media dream come true.

A sample from a newspaper, *Bengal Times*

> ...The big question is how long can the singer keep the identity of the child's father a secret without coming under serious fire herself. 'We have even been told that the father is a prominent politician and therefore is being shielded, which the mother has denied,' said a member of the investigating team, not wishing to be named.
>
> Little is known of Drishti's relationships in her social circles. Her closest friends are refusing to speak to the media on the subject. But those familiar with her life report that she has had several partners over the years, including a two-year-relationship with Devraj Mukherjee, lead singer of Devasthal, when they were starting out on the Indie music scene.
>
> Devraj was unavailable for comment, but they are reportedly still friends.
>
> Drishti is known to be fiercely independent and secretive. 'Many women did not trust her around their boyfriends or husbands. She was attractive, and without scruples,' said a member of a city band who wished to remain unnamed.
>
> There are rumours of affairs with married men. While some say that she doesn't have any regard for norms, others see her as a social climber with aspirations to marry money.
>
> A smaller group of the Page 3 set view her with compassion. 'Being a single parent isn't easy,' said designer Ekta Sharma, herself a divorced parent of two. 'People are always quick to judge, no matter what the circumstance. This is a terrible tragedy

> and we can only hope for the safe return of Tara.' Artist and social justice activist Jeet Q said he was not surprised by the whispered accusations. 'She is a young, beautiful woman who chooses not to live by the rules. People just don't understand her.'

Elsewhere, across eight columns, former 'friends' held forth on her parenting skills. 'I visited her once, to meet the baby,' said friend Moumita Chakraborty, 'The whole time she just sat there, crying. Tara was sweetly sleeping, but Drishti didn't seem happy. Why have a child, that too alone, if you can't handle it? It is like she wanted to be cool so she decided to have a baby, and then once the baby came, she didn't know what to do with herself.'

...This, from another 'friend': 'Everything she'd do for effect. She'd go everywhere with that child, to bars, restaurants. Breastfeeding everywhere. Like she forgot where she was. Which country did she live in? She'd cover up, but why this need to be too modern? It made us so uncomfortable.'

If these claims had been made in private, Drishti would have ignored them. But they were in all the papers, and that made Drishti care about the impact they were having on the police.

Another Drishti – one other than the authentic, if slightly eccentric free-spirit – was being conjured up. This was a coldly calculating and attention-hungry creature, using her child to set herself apart. Whether this image fed off the changing direction of the police investigation, or if it was the image that steered the investigation towards Drishti, it was not clear. But they moved in lock-step.

The investigation of Tara's disappearance was not the first effort to reveal the identity of her father. Single mothers are rare enough in 2019; in 1998, they were almost unheard of in middle-class Calcutta. This made Drishti's personal life a subject of scrutiny well before tragedy struck.

Drishti had been the focus of a smear campaign once before, instigated by the Preserve Calcutta Heritage Committee. In the days after the protests that led to riots in the streets, the public seemed to think the identity of the child's father was something it deserved to know. But even then, the media had been given little to satisfy its hunger for information. Her friends and family were in the dark, and those who may have known – or guessed – stayed mum. Which only fuelled more furious speculation.

The attention was not only from her detractors. Drishti's fame had won her groupies, too, some of whom tracked her across cities, and who pored over every detail published. This was before the Internet made this sort of thing simple. There were several fan theories about Tara's parentage; the most colourful being that Drishti had been impregnated by the scion of the nation's most illustrious political family. The only basis for this seemed to be a photograph of the two of them together at a dinner prior to Tara's birth. Another school of thought believed the singer had been in a clandestine relationship with Bengal's brightest cricket star – a married man with a wife and son.

While sensational and ludicrous, most of these rumours were ultimately harmless. Except when taken together, they gave exactly the sort of impression that scandal mongers were trying to create – that Drishti was a shameless social climber with no scruples. Who knew what such a woman was truly capable of, particularly when she was a bad mother to boot?

As public opinion reached critical mass, Tara and Drishti became dinner table conversation across the city. At a restaurant one evening, I overhead this exchange between a group of five friends:

'Such a bitch she is. What kind of a woman can do that to her own child?' said one man.

'Sachchi mein,' said one of his female companions.

'Do what? These newspapers are full of crap. The media will say anything they want nowadays. My friend's older brother is in a band and knows Drishti quite well, and he doesn't believe any of it.'

'Yeah, because she is fucking hot!'

'Yeah man, if he knows her so well, who's the dad?'

3 March 1997

Drishti was lying in bed, sinking into the hard mattress covered by a soft, cotton quilt. Usually, it was a blissfully soft place to rest, but that afternoon, it felt too soft, too hot, too stifling. The windows were shut against the midday sun, the curtains drawn, but the near darkness did nothing to help. The air was so heavy that she felt as though it had joined the baby in sitting on her lungs in squeezing the breath out of her.

She pulled up her shirt, pushed her shorts down so the waistband sat on her pelvis. She ran her fingers over her belly. It was sticky with sweat, swollen now to the point of discomfort. She fingered the ridges on her skin under her navel – a part of her body she could no longer see – and knew that the stretch marks had finally come.

The very act of being on her back was a source of pain, but she couldn't bear to roll over onto her side. She needed the air of the fan flowing over every inch of her stomach.

Finally, she shimmied her shorts off with all the grace of a rampaging elephant, and it was with some effort that she got them clear of her ankles. She closed her eyes and willed a nap to descend, but sleep had been elusive since the fourth month of pregnancy. Suddenly it felt as though the baby was kicking straight into her diaphragm, swift and decisive punishment for daring to contemplate rest.

As if her physical state weren't enough, Drishti had been feeling unsettled all day. She had received a call that morning, and had experienced a moment of true fear. It was from one of the only common acquaintances she had with *him*, and she couldn't risk word getting out. Half a world's distance between them had seemed enough to insulate her from exposure, but ever since she had begun to show, she had experienced moments of pure panic when she was out and about. The father of her child might not be from Calcutta, but he had friends here, and she was well aware of how tiny the world was for people of a certain kind. What would he do if he got wind of it?

By the end of the call, she had been fairly certain that their common friend had not had any news after all. Not only did he not ask Drishti anything, he didn't even ask the suitably vague fishing questions she had become accustomed to fielding from acquaintances trying to fill in the blanks of their colourful fantasies about who had fathered the bastard child growing inside her.

She didn't like the word father for him, and she had not wanted him to know. She had not thought about how he would feel if he did find out, not because she didn't care but because in the ultimate analysis, it wouldn't stop her either way. Who was she to him, after all?

Except that she now had a piece of him. Forever.

They had had moments where they might have been. Something. And it had been exhilarating. But then there had been a dance of distance, of choices that couldn't be unchosen, of the others who had walked in and out of both of their lives. His more than hers.

What had stopped him from leaving his wife after they'd been together that weekend? Because he definitely hadn't been thinking of her when he had been inside Drishti.

But she'd never asked him, and she never would. She could have, only a month after they'd been together, when he had been passing through town on his way back to the States. He'd called her again, and she'd heard it in his voice. The desire. But also the doubt. He'd been with his wife since he'd been with her.

But she couldn't see him. Not alone. Not then. Not when she already knew.

He had given her no notice that he'd be back in town. He had said it was an unscheduled stop, but she wondered if it was by design, that he was in fact avoiding her. If so, he got what he wanted. The only day he had to spare was also her cousin's wedding, and there was a party at her parents' house which she couldn't get out of. So she had asked him to come there instead, expecting him to refuse. But he didn't. He showed up, dressed in spotless kurta and pyjama. It was the only time he had ever been inside her world; insofar as it was her world.

And instead of being silent and resentful, there he was, with his hands all over her guitar, at the centre of the room, playing U2 and forcing her to sing. Something she hated doing for the family. But the young cousins had grown up to be less annoying than she'd remembered, and the requests kept coming and it was like they had been singing together for years and years.

She couldn't be angry while she was singing, but when he followed her into the kitchen to get some water, as he leaned against the counter, all the fury she didn't know she felt rose up.

'How can you sit there, acting like nothing happened?' she snapped.

'Why do you say that?'

'You disappeared.' She hated how she sounded.

'You made it clear you didn't want to hear from me.'

'Yes, but that has never stopped you before. And you called me today, didn't you?'

He shook his head, bewildered. 'Drishti, so much was said that you now forget.'

'Don't you fucking dare. I remember everything.'

Three words. Three innocuous words that gave away more than she had been prepared to give. But what had changed, really? She had loved him, always, and she had known it. He was still with another woman, and so it would remain. Because Drishti wanted it that way, and she was sure that, deep down, so did he.

Then why did she say what she did next? 'If it had meant so much to you, you would have been here, because you wouldn't have been *able* to be anywhere else.'

Even if he might leave his wife, he'd never leave his life.

He didn't reply, but she saw her anger and her lust mirrored in his eyes and she knew that if her aunt hadn't walked into the kitchen just then, she would have been in his arms and everything might have been different.

Instead, she had rushed out to the sitting room, scanning the sea of faces at the party, seeking the old safety of those she loved, to remind herself what was to be gained by their lies, their silence. But it was a hard sell, for it had never meant anything to her, this illusion of propriety. The compunctions were his, the family too, and she could not wrench them from him.

If anything, their argument was a reminder to her that she didn't want long-term relationships for a very good reason: expectations. Of her, by her. They twisted what was beautiful till it was beautiful no more.

She awoke with a start, sopping wet with sweat. For the first time, there was a longing she could not, or would not, consider.

She got up and took a shower, but the water too felt near boiling.

The next day, she went out and ordered an air-conditioner.

Day 10

How Much Blood?

Ahana's orders to stay away from the office had, thanks to the interview with Drishti, been summarily and mutually revoked. Instead, she was there till the last cars left and the office went into mandatory shut down at 3 am. The rushed version of the article went out with the early edition, a more refined one in the next. By the time she was in the car on the way home, her arm and shoulder were throbbing worse than the day of the assault.

The following morning, she was under orders to visit the doctor, send in the medical reports for the official complaint to the Press Council of India, and take time off.

At the clinic, they redid the X-ray, and once again found no problem with the bone. 'It's soft tissue damage, but you need to rest,' the doctor said. 'For a week.'

She knew that wasn't a possibility, but even that day off proved to be elusive, for just as she was leaving the doctor's office, she got a call, and it was from Drishti.

Ahana's stomach clenched as she saw the name on her caller ID – she had no idea what Drishti had thought of the piece that morning; she hadn't had the courage to ask.

But Drishti had far worse to worry about. 'Ahana, they are here again,' she said in a panicked whisper.

'Who?'

'The police. They are going through Tara's room – something has happened, I just know it! They aren't telling me anything.'

'Give me ten minutes. I'll find out what I can and call you back.'

She quickly paid her bill and called Manash from the taxi. 'Can Probal call the police to find out what is going on? Drishti is frightened.'

'Yes, but also come in now. Sorry to do this to you again.'

'I'm already on my way.'

Ahana couldn't keep her ten-minute promise to Drishti. She didn't hear from Manash, and by the time she reached the office, the usual crowd had assembled in the conference room. As she sat down, she saw from their faces that the news was not good.

'They are considering the possibility that the story is quite different from what they originally thought. Drishti is a suspect now,' said Manash.

'Suspect for what?'

'They think Tara might have been abducted by Drishti, or perhaps that this is in fact a murder case,' said Atanu, grim.

'What?' she gasped. 'Why?'

'There are so many inconsistencies in the stories, so many things that just don't make sense.'

It was exactly what Drishti had warned her against – but murder? 'I don't understand. Do they have any evidence that Tara is dead?'

'No.'

Relief flooded her body.

'But there is a witness who says he saw Drishti at a hotel an hour before her show,' said Manash. 'She was visiting a man there.'

'Who?'

'They haven't released the name to us. But it seems the ID that he's given to the hotel isn't valid.'

'It's fake?'

'Might be. It was a driver's license with a Delhi address that is no longer where the person or his family lives. It was a rental property that has since been sold by the owners, so they have not been able to trace the family.'

'Who do they think it is?'

'Officially, they aren't saying. But unofficially, they think it is a lover, most likely.'

'So? She had a date. Why is this significant?'

'She had not lied about her morning meeting with one boyfriend, so they are wondering why she was lying about the other. She has maintained from day one that she went straight from her home to the hotel.'

'How do they know it was a lover?'

'The maid describes a man who fits his description, who landed up at the house the previous night. He came just when

Sumita was about to leave for the day, so it was about 8.30 pm. For some reason, Drishti didn't want him in the house, and so she told Sumita to stay while she went out. She said it sounded like they were arguing, something to do with Tara. Apparently, they went downstairs and continued their fight in the parking lot. She was back up in ten minutes, and seemed very upset.'

'The maid didn't hear anything more specific?'

'Apparently not. They didn't seem happy, is what she has said so far. Police are working on her still.'

'How about a description?'

'Dark skinned, white hair.'

'An old man?' asked Atanu. 'That doesn't seem to be her style.'

'Everyone seems to be her style,' said Probal, and Atanu and Manash laughed.

'He isn't old,' said Ahana. The man from the bar. 'The same man had come to the Victoria to look for her a few days ago. He spoke to one of the staff members and got her number. Drishti was apparently very angry.'

'How do you know this?' Manash asked sharply.

'One of the bartenders told me.'

'Why didn't you bring it up earlier?'

'I had no idea how it was connected to anything till now.'

'Ok,' he said, 'as far as we know, this is information that not even the police have. We have to go big with this.'

'Could we try to get the CCTV footage from the Victoria?' asked Ahana.

'They will release it to the police if they ask for it. But to us?' Atanu said.

'Let me give it a shot. I know the owner a little,' said Manash. 'But I don't think we can count on it.'

‘Which hotel was the man staying at?’ asked Ahana.

‘The Chowringhee,’ said Probal.

‘So he has money,’ said Manash.

‘Maybe we can get something from them?’ suggested Ahana.

‘Five-stars usually have tighter standards,’ said Manash. ‘Do you know anyone there?’

‘The PR woman. She’s a nightmare though.’

‘Karishma, right?’

‘Yes. Why don’t you call her too?’ Ahana suggested. ‘She will take it more seriously than if I call.’

He nodded.

Ahana shrugged. ‘I still don’t understand how any of this translates to Tara being dead. What am I missing?’

Manash leaned back in his chair. ‘We only have Drishti’s word that Tara was fine and asleep when she left the house the night of the disappearance. The maid said she didn’t see Drishti when she left. And that she didn’t see Tara either, after they went into the room for bedtime. No one can corroborate Drishti’s version of events. And now, there are holes in it,’ said Probal.

‘Why would Sumita have seen Tara if she had already been asleep when Drishti left the house?’ asked Ahana.

‘The point is that it is Drishti’s word, and her word alone – and her word has very little weight if she is caught in a lie, which she finally has been,’ said Manash. ‘Anything is possible all of a sudden.’

‘Such as?’

‘That Tara is dead. Killed, or that some kind of accident took place.’

‘That’s crazy!’

‘Is it? How can you be sure?’ asked Manash. ‘It is true that the only person who says Tara was in her room that night is Drishti.'

'If no one entered the house, then why was the bedroom door open later when the maid came out of the room and went in to check on her?' Ahana asked.

'Could have opened on its own. Doors do that sometimes,' Atanu pointed out. 'Maybe it was open all along, and the maid didn't notice.'

'But none of the rest of it makes sense.'

'It does if Drishti was trying to paint a very specific picture in the mind of the police,' said Manash.

'She's not like that!' said Ahana, unable to keep it in any longer. The one thing she had not wanted to say.

She caught the looks of pity on the faces of Manash and Atanu, the smug look on Probal's. 'It is like they are coming up with a story that lets them off the hook for not finding Tara,' she said.

'There is some evidence to back it up,' said Atanu softly.

'Like what?' she said.

'Traces of blood,' said Probal.

'All of a sudden they produce blood after saying for days that there was no sign of violence?' asked Ahana.

'How much blood?' Manash asked Probal.

'I don't know, they haven't said as yet.'

'Was it enough blood to indicate a nosebleed, a small cut or a violent crime? She did live there, after all, there are other possibilities,' said Ahana, hating how shrill she sounded.

He shrugged. 'They are working on this angle now.'

Atanu leaned back in his chair, arms stretched back, hands on the crown of his head.

'The timing does seem convenient, doesn't it?' he mused. 'Such a sudden swing in theories, based on nothing more than traces of a child's blood in her own home, and a sighting of her mother at a hotel.' He looked from face to face sitting across from him in the unblinking manner that usually made Ahana squirm. Now, it could not even touch the raging emotion inside her.

'They aren't looking into this man for the kidnapping?' he asked Probal.

'They are. They are also considering that he may be the father.'

Manash turned to her. 'I still don't understand why Drishti isn't willing to come clean with the identity of the father.'

'Must be married,' said Probal.

'Maybe,' said Ahana with a shrug, 'Though that sort of thing doesn't bother her. She sees it as a distraction, a waste of time, since she knows it couldn't have been him. She also does not see it as anyone's business.'

'But he is now a suspect. That makes it very much the business of the police.'

Ahana left the meeting and stopped in the hallway to catch her breath. In the span of twenty minutes, Drishti had gone from a tragic figure to prime suspect in the disappearance of her own daughter.

And Ahana would be the one to break it to her. She knew she'd have to be careful with how much she said; she didn't want to tip Drishti off about the police's new direction. No matter what she felt about the situation, she had to establish some boundaries. But at the same time, Ahana felt she owed Drishti something – though she was not sure what.

When Ahana finally called back, the police had left, and Drishti seemed calmer.

'I can't say exactly what they were looking for,' Ahana said, choosing her words with care, 'but I do know they have been looking into a man who had visited your house the day before Tara went missing.'

There was a beat. 'Yes, they do a lot of wondering about the men in my life,' she said with a harsh laugh. 'Much more than I ever did.'

'Drishti, I am telling you this as a friend: the secrets aren't doing you any favours at this point. It is going to have to come out. Especially if you want to stay out of trouble.'

'You might be right. But you know what? They haven't asked me about that man, or anyone else yet. The police are no better than the gossiping aunties in the building.'

'What about the father?' she said softly. 'They've asked you about him before – was it him?'

Drishti was silent.

'You saw this coming, Drishti. That's why you spoke to me yesterday. You were right; things have changed. Give them what they want – they won't let go till you do.'

She hung up. Ahana stood in the tube-lit hallway, her hands trembling and her body covered in sweat, despite the AC blasting right above her.

The puzzle of Drishti's life was cobbled together as much as it was concocted, prised as much as it was stolen. As Drishti became the primary suspect in the kidnap – or murder? – of her own child, every detail became fair game.

The *Tribune* finally ran the description of the man from the bar, believed to be the same man who landed up at Drishti's doorstep the night before the disappearance, the same man she had met before the show, on the night that Tara went missing. The bartender's account – his description of the man who had come for Drishti and her reaction on learning about it – were significant revelations at the time, and the police did follow up with questions of their own.

The police also released news of the sensational revelations from the maid's latest interview; and the media covered little else the next morning.

'Day 0', as one national channel called it, began when Tara and Drishti woke up around 7 am, and Drishti dropped her daughter off at school by 8.20 am. Then she went to buy vegetables (cauliflower and brinjal) and meat (mutton leg); the next day they were expecting friends to come for dinner. She was back at home in time for the cook to arrive at 9.45 am. ('Why would she be buying mutton that day if her friends were coming the next?' asked one anchor. 'On a Thursday, where would she be buying meat anyway?' asked another. 'How could she be shopping for a dinner party the day she planned to abduct her own daughter?' asked no one.) The maid was cleaning the house at that time and remembered that Drishti received a phone call soon after, quickly showered and left again.

When she returned, it was noon. According to Sumita's account, she had a cup of tea and did some work on her computer, which was in her bedroom. At 1 pm, she left to pick up Tara, and about thirty minutes later, they came back and had lunch together. Sumita tried to put Tara down for a nap, but she wouldn't sleep, so Drishti and Tara did some painting together. It was a beach scene – they had recently got back from Goa – and the artwork had gone on the refrigerator alongside its companion piece made the day before.

Sumita then took Tara down to the park, and she came back in time for the child's bath at 5.30 pm. Tara had dinner around 6.30 pm, and was asleep by 7.30 pm. And then Drishti left for the evening.

The question of where she had been in the hour or so preceding her concert was the big one. Manash had been unable to get CCTV footage from the owner of the Victoria or from the public relations manager at the Chowringhee, but the information about the mystery man had been passed on to the police. There was a gag order on communication with the press, enforced by DCDD II Vinayak Agarwal, but details did not take long to leak. Drishti had maintained from the beginning that on the night of Tara's disappearance, she had gone straight to the hotel for the show, but this no longer appeared to be true. She had very clearly arrived at the Victoria at 9.30 pm, just in time for her set. It would have taken her a maximum of forty minutes in evening traffic to reach the hotel from home. Even giving her the benefit of the doubt, there was an hour of unaccounted time.

Her morning meeting, which she made no effort to hide, was with Suresh Vardhan, well known in social circles to be a player. He and his wife lived separately though they were still married, at least legally. She went to his home, and there was much speculation that they were a couple. Drishti and Suresh neither confirmed nor denied their relationship status, but did admit to being together at the time, and there was CCTV footage from his building proving it.

During that news cycle, the speculation went two ways: Drishti was being quite open about an assignation with a married man the very morning of her daughter's disappearance, so whatever she was hiding about the evening meeting had to be worse, much worse. There was the camp that went so far as to say that she must be a prostitute; simply being a woman of questionable character couldn't cover the true debauchery of taking two lovers in the same day. There was another opinion – seemingly shared by the police – that the second meeting was not a date, that she and the silver-haired man at the hotel had conspired in some way, that she had removed her own daughter from the bedroom already – alive or dead – and together they had either faked her abduction or disposed of her, and concocted an elaborate scheme to hide it.

'I was not in the hall when Drishti madam left the house, so I didn't see her go,' said Sumita in her statement to the police. 'I didn't go into the room to check on Tara. Why would I? Only if she had called out I would have gone in to check on her.' Tara had been asleep in Drishti's room, as was her custom. Tara had her own room with her own bed, but it was seldom used, except for daytime naps.

Sumita also said that Drishti usually called out to her before leaving the house. But that day, she didn't. Instead, she hurried out without saying goodbye or leaving any instructions.

'Drishti had a car. What would be easier for her than to carry her child sleeping – or otherwise – downstairs, cover her with a blanket in the backseat, and take her elsewhere?' she went so far as to suggest.

The speculators had sorted out the how. Now the question was, why?

Those that still believed that Tara had been kidnapped, advanced a theory that it was all an elaborate scheme to extract ransom from the father of the child, or perhaps Drishti's own father. It was suggested that both the men had refused to support her and this was the only way. In actual fact, Drishti's own father had been ready to support her, and she had never asked the child's biological father for support. But the reportage of the time had scant regard for the facts.

The proponents of the parallel theory had Drishti murdering Tara in her own bed. Why would she do such a thing? Perhaps the post-partum depression had made a comeback; perhaps Drishti was simply tired of being a single mother and this was a way out, perhaps she was in a serious relationship with the silver-haired man and this was a demand he placed on her; perhaps she was pure evil.

'Drishti didn't seem herself that evening,' said Indra Kedia, a member of the audience at the Victoria on the night Tara disappeared, as interviewed by *Tarar Khonje*. 'She was flustered even before the call came from home.'

Her bandmates and Bunty both rubbished these claims. But Drishti's friends were considered the least reliable sources, being biased at best and accomplices at worst.

'The police came to my home,' said Bunty. 'My presence at the thana that first night made me a suspect. They seemed to think we were involved romantically.'

Bunty had additional reason to be fearful of the police in those days – he was gay and he lived with his partner Ashish Soni, a prominent city banker. 'Ashish wasn't home when the police came,' Bunty recalled. 'I told them I had a flatmate, and though they did take his name and details, they didn't get around to contacting him.'

Things were moving fast in those days.

Day 11

Good Wife

Ahana felt unsettled and upside down. Back in office the next day, her arm finally better, she needed to regroup, to find a new angle. So she began to plough through the boxes of letters from fans that Drishti had sent over to her parents' house that morning. She'd forwarded some emails, too, the ones that seemed noteworthy. Any fan who wrote repeatedly, or had made overly personal comments. The letters pertaining to the political protests and subsequent case against her were also all in the box.

'Indecency' is what the Preserve Calcutta Heritage

Committee had accused her of, a year before. The letter was dated just a week after she had appeared in a concert hosted to protest police brutality in North Bengal. The letter described her outfit on the occasion as objectionable – it was jeans and a sleeveless tank top. Her dancing – which any objective witness would have described at best as keeping time – was allegedly an affront too.

Ahana looked through the *Tribune*'s digital archives to find any mention of other complaints made by the PCHC. And there they were – protests against singers, actresses (never actors), and writers. She wondered at such dedication to a cause. Prabir Das would be in his sixties at least, perhaps even older. While it was tempting to consider him as a suspect, perhaps in cahoots with younger, more able-bodied activists, it just didn't seem right. He seemed to be nothing more or less than a crotchety old man with too much time on his hands. And the police had ruled him out anyhow.

So it was on to the fan mail. In all, there were hundreds of letters dating back several years. Ahana wondered that Drishti had kept them all. Many were innocuous. There were several writers who had kept up a flow of correspondence, a couple of whom were early fans who watched her career grow with pleasure. A handful of letters made a reference to the Drishti Sengupta Fan Club. Ahana had no idea such a thing even existed and kept these letters aside. There was another angry fan who accused her of selling out by 'going Bollywood', abandoning her unique sound. Then there were letters from fans who had seen her on TV and in the press, speaking about being a single mother, who expressed displeasure.

These caught Ahana's attention. There was one fan in particular, whose letters after learning about Tara's birth status was particularly disturbing:

Drishti,

I saw you walk into your building the other day. You ran your hand through your hair, and I wondered why I ever thought you were beautiful. Your hair is too short and your skin is too dark for you to be a beauty. And I realized that what I want in a woman is so different from you. I want a woman who would be a good wife, and I don't think you would ever be that. Then I saw you leaving with your child, and I knew there was no point wasting my time on a shameless woman like you.

A former fan

It made Ahana's skin crawl and she quickly called Drishti. 'Have you heard from this guy again?'

'No,' said Drishti. 'I don't think so. That letter describes a news story that happened just a month prior. So although it sounds like it, I don't think he was watching me in person, just on TV.'

'Oh.'

'Yeah. I should have kept my mouth shut.'

Ahana cringed. She could ignore it no longer. 'I assume you saw the *Tribune* piece this morning.' Probal's piece on Drishti's newfound status as suspect in the disappearance, and possible murder, of her own daughter, had dominated the front page of the *Tribune* and every other city newspaper.

'Yes. It's the job, I get it. I don't expect you to champion my cause, Ahana. It's not I who needs a champion. I just need you to remember Tara.'

Ahana got back to the carton, and discovered a photo collage at the bottom of the pile, containing Drishti's photographs from magazines and newspapers. Two A4 sheets covered with clippings. On one, there was a line of text at the bottom:

'Not everyone understands you. But I do.'

Ahana studied the photos – they started as far back as five or six years ago. Most of the photographs Ahana was familiar with, thanks to the media flashing every available image of the singer with every news bulletin. But there were some that seemed new. Ahana checked the date on the envelope; it had been sent about a year ago. The new photographs – a series of three taken during a concert, from slightly different angles – looked to be from the Victoria. Ahana realized that they weren't clippings at all but actual photographs on cheap photo paper. The sender hadn't provided any name or contact details, but there was a return address on the envelope for a street in Calcutta she wasn't familiar with.

That was when Manash approached her. He looked over her desk, covered in letters. He picked up the collage.

'What are you doing? What are these?' he asked.

'Fan letters Drishti received over the past few years.'

'Anything interesting?'

'Some of this stuff is seriously creepy, like that collage, but no smoking gun.'

He sat on the seat next to her desk and sighed. 'Look, I know you are trying to help, but this is a job for the police detectives.'

'I just wanted to see if I could find something.'

'I understand – it is hard, especially since you know her and all that. But you need to find a way to separate yourself from it somehow.'

'What's the harm in looking? The police have taken some of this stuff too.'

'The harm is that you will burn yourself out. You don't have the tools or the skills to launch a parallel investigation. What you need to do is stay focussed on your sources as the situation emerges. The interview is the primary tool for you as a reporter. Use it.'

She bristled. 'Ok.' And then, in her own defence, she asked: 'Have you heard of the Drishti Sengupta Fan Club?'

'No,' he replied.

'There seems to be one,' she said, pointing to the pile of letters.

'Good,' he said, 'Check them out.' He stood up. 'You have exceeded everyone's expectations,' he said gently.

'That is great for me, but Drishti is being accused of killing her own child.'

'That is not your doing.'

'Is the CBI coming in on this?'

'There is still some fighting. But it looks as though it is going to happen, the CM is backing down finally.'

Ahana headed to the tea stall on the street in front of the building, in an effort to fortify herself. Instead, she ended up with a lungful of dust from the road, and tea that was too sweet. She lit a cigarette and fielded several questions about the 'Drishti interview' from journalists who were standing around. As she slurped her scalding tea in an effort to get out of there as fast as she could, she got a call from an unknown number.

'Hello?' she said.

'It's Sagar.'

She was so surprised she didn't reply at once.

'Hello?'

'Yes, I'm here. You got yourself a cell phone,' she said.

'Nope. Just borrowing a friend's till I get my landline. I needed to speak to you about something.'

'Now?'

'In person.'

'Would you like to come to the office?'

'No. Somewhere more private.'

'I can come to your place tomorrow,' she suggested.

'It is fairly urgent. It is about Drishti.'

She would have suggested the bar, but given his status as recovering alcoholic, she thought better of it. 'My place?'

'If you are comfortable with it, I can come there now.'

'I'll text you the address.'

Sagar was coming from his *mofussil* home, so it would take him at least an hour and a half to reach. Which suited her well, because she needed some time. She told Manash that she had to go. 'I have to meet someone. An interview,' she said with a wry smile.

He grinned. 'Well done. Who is it?'

'It might be nothing,' she said. 'I'll tell you if anything comes of it.'

He nodded. 'If all your targets bear fruit, you know you aren't pushing yourself enough.'

As she picked up her bag, she winced.

'You are in pain, still?' he asked.

'A little.'

'Don't come back then today. You have to rest.'

Just then, Probal approached Manash's desk. 'Leaving?' he asked her.

'I've got a meeting.'

'You might want to see this first.' He pulled a document out of a folder and handed it to Manash.

'What's this?' Manash asked, his eyes wide.

'Tara Sengupta's birth certificate.'

Ahana got home and collapsed into a chair in front of the TV.

She had no clue what she was watching for the next thirty minutes, but she finally stirred in time to straighten up – her maid had come and cleaned while she was gone, but there were still books and clothes scattered everywhere. She was just getting the tea on when the doorbell rang.

She opened it and there stood Sagar, at her home for the first time, dressed again in kurta, jeans and chappals. Her heart was pounding as she invited him in. 'Take a seat,' she said. 'Tea?'

He nodded, but instead of sitting, he followed her into the kitchen. It was small enough without his tall frame in there. She felt inordinately aware of every single action and was mortified to find herself jittery.

'How was the drive?' she asked.

'You get used to it.'

'I think commuting is the one thing I'd rather do without.'

'Well, I don't commute on a daily basis. At least not yet.'

'You said you were on a break.'

He nodded. 'Haven't decided what is next.'

They took their cups and went to the living room, where her arrangement of cheap mattress covered with bedsheets and throw pillows was what passed for a sofa, with a couple of cane chairs on the side. She loved her home, sparse and bare as it was.

Sagar sat on the mattress. She thought it would be awkward sitting on the chair and looking down at him, so she carefully arranged herself on the other side, as far away as possible.

And then, suddenly, without warning, he spoke.

'I am officially Tara's father.'

She knew his eyes were on her. She took a sip of her tea before she spoke. 'What do you mean, officially?'

'You don't seem surprised.'

'Did you expect me to be?'

'Touché.'

'How did you know my colleague had unearthed the birth certificate?'

'Because the school clerk called me and tried to extort me for his silence.'

'Really?'

'Your colleague paid quite handsomely for it. The price to outbid him was beyond my modest farmer's means.'

'Jesus.'

'Yeah.'

'So why are we here?'

'You know half of the story. You might as well know the rest of it.'

'I would like to record this.'

He thought about this for a moment, and then gave a nod. She pulled her recorder from her bag, and turned it on.

'Drishti had been very clear that she didn't want the biological father's name on any paperwork. Which meant she never could apply for a birth certificate for Tara.'

'Why not?'

'You need both parents' names, and in the event the parents' are not married, there is a long, convoluted process involved. So Drishti went without it, for as long as she could, which was till it was time for Tara to go to school.'

'Then?'

'There is a provision for single mothers to get a birth certificate: they need to essentially get guardianship of their own child by getting a letter from the father saying he doesn't object to it.'

'Ok. Ridiculous, but ok.'

'Drishti didn't want to tell the real father. So I was the stand in.'

'How could you do that?'

'It was all quite simple – it isn't like they wanted a DNA test or anything. I simply said I was the father and that Drishti could be granted guardianship. There was an affidavit, if I remember correctly. Which is how my name came to be on Tara's birth certificate.'

'Ok. So why are you telling me this now?'

'The police know about this now. Drishti didn't say anything because she didn't want to get me involved, but I don't see a way out anymore.'

'You want to go public with this story?'

'It is coming out anyway. I need you to get the whole truth out because it is about to get much more messy.'

'Do you think the real father had something to do with this? Is that what is going on here?'

He didn't say anything.

'Who is it?'

'Honestly, I don't know. Drishti is the most frustratingly pig-headed woman I have ever met when she wants to be. Drisnti is going to be arrested, and she can't even see it. But if she goes to jail, who will fight for Tara?'

'If you know who it is, you should speak out now.'

'I don't. Either way, these are not my secrets to tell.'

She threw her hands up in frustration. 'Again with the secrets! There is no room for secrets in a murder investigation!'

He stood and paced the room. In a moment, he turned to her. 'Put this out there. What I said. It is true after all.'

'And then?'

'If the police come for me, maybe it buys her some time.'

'She needs to come clean.'

'She thinks that all this stuff about paternity is a distraction that is keeping the cops from looking for Tara.'

'At the moment it is just the opposite. Are the police likely to let go till they have put together the pieces?'

'Hopefully she sees that now.'

'I would need to speak to Drishti about your account, to get her version of the story.'

'Go ahead. As I said, it is the truth.'

'What if she says that you are indeed the real father?'

He gave her a look she couldn't read, rubbing his day old stubble with his long fingers. 'It is against her code to lie.'

'Tara's birth certificate says otherwise.'

'That's different – she wouldn't be held hostage by the system. The law about single mothers is archaic and misogynistic and she sees no harm in what she did because it was a way around that. But, she would never throw me under the bus to save another man. Or whatever else she thinks she is doing by keeping her mouth shut about his identity.'

'Well, now I really do need to know what the nature of your relationship with Drishti has been.'

'Oh, we were never together. I have known her for years and years, and she came to me after giving birth, when she was in the throes of post-partum depression. I referred her to a friend, because I couldn't be her therapist. And then, I chose to be the fake father of her child. I saw myself as a godfather.'

'And you really don't know the name of the real father?'

'No,' he said. 'Believe it or not. Drishti is very good at keeping secrets. But the police have asked her for a narcoanalysis. They will get it out of her one way or another.'

'If she is innocent, what is the problem?'

And then she saw it, the flicker of doubt.

'Oh my god, you're not sure she is innocent, are you?'

'That's not it.'

'Don't lie to me. Again.'

'It is not a matter of guilt or innocence. We are all guilty of something. The question is, of what?'

30 August 1996

Pulling up her shirt, taking her nipple in his mouth there, right there, was the most exhilarating moment he could remember. Despite the darkness, he knew that anyone might see them, and it fuelled his lust. As though he needed it. But to her, it seemed to make no difference. So self-contained was she in that moment, as she seemed to be in every other, that the possibility of others witnessing their act, already a transgression, didn't matter. And a little part of him would, and had, always hated her for it. His adultery could never taint her.

His mouth on her breast, his eyes open, he thought he saw movement, somewhere. Nothing more than a flutter. It could have been leaves, it could have been a curtain, it could have been a cat.

He pulled away and saw in her eyes that stopping wasn't an option. She would have thought nothing of continuing, on the park bench in her complex, where they had come to 'chat' after her show, if that were possible. As though anyone could have kept him away from her after that kiss on the golf course.

'Can we go upstairs?' he said.

She straightened her clothes and stood up, taking him by the hand and walking towards the building. As soon as the lift doors had closed, his mouth was back on hers.

They didn't leave the house for three days after that. He couldn't remember the details of those drunken days, looking back. Sex, of course. And lies. Nightly lies when his wife called, calls which he was very careful not to take in front of Drishti.

The chronological chain of events might be lost, but they

had never really mattered in the first place. Their essence was imprinted on his soul. And then there were fragments from their letters, from their earliest encounters, memories laid on top of each other, to complete the image he carried of her and those days spent wrapped around each other. Time had no meaning when it came to Drishti.

What had made it so hard for him to get up and get as far as possible from that flat? He had known even then he wasn't going to leave his wife. But if she had expected him to, he wouldn't have been able to stop himself.

'It doesn't need to be perfect to be good enough,' he had said.

'But that just sounds like you are settling.'

'How is that a bad thing? All it proves is that you are willing to adjust to reality. To adapt. Perfection is only ever about how you would wish things to be, regardless of the facts.'

'Reality and fantasy can never be one?'

Had she actually asked that, like a fourteen-year-old with her first crush? Was she really so naïve, so idealistic? 'Fantasy, once real, fades fast.'

And on and on went their conversations. Round and round the same circles, with him pushing her to demand more, and her pushing the very notion of him away.

What is it about love on the brink that is so wildly addictive? Every look, every breath, every intonation, charged with possibility. The lip-swelling, nipple-hardening, blood-pumping anticipation of touch; the hunger that the first fleeting moments bring, heightened by every breath till there is only one possible end. Or so you hope.

To live in that moment is to know desire, but also to ignore its aftermath. It is to be so close that the body forgets the mind. It is to be free.

'This is the moment I want to live in. Any further will simply ruin it,' she said.

'That works in one of your songs. Not in real life.'

'That's why I walk away.'

'Walk away from this. If you can,' he said, kissing her.

And then there is a moment where desire tips over. To stretch it out makes it an ugly, violent thing. And he was a fool for holding on, in the absence of the softening glow of love. But he wanted to live in its beauty. If only for a night.

Day 12

The Final Piece

Ahana had worked, during one of her summer placements from business school, in the back office of the Chowringhee. She had returned there, degree in hand, for her first real job, occupying the lowest possible position of business sales executive. The sheen had worn off fast when she found herself selling loyalty cards over the phone to rich businessmen. When she received a more lucrative offer selling soap in B-towns across the east, she had jumped at the chance to get out of what had become her own private, 5-star prison.

But she still had friends there, a fact Manash had forgotten and which Ahana had kept on the down low. Once it was known you had contacts in a place, you were constantly expected to milk them till the udder ran dry.

Now, she knew it was time to call in whatever favours she could. The Tara case had put her on a path she had not foreseen. It also gave her the chance to fail in ways she could not have as a lifestyle reporter. She knew the price for being wrong: she could see it in Probal's preening form. He resented her interview with Sagar, taking some of the victory out of his acquisition of the prized birth certificate, though he hid it under the same superciliousness he applied to everything.

So when Ahana walked into the lobby of the Chowringhee, there was more at stake than there had ever been. She went straight to the front desk manager, who had been told to expect her.

'Salil,' she said, introducing herself. 'Sanjana may have told you I'd be coming?'

'Yes,' he said. There was the merest pause before he flashed her the company-required smile. 'I'll be with you in just a moment.'

Salil went to attend to a guest who was standing at the desk. It was 3 pm, and the check-ins and check-outs for the day would have mostly happened already. She waited. She could tell he was biding his time; even after the guest left he was fiddling around on the computer. Then he finally looked up, smiled again, and returned to her.

'Sanjana asked me to help you,' said Salil, voice low. 'But I don't know if I can.'

She gave him a sympathetic smile. He seemed terribly young. 'I know it's tough, but it is for a good cause – to help find a missing child.' She felt a stab of guilt.

'I could lose my job if someone found out it was me.'

'You know I won't tell anyone. We protect our sources at the *Tribune*. Think of that girl – this could really help find her.'

If you tell the lie enough times, it starts to look and feel like the truth.

He nervously looked around. 'I have a family to support.'

'And that won't change. Look, I used to work here too. There is no way they can track this back to you.'

'I don't know.'

'You see how much the police are doing – they are doing nothing. If we all wait and do nothing as well, what will become of Tara? Help me find this man, and in the process you help her too.'

'I'll have to think about it.'

She felt him slipping away. She thought of Probal.

'Look, Sanjana tells me you like music. How about if I get you passes for the A.R. Rahman concert next month? Two tickets. Good seats.'

She saw a gleam in his eye. 'Can you make it four tickets?'

She pretended to think about it. 'That will be harder.'

'Then I can take my parents too.'

She smiled, suddenly munificent. 'Okay. Done.'

'Okay,' he said, looking around again. How she wished he wouldn't do that. 'You wanted his name?'

'Yes, that is all.'

'Give me an hour. I'll message it to you.'

That hour came and went and there was no news from Salil. Her texts went unanswered, and she had to assume that he had chickened out. She was on the phone for the rest of the day, following up with all her sources, looking for any stray leads that might unlock a new direction. She did her best to avoid Probal.

And then, at 6 pm, when she thought she'd have an early night, she heard Atanu's bellow.

As she ran into his room, there, on the TV was a picture of Tara. She wore a blue dress. BREAKING NEWS erupted across the bottom quadrant of the screen, and then there was a split screen too, and Ranadeep was on TV, beside the photo of Tara. 'The picture sent to us over email,' he announced, 'along with one line: "She's alive".'

Ahana was flooded with relief a moment before the confusion hit.

'What could this mean? There is no demand for ransom, no mention of how she might be returned to her family. The photo, as far as we know, was only sent to *Tarar Khonje*, and not even to the parents,' bellowed Ranadeep.

'We appeal to whoever sent this – bring Tara back to her mother. Reunite this family and end their misery.'

'Have you seen this photograph before?' Manash asked her.

She shook her head. She'd gone through every public picture of Tara every day since the search had begun. This was not one of them. She looked more tired and skinny than she did in other photos, though she seemed clean and healthy.

'There is nothing to indicate when it was taken,' said Atanu.

'Aren't they supposed to make victims hold up a newspaper or something?' she said.

'The kidnapper doesn't watch the same movies as you,' said Atanu. 'Start your follow-up,' he said.

Probal spent the next twenty minutes trying to get hold of his police sources, who finally confirmed that the photograph had only been sent to the news channel. Now only Drishti could tell them if that photo was a new one, and she was not answering Ahana's calls.

She dialled, once, twice, and could feel every shrill ring down to her toes. Ahana closed her eyes and all she saw was that photo, and she knew that right at that moment, Drishti was looking at it too. Even the effort to intrude on that moment left her revolted. After the sixth try, she gave up.

But finally, someone did respond. Ahana's cellphone sprung to life with a message from Salil. She opened it, fingers trembling in anticipation. It contained only two words. 'Vidyut Desai.'

Vidyut Desai? The name was vaguely familiar.

She did a search of the digital archives and found nothing. Next, she stood in line for the only computer on the floor with Internet access, waiting behind three others before she finally had a crack at it.

She typed in the name and the results were many. But it only took her a few moments to figure out exactly who Vidyut Desai was.

She called Manash over to the computer. She had an article open, with a photograph.

'Silicon Valley millionaire?' he said, scrolling down, stopping to study the photo. He had distinctly salt-and-pepper hair, set off by beautifully even, dark skin. His face was slender and his nose sharp. His hair was cut short, and he had a lean, compact look about him. He was very attractive, and he matched the bartender's description perfectly.

'This is the man?'

'I think so,' said Ahana. 'Though I can't find anything to connect him to Drishti, or even to Calcutta.'

‘They could have met anywhere,’ he said. ‘She must perform all over.’

‘That’s only recently.’ Ahana couldn’t take her eyes off the photograph. ‘He could be the father. Tara looks like him.’

Manash nodded. ‘If he is the father, the entire ransom thing makes more sense.’

‘The kidnapper knew who he was.’

Manash shot her a look, and she knew he too was now viewing Drishti as a suspect.

‘But where is the demand?’ she asked. She pulled up a black swivel chair beside him and collapsed into it. ‘Perhaps it has been made privately and we don’t know?’ he suggested.

‘What can we write that is not speculation?’

‘Not a lot. But we can reveal his identity.’

‘The police must know – they have this information.’

‘It is possible. But maybe they haven’t made the connection. Any chance of getting Drishti to comment?’

‘I tried calling her – no answer. I also tried calling Vidyut Desai.’

‘What? How?’

‘His Palo Alto office phone number was listed online.’

Now he really looked impressed. ‘Shabash. And?’

‘His office told me that he wasn’t available. That he was out of the country.’

‘In India?’

‘That they wouldn’t say.’

‘Well done, Ahana.’

‘Still not a lot to go on.’

‘It is enough. Drum it out. Good work.’

The unmasking of Vidyut Desai had the power to shift the way the entire case was perceived.

If *he* was the father, it would explain Drishti's desire for secrecy: he was married and amid tech circles, famous for being a maverick, a serial founder of companies collectively valued at over a billion dollars. It would also explain why Tara would be the target of a kidnapper, and this was the refrain that exploded across screens after the *Tribune* article hit the stands. How could Drishti keep this explosive fact from authorities when it had real bearing on the case? It could only be because she was, in some way complicit. Vidyut was, after all, a millionaire many times over. There was suddenly a lot to lose, and gain, for anyone potentially involved, including Drishti.

Several conspiracy theories were born in the days that followed, and lingered for years to come. 'Faked kidnapping gone wrong', was the big one, the obvious one. Perhaps Drishti had made financial demands of him, and, finding him unsympathetic, had orchestrated this charade to get him to pay.

A sample: 'Drishti tasted fame and fortune, but all too briefly. The money from her hit songs had dried up and she learned that bringing up a child is an expensive affair. So she reached out to the father. Frightened of exposure, he went into denial mode and refused any help or any association with Tara. So, Drishti created this fake kidnapping scheme. There may be others involved, but she herself is the mastermind.'

But the frenzy grew greedily to accommodate an even more

scandalous possibility: that Vidyut and Drishti were in on it together. Say he wasn't Tara's father? Say the child was suddenly the third wheel in a cross-continental adulterous romance? Then what? Or perhaps the two of them had killed the child to protect Vidyut's considerable fortune. If his wife sued for divorce, he might lose millions. If Drishti and Vidyut had been in a clandestine relationship for years, the child was inconvenient evidence of that affair. The reports purported that Tara could have been in the car, dead, when Drishti had left her home that night. That the photograph that had been sent to *Tarar Khonje* was from an earlier time, designed to relieve Drishti of the pressure building up around her. How the faked kidnapping could help conceal their involvement was anyone's guess. But no one cared about motive when the scandal was so very lucratively scandalous. They were in love, so desperately in love, and that can sometimes make you sloppy. Not to mention murderous. Though it was hard to argue for Drishti's innocence in those days, the hypothesis presented by the shrill media hardly stood up to scrutiny.

Drishti had said, and records confirmed, that she had given her car to the valet at Vidyut's five-star hotel. The hotel had provided CCTV footage to the police as well, and sources said there was no sign that she was overly concerned or distressed at this time, and there was definitely no sign of a child in the car. But none of it was any use to Drishti, as it made no difference to the actual investigation. Those were the days before mandatory security checks in hotels, and so the police said it could not rule out that Tara's body was in the back the entire time. So cold and calm was Drishti, allegedly, that she thought nothing of handing over the car keys to a stranger with her dead child in it.

The searches also stepped up pace – Drishti's flat, her parent's home in Salt Lake, Vidyut's hotel room and the taxi he took to the airport. Apart from Sumita, they found another eyewitness to the argument between Drishti and Vidyut at Surya Apartments: an elderly lady on an evening walk. She hadn't seemed to think it was a fight at first, but after a few hours with the police, her statement fit into their story far better: there had been raised voices, there may have been a push or two, both ways; at the end of it, there had been an embrace. Why conspirators in such a heinous scheme would choose to argue in public was never questioned.

With facts thin on the ground, anyone's theory could hold water, even if only for the space of a fifteen-minute news broadcast. Or at the police headquarters. Drishti's arrest seemed imminent.

Day 13

True Fan

Ahana fled her parents' house after a morning of bickering between her mom and her aunt about ashirbad – the formal blessing of the bride-rituals according to 'her' side of the family. Her mother insisted that she was on top of things, and her jyethima, arbiter of all matters family as the 'elder', insisted she was getting it all wrong.

Far worse was when Ahana tried on the blouse that had come back from the tailor, and the sleeve would not go over her still swollen arm.

'Bonnie, this just won't do!' screamed her mother. 'The

engagement is just a breath away!'

'There is still time for the swelling to go down.'

'And if doesn't?'

'I'll wear jeans.'

A barrage of frustrated regret at having mothered her whizzed by Ahana's head as she was getting ready to leave. She escaped to the comfort of fumes spewing directly into her face in the black-and-yellow taxi that she boarded five minutes later.

Finally, when she reached her destination, she had a pounding headache.

'I won't go into that goli,' the taxi driver said, pulling over abruptly.

'Please, dada. It's not a goli, it's a road.'

He was impassive. She handed over the money.

'Khuchro nei,' he barked.

She rummaged through her bag. No way would she pay extra. She handed him notes and more coins than was perhaps decent and jumped out – and straight into a puddle.

She cursed as she shook her chappalled and now-wet salwared foot, and began the trudge down what was unmistakably a goli, with puddles of unknown depth on both sides. She tried to walk down the middle of the road, but was constantly pushed into the water by passing carts, hand-pulled rickshaws, cars, and then, improbably, a 16-wheel flatbed truck.

She had to stop to ask for directions a few times, and was finally pointed towards a narrow black gate. She pushed it open and walked up three thick black stone steps into a narrow corridor.

There was no sign, but it matched the description of the offices of the Drishti Sengupta Fan Club, the phone number of which she had tracked down the night before. She had contacted the founder and he had provided only the vaguest possible answers to her questions then, but had far more enthusiastically invited her for a meeting the next morning. She had hoped to finish the business over the phone, but that wasn't to be.

There was an office at the end of the hall, with a two-panelled door of green-painted wood. Ahana pushed open one side and peered in. The walls were thick, the windows small with metal bars across it. It smelled of damp and drain.

She didn't know what to expect from the convenor of a fan club. What she found was a man, possibly in his late thirties, sitting behind a desk crowded with papers and boxes. He looked surprisingly corporate, dressed in a white shirt and grey trousers.

'Rahul Bhaduri?'

He nodded. 'Come come. You got wet.'

'Yes,' she said. 'Waterlogging.'

She took a seat on the plastic chair opposite him. There was a large framed photograph of him with Zakir Ali Khan on the wall, another with several newspaper clippings. 'You are the president of the Drishti Sengupta Fan Club?' she asked, taking her notepad and pen out of her bag.

'Yes. Founder-president.'

'How did you become such a fan of her music?' she asked. It seemed an unlikely fit.

'Actually, we first started the fan club for Zakir Khan sir. And from there, we started clubs for other personalities, according to members' wishes.'

'How many of them are there now?'

He took mental stock. 'Twelve, thirteen?'

'That's a lot!'

He gave her a smug grin. 'Ours is a very large organization.'

'How do you manage it all?'

'There is a secretary as well.'

'And who are these other stars for whom you have clubs?'

He rattled off a list of the most popular actors of the time, and a couple of actresses too. There was one other musician, responsible for at least half of the biggest hits of the past thirty years.

'Drishti definitely seems like the odd one on that list,' she said.

'Why?'

'She is hardly as big a star as the others. She is just beginning her career.'

'You are right,' he said, as though he had never considered this before.

'Can you remember how it came about?'

'It is not so long ago. That song of hers picturized on Neha was just too good. We were all very big fans of that movie.'

'And there were protests around her too at about that time.'

'Yes, I remember that. That was a bit of a problem.'

'Why?'

'Some of our members felt we should shut down.'

'Why is that?'

'See, madam, we are not a political organization. I said this to the reporters at the time also, we are simply fans of music and films, and we want to celebrate the artistes that we feel strongly about.'

'But you were her fan club – no need to have gotten involved with the politics.'

'Some of our members attended the rallies supporting Drishti. They were featured by some news channels, which others did not like.'

'Did any of the objections have to do with her status as a single mother?'

He shook his head and clucked. 'We do not get into the personal lives of any of our stars.'

'Really?'

'Never. Not when Zakir sir was accused of abuse by his wife, not when Sona ma'am had that accident in Goa. We don't want to encourage the kind of fan who likes gossiping and such things.'

'That is very refreshing. Do all your members feel the same way? Do you have meetings?'

'Yes, always. Once a month. If our members don't agree with our policy, they don't complain about it in public.'

'How many people attend?'

'It depends on what is happening. Sometimes, we get discounted tickets for movie shows, that time we have lot of participants. Maybe 400, 500 people come. And some of our groups are quite active in other projects. Like when we put up the Zakir sir bust in Tollygunge, and when we had the Prakash Roshan puja, when he was in hospital and seemed very serious.'

'Are there separate meetings for each of the fan clubs?'

'The bigger ones, yes. But the Drishti group does not meet separately – usually it will be a few members meeting on the sidelines of another event.'

'You have never done any event just around her?'

'No, but with her child going missing, there have been a lot of emails going around. About how we can help, whether we can approach the police to volunteer.'

'And?'

'Finally, nothing happened, but we did send her an email with our support for her.'

'Did she respond?'

'No.' He seemed miffed.

'And now that she is the focus of the investigations?'

'There have been suggestions that we shut the club once again.'

'What would that involve?'

'We've never done it before, so I really don't know. But I have said we will wait and watch. Fans don't abandon stars because the rest of the public do. That is the difference between a true fan and everyone else.'

She smiled at this, surprised to find herself charmed. 'I'd like to show you some letters that Drishti received,' she said, reaching into her bag. 'Could you please take a look at them and tell me if you recognize any of the senders?'

She had prints of a few of the more sketchy emails, the photo collage, as well as some of the hand-written letters. He looked through them, shuffling past the letters and looking at the collage first.

'Good collection,' he said with a nod.

'Do you recognize the last few pictures?' Ahana asked.

'These are photographs?'

'Yes.'

'No, like I said, I have never been to any of her shows.'

'What about the postal address it was sent from?'

He took the envelope from her and looked at the return address.

'No name?'

'No.'

'I can't recognize the address just like that, na.'

'Do you have a database of members' addresses?'

'Yes, but it is not complete. Nowadays we coordinate through SMS and email, mostly.'

'Could you check for this one in there?'

'Yes, that I can. But you will have to give me some time.'

'Do you think you might be able to give me names of the members who attended her concerts?'

'Several have. She is a Calcuttan, after all.'

'Why didn't you?'

'Honestly I don't care for her kind of performance,' he said.

'Then why did you start the fan club?'

'I am not the sole decision maker. It is what the members wanted. We have a nomination system.'

'How does that work?'

'Five members have to nominate a personality, and then they can form a sub-group.'

'Do you remember the names of the people who nominated her?'

'No, but I will have it down somewhere.'

'I'd appreciate if you could share those with me as well,' she said. 'If members are going to shows, they must also be sharing their experiences, their photographs within the group.'

He nodded.

'Do you remember seeing any photographs like the ones on that sheet?'

'It is possible. With so many emails and letters, it is hard to remember them all. Our Zakir Khan Fan Club alone has 5,000-plus members from over twenty different countries!'

'That's really impressive,' she said.

'And we do so much work, so much social work!'

'Is that right?'

She listened as he catalogued the projects undertaken – feeding orphans in the name of one star, road cleanings to mark the seventy-fifth birthday of another, and of course, bust erection and beautification of the small park on which it stands. Finally, when he seemed to have exhausted the list, she spoke again.

'Would it be possible to check the letters and email of the Drishti Sengupta Fan Club, to see if there are any more such pictures?'

'Yes, I can, but that also will take some time. I don't have a computer at home. I will have to go to a cyber café,' he said by way of explanation.

'I appreciate the effort,' she said. 'This is for Drishti – or more importantly, for Tara.'

He frowned. 'You will be writing about us?'

'Yes,' she said quickly.

'Do you think one of our members might have something to do with her disappearance?'

'No, but we'd like to look at everything we can get our hands on.'

She couldn't tell if he was relieved by this or disappointed.

'Ok,' he said with a shrug.

'By when do you think you might be able to take a look?'

He turned around to look at the sweet-shop-freebie calendar that hung on the wall next to him. 'By next week?'

Her heart sank. 'Any chance of getting it sooner than that? It is a little urgent, given the situation.'

'Ok, I will try. Perhaps by tomorrow. Evening.'

'Thank you,' she said. 'I will give you a call then. You can keep those letters,' she said, pointing at the papers on his desk, 'but I will be needing the collage back.'

He took a long look at it, pulled out a paper and pen and jotted down the address from the envelope, and then he handed it back to her. 'I'll let you know if I find anything.'

'Thanks. I appreciate it,' she said, standing up.

He stayed seated. 'Have you heard of Syzygy?' he asked abruptly.

'Er... no.'

'It is a range of beauty and health products which have amazing benefits. I am a dealer for these, and if you could spare just five minutes to hear about them. They are truly life-changing.'

She looked discreetly at her watch. Then she tucked the collage into her bag and sat back down. 'Sure.'

Rahul opened one of the boxes in front of him. 'See, it works like this...'

Twenty minutes later, Ahana was finally on her way, with an 'energy tonic' in her bag that sounded suspiciously like it had something to do with male erectile dysfunction. It was time to go to the hospital.

Ahana had only vaguely heard of narcoanalysis when Drishti volunteered to submit herself to one at the police's request. It sounded in equal parts terrifying and ridiculous, and for the same reasons: it was essentially truth serum, something you'd expect to hear about in a spy thriller. She couldn't imagine how or why this was a legitimate technique used by law enforcement.

When she arrived at the hospital, Sagar was already there at the reception. He stood up when he saw her.

'Hi,' she said, feeling out of sorts after their last meeting, but thankful that she had mostly dried off on the way over.

He just nodded his head.

'Is she here yet?'

'No. In a little while.'

'This isn't going as planned, is it?'

'No, not at all.'

'Are they going to let you in there?'

'Drishti has put in a request. They haven't said anything yet.'

'She isn't angry with you about the birth certificate reveal?'

He shook his head. 'She has no time to be angry.'

'Did the police contact you after the article appeared?'

'No. And then everything changed with Vidyut's name getting out there.'

She bristled. 'The police knew that already.'

He shrugged. 'After Drishti agreed to the narco, I think they decided to wait and see what they got from her.'

'Do you have any experience with this sort of thing?'

'Only academic.'

'What will they do to her?'

'They will inject her with a chemical, sodium pentathol, which will put her into a trance state. Her defences will be down, and she will be filled with a sense of wellbeing. Essentially it will make it impossible to lie.'

'How reliable is it?'

'What she says can't be used in court, but it can inform the investigation.'

She shook her head. 'Any chance of it going bad?'

'Let me put it this way: the same chemical can also be used in a lethal injection.'

She cringed. 'Why would they do this instead of a polygraph?'

'They usually do it in addition to one.'

And then Drishti walked through the doors with her father. She glanced at the two of them as she sat down in a chair, and then her father stood in front of her, as though his physical form could shield her from them, from it all.

Sagar was not put out. He approached Drishti, greeting

her father and taking the seat beside her. Ahana watched from the corner of her eye.

They spoke quietly till Vinayak Agarwal strode through the doors, looking at no one. He and his colleague walked into the bowels of the hospital, and did not emerge for another fifteen minutes. Finally, a man in a white lab coat approached Drishti. 'You are on an empty stomach?' he asked.

She nodded.

'Who are you?' asked Drishti's father.

'I am from the forensic science unit. We will be conducting the procedure.'

Sagar stood up. 'I would like to be in the room,' he said.

'Who are you? Her lawyer?'

'No, a friend. But I am also a doctor – a psychiatrist.'

'Are you *her* doctor?' he asked.

'No.'

'There is no provision for having outsiders in the room,' he said. 'You don't need to worry about her safety, it is a perfectly harmless procedure. And not even the police are allowed in.'

'How will her statements be recorded?' her father asked.

He nodded. 'There will be a video recorder.'

'A camera?' asked Sagar. As he began to argue again for being let in, Drishti stood up and touched his arm. 'Don't. It's okay. I just want this to be over with.'

Then, a man walked into the lobby and it was as though all the air had been sucked out of the room. Everyone knew who he was: hair more salt than pepper, dark skin, grey button down shirt with sleeves rolled up over jeans. His face impassive.

Vidyut Desai.

His eyes went straight to Drishti. She frowned as she saw

him, then turned away, the pain clear for all to see. All secrecy was now futile.

There was a second's hesitation in his step. And then he walked up to her. 'It's no use,' she said. 'How many times do I have to tell you it is of no use?'

'If I turn myself in now, it might put an end to this madness,' he said.

'Sagar says it will be fine.'

He looked towards Sagar, and back to her.

'But if I tell them the truth –'

'Nothing will change. Believe me. There is no winning here.'

He looked bewildered. 'There has to be some way to push back! Where is the process, where is the accountability!'

Drishti shook her head.

'You aren't in California anymore,' said Sagar softly.

'So we just sit back and do nothing?'

'Save your breath and get your version heard. Even if the police don't care about the news, the CBI might,' said Sagar. 'Someone might.' They were all grasping at straws. 'The truth has to matter at some point.'

Drishti was led away as the two men stood there and stared after her disappearing down the corridor.

After a few moments, finally, Ahana approached them. She had no choice but to try. She introduced herself to Vidyut.

He looked at her, and she felt the force of his anger. 'From the newspaper,' he said.

'Yes.'

'For some reason, these people think I should speak to you,' he said, with a nod towards Sagar.

'Drishti came to us with her story, and we helped her get it out,' said Ahana, blood pounding in her ears.

Vidyut looked at her, inscrutable. 'And how has that helped her in any way?'

'It is early days yet.'

He looked at her, eyes full of distrust. 'But it didn't work. She's right – nothing will change.'

'The CBI are in play now.' Or so she kept hearing.

'And how will that improve the situation?' asked Vidyut.

'We are hoping for a little more objectivity, if nothing else. They will not protect the local police and their actions,' said Ahana.

He seemed to consider this.

'Would you give us a statement?' she asked.

He looked at her, his dark eyes haunted. 'Yes, I will speak to you. Not because it is what Drishti wants, but in spite of it.'

12 June 2002

'Who is it, Sumita?' said Drishti, coming out of the bedroom.

'One gents has come, Didi,' she called out.

Drishti walked into the living room and her legs turned to lead.

She didn't know how long she stood there, taking in the accusation radiating from every inch of his being.

Sumita dissolved into the background. Drishti saw his lips moving, but she had no idea what he was saying. She forced herself back into the moment.

'If you wanted to keep our love child a secret, you should have stayed away from magazine covers, Drishti.'

'She's not yours.' She knew the words had come out of her mouth, but she could barely recognize her own voice.

'Why, Drishti, would you do this to me?'

And then she saw, behind the accusation, a flash of hurt. And that was even more dangerous to her. 'Get out of my house.'

'Not till you tell me what is going on. And why.'

All she knew was that he had to get out of there; he couldn't be there with Tara asleep in the next room and nothing else mattered. 'I'll meet you somewhere else. Not here.'

'So desperate to keep me away from her? Why, Drishti? What have I done to you to make you hate me so much? To make you look at me like you are looking at me now?'

'Stop,' she hissed.

'No. Come with me now.'

'I can't.' Sumita was leaving; she couldn't leave Tara alone.

'Then we talk here.'

Drishti pursed her lips, turned on her heel and went into

the kitchen where Sumita was hovering. Drishti knew she had been listening to every word, and she knew enough English to catch some of it.

'Can you please stay a little longer? I will just be back.'

'Yes, Didi.'

'I'll just be downstairs.'

She took a deep breath and went back out to the living room. 'Let's go,' she said.

'Where is she?' he asked.

She tried to respond, but her mouth wouldn't move.

Downstairs, Drishti led him to the back of the building. Too late she remembered that they had already been to the park together, once. Under very different circumstances. She turned her back to the playground and focused all her attention on Vidyut. If he remembered that spot, five years on, it was lost under the anger.

'What the fuck, Drishti?'

'I really don't know what you are talking about.'

'She is mine. Don't try to deny it.'

'No.'

'The timeline matches, and I could have picked her out of a line-up as my child, she looks so much like me, like I did when I was her age.'

'That is your imagination. Wishful thinking.'

The pain in his eyes was unmistakable. 'You think I wish to have a child in the world with whom I have no contact?'

She pushed back. 'She is my child.'

'Unless you are promoting some sort of "immaculate conception" theory, she has a father.'

'Yes, and it's not you. I'll show you her birth certificate, you'll see for yourself.'

'I want a paternity test.'

'No.'

'I'll take you to court to get it if I have to.'

She closed her eyes. When she opened them again, she had traded panic for anger. 'Go back to your life, Vidyut. You're married, why don't you have a child of your own if you want one so badly?'

'What I choose to do is none of your business,' he said, voice like ice. 'You have no right to keep my child away from me.'

'You have no right to come here years later and make such claims.'

'You act like I abandoned you!'

'You were married!'

'A fact you are using to keep me away from my child when it is you who pushed me away.'

'She's not your child.'

'A paternity test will prove that one way or the other.'

'No.'

'Why? Have you convinced some other man that he is the father?'

'You have no idea what you are talking about!'

'I think I do. Whether you want me to be a part of your life or not, Tara has a right to know her father.'

'Do not say her name!'

'Why, Drishti? What are you so afraid of?'

Drishti crossed her arms. It was only then that she noticed a couple of evening walkers watching them. This was not the place. Even she knew that. 'What do you want from me?' she said, softer this time.

'The truth, for starters. Sleep over it,' he said, pulling out a piece of paper from his pocket and scribbled something on it. 'This is where I am staying, the room number. I am there till tomorrow night.' She held out her hand to take the paper, but he pulled it away and scribbled on the back. 'Here's my local cell number, too. If you don't call by tomorrow, you can expect to hear from my lawyers.'

Drishti didn't sleep much. All night, she tossed and turned, and every time she dozed off, she woke with a start to check on Tara, who slept blissfully through it all, snuggled up beside her in bed. Drishti hugged her and it filled her with calm. Her own private talisman.

By morning, she knew what she had to do. She went to visit Udit Dalmia. She knew he had decided to stay with his wife only for custody reasons. He was the only person she could think of who might be able to advise her on what Vidyut's re-entry into her life could mean. Legally speaking.

'Was he really a bastard?' he asked, after she explained, haltingly, her predicament.

'No.'

'But he was married.'

'Yes.'

'He didn't want to leave his wife?'

'I saw no reason to ask him to.'

'And you didn't tell him.'

'No.'

'That's harsh, Drishti.'

'When he was with me, there were no promises, no intentions of a future together. This was the future I wanted. Why must it be shared with him?'

'Look at it from his perspective. He wants to know his child. Isn't that the decent response?'

'Me and Tara, we are perfect together. I don't want any

one. I don't need any more.'

'But Tara might,' he said. 'I can't imagine my kids growing up without me in their lives. I can't imagine my life without them. And thank god they don't have to, because their mother is fucking crazy.'

It was late when she arrived at Vidyut's hotel – past 8 pm, and she knew she'd be late for her show unless she hurried.

'Come in,' he said, holding the door open.

'I need time,' she said.

'For what?'

'To prepare her.'

She could see the relief in his eyes. He almost smiled. 'I can delay my flight,' he said.

'No. I can't spring this on her just like that. She is too small, Vidyut, to understand. I need to talk to her, to explain, to let it sink in before the meeting. I need at least a month.'

His eyes never left her face as he thought about what she said. 'You have two weeks. I will come back then.'

Her shoulders slumped. He shook his head slowly.

'Will it be so bad, Drishti? What did I do to make you hate me so much?'

'I don't hate you, Vidyut.'

'All I want is to get to know my child, to be a part of her life. To let her know that she is loved, not by one parent only, but by two.'

'How does it work, moving forward?'

'It works by making an effort, Drishti. Something you have never felt able to do, at least where I was concerned. This time, you don't get to say no.'

'I have rights as a mother.'

'Yes you do. Rights I am not trying to infringe upon. But I

have rights too. And if push comes to shove, there is no court in the world that will allow you to shut me out completely. Especially once I have made clear the deception. Years and years of lies, Drishti. And for what?'

'If you try to take her away from me, you will learn what I am capable of.'

He closed his eyes, and let out a deep breath. 'Drishti, have you lost your mind? Why would I want to take her away from you?'

'We need to establish some ground rules.'

'Such as?'

'You don't get to meet her alone.'

'Not yet – I can agree to that. What else?'

'You can't talk to her about our situation. You want to spend time with her, do that.'

'Ok, what happens when she starts asking questions?'

'We'll cross that bridge when we come to it.'

'Ok. Whatever. Let's get through the first meeting, and we will take stock afterwards.'

'How often do you intend to be here?'

'As often as I can be.'

In his eyes, she could see the hope she didn't feel.

'I didn't mean to hurt you,' she said.

'No?' The anger was back, and she was sorry she'd said anything.

'How did you think I'd feel? I wasn't some anonymous sperm donor, Drishti.'

'That is not how I thought of you. Not for a minute.'

'You thought of me at all? You could have fooled me!' The gratitude he felt at her capitulation had disappeared, and she realized he had never understood her need or her desire to live life unfettered. To him, it had only meant rejection.

'Is it so difficult to believe that I genuinely wanted to have this child by myself?'

'No, it's not.' He sounded sad. 'All you had to do was tell me. I wouldn't have tried to swoop in and rescue you. But this – this is something else, Drishti. You are denying your child half her story.'

She slumped against the wall, exhausted.

The room was heavy with all that remained unsaid. Finally, it was Vidyut who spoke. 'I want you to know that I will take responsibility for her.'

'What, you mean money?'

He nodded. 'I can support her. Anything she needs. School, college.'

'I know you are rich, but I am not doing too badly myself.'

'I am not suggesting you are. But the world could be at her feet, Drishti. All you have to do is stop being so damn stubborn.'

There was so much that she could have said. That his idea of the world and hers had always been different, that Tara had everything she needed already. But it was hard to set Vidyut up as the enemy while he was standing in front of her, when all he had ever wanted was to be loved.

She nodded. 'Two weeks,' she said.

As she left the room and walked towards the elevator, her heels sinking into the plush carpet, she knew nothing would ever be the same again.

What Kind of Monster

Neither Ahana nor Vidyut wanted to go very far from the hospital, so they found a *chaat* shop nearby with a few tables. They ordered tea, which came in dinky plastic cups with too much sugar.

He sat by the window, looking out at the steady drizzle. He was very attractive, more attractive than his pictures. Even the brooding could not take away from it.

He didn't seem likely to start, so she decided it was on her to pull off the Band-Aid. 'You are Tara's father.'

He didn't flinch. 'Yes. I believe so.'

'You don't know?'

'Yes, I know. But do I have the evidence to prove it? No. On paper, she is another man's child.'

'Why?'

'I had been kept in the dark by Drishti. Deliberately. For years.'

'Why?' she asked again.

'That only she can answer.'

She wasn't sure how much time they had. The personal details would have to wait till she could grapple with the facts that related to Tara's disappearance.

'The big question that everyone is asking is why Drishti has been protecting you.'

He laughed a sad, bitter little laugh. 'You think she has been protecting me? She hasn't been protecting me. She's been protecting herself. From the moment we met.'

She was chilled by the look in his eye. 'What I mean is why didn't she give up your name when the police wanted it?'

'The short answer is that we were together just before Tara

went missing, so she knows I had nothing to do with it. But if you want to know the real reason she hasn't spoken up, it is because she has not yet publicly acknowledged that I am the father.'

'I know that, but why?'

'We were never in a real relationship, and she wanted me to have nothing to do with her child. My child.'

She could hear the anger and she knew it would take time to push past it enough to make sense of the story. 'Can you start from the beginning please?'

Ahana could see him weighing something – his anger towards Drishti? His mistrust for her? – before he spoke.

'Some of this needs to stay off the record.'

'Ok.'

'This next part is not for public consumption.'

She turned off the recorder.

'When I first met Drishti in 1993, she was young. Hell, I was too, but she was still a master's student. I had already been working for several years in the US, and had only come back to the country to be closer to my mother, who was suffering from cancer at the time. We had an instant connection, but soon after we met, my mother went into remission and I returned to my home in California.'

'Were you in a relationship then?'

'No,' he said, shaking his head. 'I could not imagine a person more impossible to pin down, and so happy about it. And yet, being with her was like every single rom-com cliché, so much so that I couldn't take it seriously – it was bound to turn out to be too good to be true at some point.

'After our first meeting, I wanted to find out if there was more. Staying in touch in those days was hard, we had email in the States, at work, but it wasn't yet prevalent in India. So we would actually write letters, and I would call whenever I could. It would be fits and starts of intense communication and then silence for months. About six months in, I asked her to come visit me in San Francisco. By that time, I believed there was something there. But she said no, and continued to say no every time I suggested it. I didn't get it. But there is only so much rejection a man can take.'

He ran his hand through his hair. 'And then I met my wife. Sandhya. We were pushed together by everyone – family, friends, and just common sense. It seemed as though it was the right thing for both of us. We were friends, and I was ready to settle down, and though I think I always knew the spark wasn't quite there, I thought the other stuff would make up for it.'

'You were colleagues?'

'No. But we were in the same industry. She was as passionate about her work as I was. We were from the same community, and our parents were connected. We had so much in common.'

'And that was when your first company made it big.'

'Yes. I was busier than I had ever been. I didn't have time for Drishti's drama, and eventually I cut it out.'

'Drama?' She wasn't sure why the word bothered her so much, but it did. 'It sounds like it was the opposite of drama.'

He raised a skeptical brow. 'How do you figure?'

'She wanted nothing from you.'

Something in his gaze changed. 'Which would have been perfect if I wanted nothing from her.' He sounded angry.

She paused, waiting for him to compose himself. 'Gosh, is that what it looks like from the outside? Like I was some desperate stalker?'

'Not stalker.'

If he heard her, he ignored it. 'I guess that is one way of looking at it. Whatever feelings she had for me weren't strong enough to last the test of time and distance.'

'But you did get together eventually.'

He nodded. 'I came back to India, what was it? Must have been a couple of years after we first met. That is only the second time I met Drishti, for all of an evening. In a crowd of my former students. I thought that would be it, except that as soon as she walked into the room I knew it was only going to make it worse. I thought she felt the same way, too, but our efforts to communicate long distance didn't get any better.'

'And then at some point you got married. To Sandhya.'

'Yes, in 1996. And I really did think that that was that. I don't take commitment lightly. Which only makes what happened next so much worse.' He ran his long fingers through his hair. It was too short to make any impact. He shook his head, staring out the window.

'It was another two years before my work brought me to this part of the world again, and that time I stayed a couple of extra days in Calcutta. I didn't need to; I told myself I was just trying to repair our broken friendship. But even I knew it was bullshit.

'My marriage was… cordial. But with Drishti, it was electric. It almost seemed inevitable that we would finally be together, someday…' He paused, took a deep breath and then ploughed on. 'It was four years after we first met. If I thought it would put the what-ifs to rest, I was sorely mistaken. If anything, it made it all worse. And that, of course, is what brings us here. It was when Tara was conceived. And that is when Drishti's lies began.'

'It sounded like you shared a lot. Why do you think she kept it from you?'

'I wish I had an answer to that. She even had the opportunity to tell me face-to-face just weeks later when I passed through town again. I realized then that something had changed. I thought I had somehow hurt her. Now I knew that she must have already known she was pregnant. She was so stubbornly stuck on the idea of not wanting to be in a serious relationship that she didn't realize she was already in one.'

'And that was it?'

'Pretty much. When I asked her if I could see her again, all she said was she didn't want me to leave my wife. I swear if she had just once said she wanted to be with me – that she was pregnant, goddammit – I wouldn't have let her do this to us. To Tara.

'Instead, I went on, in complete ignorance. She dropped communication of all kind. I wanted to scream, but on what grounds? I was the married one. All she was doing was not breaking up my marriage. Now I know why she had to shut me out. Because of Tara.'

'If you had such a strong relationship, why not be together?'

'She insisted that she didn't want a long-term relationship. Said she had never wanted marriage, and that since it was what I clearly wanted, I should have it with someone who wanted the same things I did. That she liked her life in India, that she didn't want to shift base. None of it made sense to me, but what did I really know? And what could I do but back off?

'When she cut me out, I convinced myself that perhaps Drishti was not the person I thought she was, that our time together didn't mean as much to her as it did to me. What had we really shared? 100 hours over four years? If I agreed with Drishti on anything, it was that it wasn't enough to go on. The only difference was I was so crazy about her that I would have chucked everything else to find out, and she didn't think it was worth even picking up the phone.'

'But she did think it was worth having your child.'

He looked at his hands. 'I don't think that had anything to do with me. Drishti wants what she wants, and a baby was apparently what she has always wanted.'

'How did you find out the truth?' she asked. 'And this will need to be on the record.'

He looked out the window, and gave her an almost imperceptible nod. She turned on the recorder.

'I didn't, till a few weeks ago.'

'Details, please.'

'I had been following Drishti's career of course. Fuck that, I'd been unable to look away. But it was only a couple of years ago, when her music started making headlines, that she was profiled and she spoke out publicly about being a single mother. And then she was not specific about how old the child was, so it never struck me that Tara could be mine – I always assumed the child was younger.'

'I have to say that I am finding this a little hard to believe.'

He sighed. 'So do I. I went back over everything I read, everything I knew, to make sure I hadn't been some sort of a giant ass, that I hadn't been in denial, but there was really no way for me to have known.'

'No one mentioned it to you?'

He shrugged. 'I am not from here. My family, my entire life in India was in Delhi, and I left fifteen years ago. We have absolutely no common friends. Or maybe one, who doesn't really know Drishti that well anyway. No one knew about our relationship, no one even really knew this was a possibility. And I live on the other side of the globe.'

'So how can you be so sure she is yours? Drishti has never

been shy of admitting she has had plenty of relationships over the years.'

'Just last month, Drishti appeared in a magazine with her daughter.' He paused. 'With Tara.'

'*India Now*.' Ahana had seen it, too.

He nodded. 'I just knew it. It was uncanny – I could put my own pictures as a four-year-old beside that shot and, apart from the hair, you'd think it was the same child. So I wrote to Drishti – I got her email from her website – and she didn't respond at first. Then, when she finally did, she said I was being ridiculous. But I knew she was lying. So I flew down.'

'When?'

'Two weeks ago. I came to her place the night before Tara disappeared, and finally confronted her. She wouldn't even have me in the house, we finally spoke downstairs.'

'What happened that first night?'

'We talked. Scratch that – we fought.'

'About?'

'I was furious. Can you blame me? This was my child!'

'You don't think she should have had the baby?'

'Far from it! Just that I had a right to know!'

'She didn't want you to be involved. Isn't that her right?'

He snapped around to stare Ahana straight in the face, for what felt like the first time. Ahana had to force herself to hold that gaze, burning with fury. 'What about my rights? I have a right to know my flesh and blood is out there! Tara has a right to know her father, goddammit!'

And then, just as soon as it had appeared, the anger was gone. It was as though he had remembered why there were sitting there in the first place, in that little shop with its sticky tables and smell of ghee. The child, the source of this outrage, was missing. He slumped forward, head in his hands.

'Did you threaten any sort of action?'

'By the end of it, yes. I said I would take her to court to demand a paternity test if she continued to deny Tara was mine. And that we would take it from there.'

'What happened next?'

'The next evening, she came to the hotel. She said she needed time to break the news to Tara, to prepare her, and I could come back and meet her, under supervision. It was five years too late, but it was a beginning. I was to come back in a fortnight.'

'When did you leave the hotel?'

'Just after she left for her show, I took off for the airport. You can check with the driver – I had booked a car through the hotel.'

The driver had already been interviewed after Ahana had discovered Vidyut's identity. She already knew his version of events held up – at least during the window Tara was believed to have disappeared. 'When did you come back?'

'As soon as I landed and saw the messages from Drishti.'

'She told you?'

'No, she accused me.'

'Of abduction?'

'What else? She had already proved how little she thought of me, so why not this? I called her back – she had by then calmed down – I think it dawned on her that I couldn't have taken Tara out of the country without having her passport at the very least. I came back as soon as I could. After a terrible, completely avoidable conversation with Sandhya.'

'She knows?'

'I couldn't have her find out all this through the media. She doesn't deserve that, or any of this.' He shook his head. 'I knew I was coming back, that I was going to deal with it.'

'What was going through your mind at the time?'

'I was certain it was all some sort of fabrication. The timing was just too convenient – I show up, and Tara disappears.'

'You thought Drishti was lying?'

'Yes. I thought she had invented the episode to keep Tara away from me.'

'That she had abducted, in essence, her own daughter. Isn't that a little extreme?'

'What reason had she given me to think otherwise?'

'And now?'

'When she was implicated, when she was accused of killing her own child, I realized it simply was not possible. Drishti is many things, but she would not harm her child.'

'How could you be so sure? You don't seem to have much faith in her.'

'You know Drishti, don't you?'

'Yes.'

'What do you think?'

'Not relevant,' she said. 'You admit that you were furious. That you were shocked at her keeping the truth from you. She accused you of abducting Tara, didn't she? You must not have seen that coming either.'

'Just like she figured out that I couldn't have done it, I knew she couldn't have. Wouldn't have.'

'Still, would you stake everything on your conviction?'

He nodded. 'She was standing in front of me, telling me she needed time to prepare her daughter for the meeting. That she'd allow me to be a part of her life at last. She'd have to be a monster to do that if something had happened to Tara already! What kind of a person could do that?'

'What if there had been an accident?'

'Do you seriously think that Tara was already dead, and

she went about her business – lying to my face, performing at her show – as though nothing had happened?'

'No, I don't. But it is what is being said.'

'Then what is being said is ludicrous.'

'The police think her response was cold.'

'Why would she do it? She might hide the child to keep her away from me, but what would Drishti gain by hurting her? And why come to my hotel at all in that case?'

'They feel it could have been an accident.'

'There was no sign of an accident. Of any injury at all.'

'So she covered it up.'

'By such logic, we may all be murderers. How can you disprove a theory based on nothing?'

'So that is why you are coming forward?'

He nodded.

'Have you been in touch with her since your return?'

'I tried to reach out to her as soon as I landed. She wouldn't take my calls. But we finally met yesterday.'

'I have to say, Vidyut, it all sounds rather incredible, the timing of it.' Incredible unless he was, in fact, involved.

'I know. That is, I suppose, why I am here.'

'So what's your next move?'

'I will have to meet the police, won't I?'

'And then?'

'I have no idea.'

Ahana rushed to the office and transcribed every word that was on the recorder, to be splashed across the front page almost in totality the following morning. Without writing about their history, would anyone understand why Drishti had kept the truth from Vidyut? Would anyone believe that Vidyut's arrival on the scene and Tara's disappearance had nothing to do with each other? Did Ahana?

It was late by the time she reached home and went straight to the kitchen cabinet where she stowed her liquor. She pulled out a bottle of Smirnoff left over from her last party at home. She didn't usually drink alone. There were no mixers, but found a couple of smelly ice cubes in the freezer and a brown lemon in the vegetable drawer. They would have to do.

She put the bottle and her drink down on the coffee table and was lighting a cigarette when her phone buzzed.

It was a message. From Sagar. 'Home yet?'

They had been in touch over the course of the evening, he had given her updates as to how the narco had gone. Though he had no idea what Drishti had said in that room, he had been able to confirm at least that she was in good health. 'Just got in,' she replied.

'Am downstairs. Come up?'

She instinctively looked to her window. He was there? She glanced at her watch – it was late.

'Ok,' she replied, rushing into the bathroom and splashing water on her tired face, rubbing vigorously with the towel to get some of the dirt of the day off. She heard the doorbell ring, and by the time she got out and opened the door, he was slumped against the wall.

For a moment she thought he was drunk. Then he looked at her with eyes that were drained but clear.

'Can I come in?'

She stepped aside, closing the door behind him.

'How did it go?' she asked.

'She's home.'

She knew Vidyut was with the police at that very moment – Probal had brought the official version in later in the evening. It was not looking good for either of them.

'You were right. We should have got her story out there before,' he said.

'No Sagar, one story would have made no difference.'

For a moment, they stood there in silence, a wall between them.

Then he saw the bottle of vodka on the table and flinched.

'Sorry,' she said, quickly grabbing it and moving it back into the kitchen.

'I am getting better at it,' he said softly. 'But not tonight. I hope I didn't interrupt you.'

'No, it's just been a long day,' she said, as she stepped back out into the living room.

He reached out and pushed a lock of hair back behind her ear.

She thought of the man who was, officially, her fiancée. The man she'd never touched.

And then Sagar's hand lingered on her face.

She felt the deep vein of desire rise up within her, climbing up through body, erasing the bitter residues of the day.

She shouldn't. But she was sick to death of shouldn't.

And then his lips were on hers, and she tasted his last piece of chewing gum and the sweat on his skin.

Why had she waited so long?

'Should I leave?' he asked, breaking away, his breath as fast as hers.

She pulled him down to her again.

Already Done

Transcript of narco-analysis conducted by forensic psychologist Sheila Kumari on suspect Drishti Sengupta

Q. Can you please state your name?
A. *Drishti Sengupta.*

Q. Do you know where you are at this time?
A. *In a hospital, with truth serum coursing through my veins.*

Q. Do you know why you are here?
A. *Because of Tara.*

Q. Do you know what happened to Tara?
A. *She is gone.*

Q. Do you know where she is?
A. *I wish I did.*

Q. Do you?
A. *No.*

Q. Do you know how she left the house the night she disappeared?
A. *No. Sumita... No.*

Q. What about Sumita?
A. *She was there, at home, I wasn't.*

Q. Where were you?
A. *At the Blue Banyan, for my weekly gig.*

Q. When you left the house, was Tara with you?
A. *No. She was asleep. In her bed. She was supposed to be safe there. How was I to know?*

Q. Do you know who may have wanted to take her?
A. *Yes, but it wasn't him either.*

Q. Who are you referring to?
A. *Vidyut.*

Q. And who is Vidyut?
A. *Someone I have loved for a very, very long time.*

Q. Were you and Vidyut involved in a relationship?
A. *Only of the kind that has no beginning and no end.*

Q. At the time of Tara's disappearance, were you romantically involved with Vidyut?
A. *Yes.*

Q. Is he Tara's father?
A. *He wanted to be.*

Q. Who is Tara's father?
A. *No one. She doesn't have one. It is just me and Tara, Tara and me.*

Q. Who is Tara's biological father?
A. *Ah, of course that is what you meant. That is what everyone always means. That would be Vidyut.*

Q. Why did Vidyut come to Calcutta?
A. *Because he wanted to be involved in Tara's life. He found out about her.*

Q. He didn't know before?
A. *No.*

Q. And why is that?
A. *Because I didn't want him to. My body, my choice. My body my choice. Why is this so hard for everyone to get?*

Q. Was he angry when he found out?
A. *Yes. Very angry.*

Q. Why?
A. *Because he thought I should have told him. That he wanted to be in her life now, and that he wouldn't take no for an answer.*

Q. And what did you say to that?
A. *I told him no. But then I said yes. But I wasn't ready.*

Q. Why weren't you ready if you were in a relationship with him anyway?
A. *I wasn't in a relationship with him.*

Q. You said you were romantically involved.
A. *Yes. How can you not be involved with the one you love?*

Q. You were together in the past?
A. *Yes.*

Q. But there is no relationship at the moment?
A. *No.*

Q. Did he want to take her from you?
A. *I don't think so.*

Q. But you were not sure?
A. *How could I be? He was angry. And he had money. So much money.*

Q. Did you want to take her away from him?
A. *I... I don't know.*

Q. When you left his hotel that night, what were you thinking?
A. *That nothing would ever be the same again.*

Q. And you did not like that?
A. *No.*

Q. Did you think of taking Tara away?
A. *Yes. But how could I?*

Q. Then what did you plan on doing about it?
A. *Nothing. What could I do, when it was all already done?*

The Loss of Tara

It took less than twenty-four hours for the footage from the narco-analysis to be leaked to *Tarar Khonje*. By then, the police had received the report, which had been expedited bearing in mind the urgency of the situation. Drishti's words were ambiguous enough to allow several interpretations, and the police decided which interpretation suited them. They began to build a case against Drishti as well as her former lover.

But then, in sharp contrast with the railing police and the news, quietly, thirteen days after Tara disappeared, came the ransom note.

Can such a thing be a source of comfort? For Drishti, remarkably, it was. It meant that Tara was still alive.

But that was where comfort ended.

It arrived in the form of an email, to Drishti's inbox.

'Tara is safe.

To get her back, have your father bring a black haversack with Rs 10 lakh at 10.30 pm to Rabindra Sarobar, and leave it on a bench just inside the gate opposite Menoka Cinema. He should leave at once. If all conditions are met, you will receive a message at 10.45 pm giving the details of Tara's location. You must come alone to pick her up. If there are any police at the cash drop or the pick-up site, she will not be released.'

There was an attachment – a photo, with Tara wearing the same blue dress as before – sitting in the same chair.

Drishti was at home when the email came, but it was in fact

her father who read it first. He was in charge of checking her mail, as well as the tip ID.

'Drishti!' he called out. 'Subhra!'

Drishti rushed over and read the mail, once, twice, bent over the desk, scrolling up and down several times before slumping down into the chair her father had vacated.

Her parents watched her intently. 'The police might have already seen this,' she said, pulling at her lower lip. 'They have this password.'

'As if they would be tracking it so regularly?' he said.

'If we delete it, they won't know,' she said.

'Delete it?'

'The instructions say clearly – no police.'

'But what happens if this is a hoax?' asked her father. 'Won't they need to investigate?'

Drishti later described that moment as the loneliest of her life. She hit print, and then, delete.

'Drishti!' her father said sharply.

'The photo: look at it – it isn't the same one that was sent to the news channel! Her face is turned away from the camera. This is real.'

'Are you sure?'

'Absolutely.'

'Oh Drishti,' said her mother, wiping a tear away.

'I can undo it, if we change our minds,' said Drishti, to comfort herself as much as her parents.

'What do we do now?' asked Rajendra.

'Do you have ten lakhs in your account?' asked Drishti.

'Yes,' he said. 'I will need to go to the bank.'

'Go, fast,' said Subhra. 'But we shouldn't be alone in this.'

Her mother squeezed Drishti's shoulder. For the first time in her adult life, Drishti closed her eyes and prayed.

She called Vidyut, and then Sagar.

They both arrived and pored over the email.

'We shouldn't have deleted it, right?' asked Rajendra.

Sagar shook his head. 'It's here, in the trash folder for anyone to see. We can restore it afterwards.'

'Can you tell where it is from?' He couldn't bring himself to address him by name, somehow, but it was clear that Rajendra was speaking to Vidyut, the only one in the room with expertise in tech.

'No. I can't,' he said. 'To find out, we'd need to go to the email service provider, and since it is US-based, we'd need a warrant.'

'What are the consequences of withholding this from the police when Drishti is already under so much suspicion?' said her father.

Drishti was standing behind him. 'Baba, it's ok. If this is how we get Tara back, it is ok.'

He stood up and turned to her, the fortnight's stress spilling out, at long last. 'And if it's not? Then I will lose you too?' he said, voice cracking.

She wrapped her arms around him, and for the longest time, there they stood.

'You won't lose me, Baba,' she whispered.

'You can't be sure of that.'

'Tell them I deleted it.'

They all turned to look at Vidyut.

'Tell them it was my idea. That I was here and I took control.'

The room was still, the words hanging in the air. Loaded and at the same time, utterly irrelevant.

Her father shrugged. 'As I have said before, what happens if this is a hoax? The police will need to investigate it, right?

What assurance do we have, even that they really intend to hand her back? At the moment we hand over that bag of money, we will have nothing!'

'Then we just have to hand it over and hope for the best,' said Drishti. 'If we lose the cash, we lose it. We need to do this.'

'My concern is not about the money,' he said.

'You've seen that picture, Baba! This is a different shot from the same sequence! The same person who sent that photo to the news channel also sent this – it is the closest we have come to her yet!'

'Why ask for so little?' asked Vidyut.

Drishti was not listening, but Rajendra was. 'That's a point.'

The news was out about Vidyut's identity, and his arrival in Calcutta. The kidnapper could have asked for any amount and have had a reasonable expectation of getting it.

'What if it is a trap of some kind? I still think we need to inform the police.'

'No Baba, the note is clear,' Drishti said. 'We can't take the chance. The police are not our friends in this!'

'We will need to go in two groups, going alone would be ridiculous,' said Sagar.

Drishti wasn't listening, she was filled with a frantic energy, pacing about the room. 'We need to organize the money.'

'Already done,' said Vidyut. 'It's on the way now.'

As Drishti looked at him, for a moment she considered protesting. Then she went to Tara's room and shut herself in it for the rest of the day.

At 9.45 pm, Drishti's father set off. A security guard from Vidyut's local office had been posted in plainclothes near the location, well in advance. Vidyut gave Rajendra his number.

'In case you are in trouble, call him and he will be with you in two minutes. If we don't hear from you by 10.35 pm, he will be there anyway.'

Drishti, Vidyut and Sagar were on standby.

Vidyut sat at the computer, waiting for the next mail.

Then, at 10.35 pm father called. 'No one has come.'

'How can you be sure?'

'I went back to look. The bag is still there.'

'You need to leave.'

'Are you sure?'

'Yes. Don't worry about the bag.'

Then, 10.45 pm came and went and there still was no email, and Rajendra was on his way back. Drishti was pale and bereft.

'It was a hoax,' she said.

Vidyut turned to her. 'Tomorrow morning I will go to the police with this.'

'What's the use?'

'My local manager will come with me. He has some connections – some politician. He said he would help. This mail is something to go with – a starting point for a new investigation.'

Her father arrived, and broke down. Subhra led him away into the guest room to lie down.

Sagar insisted that they eat, but at the table, the three of them sat with empty plates. No one was hungry.

And then an alert sounded – the speakers of the computer in the bedroom had been cranked up all the way, and a tinkling sound ripped through the cheap plastic.

Drishti ran to the machine and opened her inbox, hands shaking.

It was from the same sender. There was only one line:

'Why did you involve him? This was supposed to be between the two of us.'

'What is it?' asked Vidyut.

When she didn't respond, he came to the desk and looked over her shoulder.

'What does that mean?' he said.

She looked at him, terror in her eyes.

'It means he is watching us.'

Day 14

New Angle

The news of the failed attempt by the kidnappers to extort ransom exploded on the 10 am *Tarar Khonje* bulletin the next morning. Ahana had seen it, heart in her mouth, wondering how she could have missed such a crucial development. She knew Drishti would not have spoken with Ranadeep herself, and the information was far too sketchy to be from a reliable source.

Worst of all, there was still no Tara.

'The police are not at all happy with how she handled it,' Manash told her. 'Probal is at Lalbazar now and things are not looking good for her.'

'What does that mean?'

'I think we should expect her arrest. Maybe even today.'

It was as though Ahana froze for a moment. She could see Manash – his expectant face, betraying only the merest hint of remorse. None of it made any sort of sense. How could he say this as though it meant nothing, when what they were actually saying was that Tara was dead? 'But doesn't this prove there is a kidnapper out there?' she finally got out.

'You start caring about people quickly,' said Manash with a smile. 'It is not a good thing when you are a journalist.'

Quickly? Were her feelings of sadness – grief, even – misplaced, presumptuous, inappropriate? Is that what Manash was saying?

'Just see how it looks,' he continued. 'An email, which anyone could have sent, making a ransom demand. And then no one even shows to collect the money?'

'But – '

'And then they keep it from the police. Not a good move, given the situation.'

'I see that,' she said slowly. And he turned his attention back to the keyboard, tinkering away.

It was then that Rahul of the Drishti Sengupta Fan Club finally called her back. He had, at long last, pulled out the information she had requested, and told her she would need to come and take a look to see what was important and what wasn't. He had assured her that there was plenty of Drishti-related material to see. She couldn't take anything away without running it past him.

With everything that had happened in the last twenty-four hours, the trip seemed utterly futile. But she'd go for the photographs and take it from there. She brought Amit along, to take photos of the photos, as well as of the documents, in case she found something of importance that she wasn't allowed to take away.

When they arrived, Ahana felt deflated. The one promising lead – the return address from the envelope – had not turned up in their database. But Rahul did have the list of people who had nominated Drishti for her fan club. None of them were familiar to Ahana, and the three addresses he could provide would have to be investigated separately. She knew how Manash would react if she suggested she look into the names. Today was not the day to bring it up: not when she had missed something as big as the ransom demand. A miss that was a direct result of her not grooming her source well enough.

Ahana sifted through the stack of papers and photos. There were letters from a handful of members – no matter what Rahul said, the Drishti Sengupta Fan Club was no more than a dozen people, and it was three or four of those that kept up the majority of the correspondence. She noted down the names.

And then, at the bottom of the stack was an envelope that matched perfectly the one that had been sent to Drishti. Green, wide, with one solitary sheet inside.

Ahana pulled it out with trembling hands. There were three lines of photographs, nine in all. All new images, and while the collage sent to Drishti contained photographs of her in public spaces, all of these photos were taken inside Surya Apartments. Ahana would recognize that landscaping, the vaguely muddy walls, anywhere.

At the bottom, there was another line: 'My friend Drishti Sengupta, singer of the superhit *Run for your Life*.'

Her heart raced as she took it in. The pictures were

taken from several different angles, and on several different occasions. Given Drishti's changing clothes and hairstyles, they would have to be years apart. Ahana couldn't even remember when Drishti had long hair – not since she had become famous. And there was one with what looked like a baby bump.

Drishti wasn't looking at the camera in any of the shots. They had been taken by someone without permission, by someone lurking in the shadows.

Ahana scoured the sheet and the envelope for any possible clues. There was no date on the letter, but the envelope was there, with the same return address as the other collage. It had been sent just six months ago. But none of that mattered anymore. Regardless of the address, she knew where to find the sender.

'Take pictures of all of these,' she said to Amit. 'We need clear shots.'

As he set to work with his DSLR, she rifled through the rest of the papers again. She couldn't find anything that seemed connected or with the same postmark.

If she put this collage beside the one that Ahana had seen earlier, the story of Drishti's life – at home and at work – unfolded. As did the story of a person who was watching her, whatever she did, wherever she went.

On the way, the hot midday air from the street blowing over her, she flipped through the photos on Amit's digital camera.

'We need to find out exactly where these were taken,' she said.

'This is your complex?' Amit asked.

'Yes. Shouldn't be too hard, no?'

Amit shook his head. 'I haven't been inside since this

whole drama started. But I don't think it should be difficult at all.'

When they arrived, the guard waved them in. There was still a ban on media cars, but the exception was still in place for her. The crowd outside had dwindled before that morning, but on hearing the news of the extortion attempt, the journalists were back in droves. They jostled the car as she drove in, heckling the guard as usual. She couldn't spot the *Tarar Khonje* crew.

Once inside, Ahana and Amit walked around the building. It didn't take them long to figure out that all the photographs had been taken on one side of the campus. Amit studied the angles as they slowly completed a half-circle around the building, starting at the entrance to the back of B Block, ending at the children's playground.

'This is the general area in which all the photos were taken,' said Amit.

Ahana looked around, a growing feeling of dread accompanying her growing feeling of certainty. 'Any chance this was a photoshoot? Or many photoshoots?'

He popped a cigarette into his mouth. 'I don't think so. These look like candid shots. They have been taken at several different times of day – some have low lighting as well. Not professional at all. And the quality of the camera is pretty poor.'

'Digital?'

'Yes, one of those small ones, though. At least some of them. Even without zooming, the resolution is pretty bad.'

'If you had to guess where they were taken from, what would you say?'

'This one is the easiest,' he said, pointing to the shot with the slide in the background. 'I would say,' he said, stepping back towards the building, 'from somewhere around here.'

'At ground level,' said Ahana.

'No doubt about that.'

'Are you sure?'

'Go stand where Drishti is in this photo. I'll show you.'

Ahana positioned herself on the grass in front of the sandpit, somewhere between the slide and swing. 'Here?'

'A little more to your right,' he said. 'There. Now come and take a look.'

Ahana ran around to his photo preview.

'That's it,' she said.

'And the others?'

Just to be sure, they recreated all the shots from the collage.

'Look at this shot,' said Amit. 'At the corner.'

She bent over the camera. 'It looks like… a curtain.'

He nodded. 'This was taken from inside – through the window.' He ran a few feet forward and compared the angles. 'From this window.'

'That's the bedroom,' said Ahana. It confirmed what she had guessed in the office of the Drishti Sengupta Fan Club. And yet. 'It makes no sense,' she said.

'Why?'

She shook her head. 'We need to show Manash these right away.'

Atanu made the call to the editor-in-chief, who in turn called the police commissioner, who summoned Manash and Ahana to Lalbazar to meet DCDD II Vinayak Agarwal.

The prints of the photos were on the table, spread out before him.

'Please – take a look at these pictures.' Ahana explained the context of the collages, how when they had lined up all the angles of all the photos, they pointed to someone who lived in flat no B102. The flat owned by the Banerjees, Drishti's friends. Tara's friends.

Agarwal shook his head. 'That flat, it belongs to the neighbours who used to have Drishti's keys. They were one of the first to be checked out. My men visited the house, it was closed. No one lives there anymore and the flat is up for sale. The police contacted the family at their current address, and the owner's son, Palash, opened the flat and showed it to them.'

'When?'

'The next morning – or possibly a day later.'

Giving him time to hide her, move her – or worse. 'Did they conduct a search?' asked Manash.

'That I don't know. But it is unlikely at that stage of the investigation.'

'She is a small child. She could have been hidden anywhere – a cupboard, even a suitcase!' cried Ahana.

'Someone in that flat has been watching Drishti,' said Manash quickly, perhaps to stave off an outburst. Because nothing could be worse than a show of emotion.

'She's a celebrity,' said Agarwal. 'It's not unusual for celebrities to have stalkers.'

'These photos go back to before she was a celebrity,' pointed out Ahana. 'She is pregnant in one of them.'

Agarwal looked at them again.

'Sir,' said Manash, 'Ahana has met this man at the building recently. The girl may be inside even now.'

Agarwal stared down Manash and then Ahana. She could not tell if he resented being told how to do his job, or was simply processing the information. 'Ok. We will check once more. We'll go now,' he said with a nod. 'But no cameras, no journalists.'

'Of course,' said Manash. 'This is about Tara.'

They left, and Manash cursed under his breath. 'We need to be inside. Even now he is afraid of burning bridges with the other media.'

Not just about Tara then. 'He can shut us out, even if the lead originated with me?' she asked.

'Even more so because of that. It's all about the optics.'

'I'll go to Drishti,' Ahana said.

'Yes, the real story is in her reaction. The police account we will get anyhow. Go now. Quickly.'

Ahana arrived on Drishti's doorstep, not even sure she would open it for her after everything that had happened since their last meeting, everything that had been written.

But she did, looking ever more withered, her shirt hanging off her as though she hadn't eaten in days, her eyes sunken and dead.

'We may have something,' said Ahana. She hadn't known what she'd say, but the words gushed out under the weight of that gaze.

'What?' Drishti asked. Hope had finally deserted her.

What if Ahana was wrong about everything? 'The police are investigating a lead,' she said.

Drishti's gaze did not change. 'Come in.'

Inside, her parents sat on the sofa. Ahana smiled awkwardly at them, but they did not reciprocate.

'Have you heard of the Drishti Sengupta Fan Club?' Ahana asked.

Drishti nodded.

'I took some of the photos you received to them – the collage – and there was a matching one in their records. It seems that you may have had a stalker.'

Drishti's brow shot down. 'What? Who?'

Ahana paused, steeling herself for whatever would come next. 'Palash Banerjee.'

Drishti's frown deepened. 'What do you mean? Our Palash Banerjee?' she asked, pointing to the floor. He lived three floors down.

Ahana nodded. 'The photos I found seem to have been taken from his house.'

'He was watching me?'

'Possibly.'

'But his mother –' she broke off.

'Yes?'

'Her mother has been calling regularly to check up on me.'

Drishti looked at her parents, who had stood up and were moving towards her.

'But why would he do this?' she asked, bewildered, as her mother put an arm around her waist. 'Theirs is the first door I knocked on,' she gasped. 'No one opened!'

'Has he ever made any... overtures?'

'No, never!'

'Was he around a lot?'

'Yes, but...'

'It doesn't matter, Drishti. We don't know anything for sure yet. Let's wait. We should have more information soon.'

When Drishti heard the police would be coming, she spent the next ninety minutes hanging off the balcony. Her parents took turns pacing the living room.

Finally, the men arrived. From their vantage point, they could see the brown van being parked around the corner. A man in plainclothes came out, and spoke to the security guards at the entrance, and then three more in uniform joined him – with rifles cocked at the ready, batons hanging from their belts.

Drishti cupped her hands to her mouth, wide-eyed. First the plainsclothes officer went inside the B Block entrance, and then he emerged and walked quickly around the flat. Then the uniformed guards followed, straight into the building.

Drishti and Ahana lost sight of them for what felt like an age. And then two officers quickly circled the building once again, peering into windows and listening with a device that looked like a stethoscope. They went around the front and stood guard at the entrance.

Moments later, there was a crashing noise, and Drishti cried out. Ahana grabbed her arm to steady her, to steady them both. It wasn't a gunshot, it was a duller sound, and Ahana imagined them kicking down the door. Minutes passed, there was nothing to indicate what exactly was happening just a few floors below, and Ahana could hold back Drishti no more. She ran for the front door, wrenched it open and shot out, Ahana at her heels.

Drishti sped down the three flights of stairs and in through the broken door. The policeman standing there did nothing to stop her.

Agarwal was in the hall, empty except for his men.

'She's not here, Drishti,' he said, his expression inscrutable.

Drishti's gaze was firmly fixed to a spot on the floor. She walked up to it. Lying there in the dust was a pink rubber band, with a little pink bow. She fell to her knees, clutching the tiny hair tie to her chest.

'She's not here now, but she *was*,' she gasped. 'She *was*.' Her head bowed, shoulders wracked by the pain she could not contain anymore.

Ahana and Agarwal were silent as her sobs tore the room apart. And then, all of a sudden, it was as though she had sucked it all in.

She wiped her face and stood up.

'Is there any sign that she is not okay?' she asked quietly.

'I really don't think you should be here,' said Agarwal.

'Damn you. You will tell me.'

'There is a little blood. Not a lot.'

'A nosebleed?' she asked, her voice suddenly small and childlike.

'We hope so. But now we know who it is, we'll get him.'

'You've already visited their other house?'

'Yes. But it will be searched now. Properly.'

'I'm coming.'

He was going to say no, but didn't quite manage to get the words out.

Ahana and Drishti rode in the back of the police van. It was about fifteen minutes away, off Rashbehari Avenue. No one said a word.

It was a smaller complex, just a standalone building, and it took less time to secure. The guard was told not to let anyone in. The routine was repeated – knocking, surveillance and then when the flat looked empty, the door broken down. There was no sign of Tara or anyone else, no sign that Tara had even been there. Afterwards, the guards reported that mother and son both had not been seen for a few days, though the mother had made at least one trip back a couple of mornings before.

The police dropped Drishti and Ahana back to Surya Apartments, where a forensics team was at work. The guard who was at the door was firm this time around – they weren't going to be allowed in; no one was. They hung around for a minute, and then Drishti, looking on the verge of collapse, went upstairs. Ahana stuck around for a while longer. At the back of a dusty cupboard, they found a stretch of rope, with traces of blood and skin on it. And the white nightgown Tara was wearing when she had gone missing.

The Loss of Tara

The following twenty-four hours witnessed the rush of activity that could have been expected at the beginning of the investigation. There was no sign of Palash or his mother, so the Banerjees' entire lives were torn apart. With hard evidence that Tara had been in their flat in Surya Apartments, the police went to Palash's workplace, questioned his friends, of which there were few, and visited all the family they could identify.

Rapidly, a picture emerged of a man who was very much a loner and something of a misfit. He had held down a job, the same job, at an accounting firm for more than ten years. He had not managed to clear the chartered accountancy exams, and after several attempts, had given up on that dream. The previous year, at his parents' insistence, he had enrolled for a distance executive MBA programme, but then his father had been diagnosed with a particularly aggressive throat cancer that had taken every available moment of his time for about eighteen months. Despite every effort, and several trips to Bombay for treatment, Mr Banerjee had lost his battle against the disease in April of that year.

Palash went back to work after a fortnight, and had not seemed worse off than expected, according to his co-workers. He was quiet, but that was not unusual for him. No one at work would admit to being his friend. They said he would come punctually at 9.30 am every morning and leave by 6 pm every evening. He'd bring lunch from home in a steel tiffin carrier, and sit and eat it at his desk, turning down invitations to go out with his colleagues. Eventually, the invitations dried up.

There was only one friend from school with whom he was in touch, Bibek Dey. But he too said he had not heard from Palash since just after his father's death. Bibek lived in Siliguri and though he had not seen Palash in years, he still had some insights to offer to police.

'Palash has mentioned Drishti, yes. He seemed quite proud that they were friends, especially once she became famous. He would boast about it sometimes. But he never spoke about his feelings for her.' However, on other fronts, he was more vocal. 'He would talk about his photography quite a lot, how he was trying to develop his skills. When I suggested that we plan a trip so he could practice nature photography, and that he should come to Siliguri, he said no, he preferred human subjects.'

And there were human subjects aplenty, as discovered by investigators after a search of Palash's new home. There were entire envelopes dedicated to Drishti. There were others too, all women in the building and elsewhere. There were pictures taken at the Nandan grounds, Maidan and Victoria, many of couples, all unaware they were being watched.

There was one series that was a departure from this pattern. Drishti and Tara in the Banerjee home at Surya Apartments. There they sat, Drishti on the sofa, Palash's mother beside her with Tara on her lap. They seemed to be there for dinner, perhaps a parting meal before the Banerjees moved out. In one photo, Drishti smiled a small, tight-lipped smile, which told Ahana that she wasn't quite comfortable. But Tara was exuberant, arms flapping in the air, a blur of brown against the powder-blue of the wall. Sulagna Banerjee was unsmiling and stiff.

In others, they were less aware of the camera. It was odd how Tara held her head at precisely the same angle as her mother, and she had the same self-possession that had goaded a city into declaring Drishti a criminal, a deviant of the cruelest kind.

Forensics discovered a diary which Palash maintained on and off. In it, he chronicled his fledgling feelings, dating four years back, when his mother had struck up her unlikely friendship with Drishti.

'Ma is watching Tara today. Drishti has a doctor's appointment, and she will be picking Tara up at 8 pm after she is done. That might mean she will stay for dinner, as Ma usually asks her to. She often says yes. Being Saturday, I don't have office. So I went to the gym, which I have been trying to do more and more nowadays, but never manage to have the time for. Still, today I thought it would keep my mind off this evening's visit. I lifted more than I ever have before. 46 kgs! And then my nose started bleeding. This is the tissue I used there.'

The bloody tissue had been preserved between the pages.

And then the next day:

'I was thinking of showing Drishti my diary. What if she feels the same way I do?

After all, the blood on the tissue is blood I shed for her. Why shouldn't she know that? But then I watched her as she sat there with the wavy brown hair, and thought, she isn't really even beautiful. What was the point – she would never be a good wife to me. Or anybody. She has already proved that she is a loose character. I had seen that for myself even before Tara. So I did not show it to her.'

Over the years, there were other diaries with a few more sporadic entries. There was a clear connection between some of the language and some of the fan mail Drishti had received. But nothing as clear as the photographs they found on the home computer and in his cupboards. He had been watching Drishti for years – while she was still a struggling singer, and throughout her pregnancy and then the later photographs included Tara. Even before he started writing about his feelings for her, he had been photographing her. Along with other women.

But it was not just women. At some point, Tara went from being the peripheral figure to being a focus of her own series. Playing in the park, at home with his mother, riding her cycle around the building.

Forensic teams searched the two homes, top to bottom, and found no indication of where Palash, his mother, or Tara could be. Investigations continued into their histories and financial records. But after the initial burst of energy, the pace slackened again.

That was when Drishti remembered having spoken to Mrs Banerjee about a plot of land that Palash had bought, which was under dispute. 'More than Uncle's medical bills,' said Drishti, 'it was this plot that had drained their resources.'

Palash had bought it, apparently, on the encouragement of a man he had described as a friend. This man turned out to be an agent who had failed to disclose that the defunct food factory currently situated on the land was under dispute. 'All I remember was that it was past Salt Lake,' said Drishti.

After taking the information to the police and watching them sit on it for a day, Vidyut went to the Calcutta Chamber of Commerce and had them pull up a list of all distressed foods factories between Dum Dum and Salt Lake. There were at least a dozen – and Drishti had no more information that might narrow down which one it was. So then they took that list to the police, who promised they would go through Palash's computer to look for more details. Vidyut volunteered to do it himself, but they turned down the offer.

Meanwhile, *Tarar Khonje* went big with the information about their new search for their 6 pm broadcast. Agarwal stopped all business and took his department to task, declaring that the leaker would be out of a job by morning.

But the damage was already done.

By that time, Drishti's desolation had turned to all-out terror. She was at home when she saw the broadcast, pacing a hole in the living room floor. 'This is not good,' she kept saying. 'What if he panics? What will become of Tara then?'

Day 15

One – Two – Three – Four – Five

While the police were still only beginning their search through the bowels of a hard drive, in search of an address that may or may not have anything to do with the case, Nimai the security guard stood outside the entrance of Surya Apartments. It was time for the now infamous shift change, during which they were on high alert. Which meant that there was even greater chaos than before. Now with three guards, instead of the customary two, they all stood about chatting. In addition, that night there was no power in the vicinity, and though the building's lights were on, thanks to the generator, the road in front of it was in darkness.

A car was approaching. Nimai turned his old eyes to it as the others continued chatting. He didn't recognize it in the darkness, so he didn't open the gate, and then it overshot, screeching to a halt at such an angle that it was blocking the exit gate. As he approached to ask the driver to move, the back door swung open. And before he knew it, a dark form was pushed out of the vehicle and at his feet, half standing, on the verge of collapse: it was Tara.

It was over in five seconds. One – stop. Two – car door open. Three – four – child out the door. Five – close again.

He reached out and caught her. He knew he should try to stop the car, but the child in his arms was deadweight.

And then it was gone.

And there was Tara, alive, in his arms. She stared at the building in a daze, tears running down her face.

'Mama!' she cried.

He stood up, cradling her like an infant, and ran inside.

Later Nimai remembered racing that girl up to her home, as she called for her mother over and over again. She smelt of stale clothes and vomit. When he rang the bell, it was thrown open with violence, as though Drishti had peered through the eyehole and seen them there, and she snatched the child away from him. For a few minutes, Drishti did nothing but cry, standing there in the doorway, a sound so devastating that he would be haunted by it for the rest of his days. And then Tara, whose eyes were dry by then, reached out her little hand and ran it across her mother's cheek. Drishti pulled away, looking at her baby in wonder, laughing through the tears.

Drishti's father, also in tears, rushed to the guard and began to ask questions about where he had found her and what he had seen.

Nimai said that all he had caught was a fragment of a glimpse of a person in the back seat of the car, face covered by a dupatta tied like a mummy's mask. He tried to see what he could of the car as it sped away – it was a silver Hyundai Santro, its license plate covered with a piece of paper.

Then Rajendra asked him to wait in the living room as he called the police, who told him the guard should wait on the premises but that Tara would need to visit the medical examiner as soon as possible. None of them wanted to set foot anywhere near a hospital at that point, but Drishti knew that they would need to find out just what had happened to Tara.

Tara did not say a word at the hospital. She held on to her mother almost as tightly as her mother held on to her, but she said nothing. She did not object to the blood tests or X-rays, to the forensics teams collecting swabs and scraping. She seemed done with tears, which terrified Drishti even more.

But that was just the beginning. Drishti remembered the days that followed as a different sort of agony engulfed her child. If Tara ever lost sight of Drishti, she would scream an anguished, blood curdling scream. Every waking moment was spent as close to her mother as possible. Tara was too young to even tell her mother when she was feeling ill. What could she possibly say about the terror of the past two weeks?

The medical results came back in tranches, the first lot of which suggested there were sedatives in Tara's system. As these wore off, nothing seemed to change, much to Drishti's anguish. She had been dehydrated, too, which had been remedied the first night she was in hospital through intravenous drip. It did nothing to bring back her tears.

But little by little, with food and love and her mother by her side, Tara started to speak. At first, it was about the little things of daily life, in that remarkable way children have of simply focussing on what is in front of them.

Perhaps it didn't help that Drishti was loathe to bring up anything that had happened during Tara's absence, but as the days wore on, the police were getting impatient and she knew she couldn't protect her child from the facts by ignoring them.

The third morning after her return, they were curled up on the sofa, reading a book. Once they were done, Drishti put it down. 'Tara, do you think you can tell me what happened when you were gone?'

She buried her face in Drishti's arm. 'I don't want to, Mama.'

'Why?'

She knew from the way Tara was looking at her askance that she thought Drishti would be angry with her.

'I can help you. Whatever it is, it is ok, Starlight.'

'No it isn't.'

And that was the end of that.

After Tara's favourite lunch of dal, rice and aloo bhaja, she tried again. 'After I put you to sleep that night, did someone come into the room?'

And then at last, playing with her spoon, Tara said, 'No one did, Mama.'

Drishti's breath caught in her throat.

'I left. I cried and cried, and when no one came, I went looking for you.'

In that moment, Drishti knew her heart would never recover. She had always known this had been a possibility – it was what she had herself believed in the early hours. That the maid hadn't latched the door and that Tara had simply wandered out.

'Then what happened?' she asked, her voice a whisper.

'Dolly needs lunch too,' said Tara, turning to the toy on the chair next to her. The spoon of dal fell, and Tara quickly snuck a look at her mother, who did not react. Drishti thought in that moment that such things, the tiny daily aggravations of motherhood, would never bother her again.

Later, with Tara in the bubble bath, Drishti tried again.

'So what happened once you left the house? You couldn't find your way back?'

'I was in the lift and I got down at the ground floor. I went out to the front, and that is when I met Palash Kaku.'

Drishti felt the ground beneath her feet give way. It was as simple as that.

She should have known. She should have known that all along, her daughter was just three floors below her.

'And then?'

'He told me he'd bring me home. But he didn't.'

From then, the days blurred, but she described being in the flat, not being allowed to leave. 'And then I got sick, and finally Didun came, and she was very angry with Palash Kaku and they took me to another place.'

'A house? Didun's house?'

'No Mama, not Didun's house.' She was angry herself now. 'It was a yucky house that I didn't like. It had a smell. And then I cried a lot.'

'Do you know where you were?'

'There were airplanes.'

'You could see them?'

'All the windows were dirty and closed so how could I see them!' she said, brow shooting down. 'I heard them. It was so loud!'

Drishti slowly finished bathing her daughter, dressed her and called the police. And next, she called Ahana.

Palash Banerjee was a hunted man.

They found the old factory, and it was confirmed as the scene of Tara's captivity. But there was no sign of her captors. It was just three kilometers from the airport.

Through the bank, they tried to identify Palash's whereabouts. It was rather late in the day, but they put an alert out at airports across the country. Railway stations too. They were able to confirm that he had not flown out of the city at least. But that left train, bus and even car, though the vehicle in which they had dropped off Tara had been turned over to the police by a cousin. Palash had apparently borrowed it, claiming that the family's own car had broken down and they had a large amount of grocery shopping to do for a pujo they intended to hold for his dead father.

Before they found Palash, they found Palash's mother as she was entering her Rashbehari home. The neighbours caught her and dragged her by her hair to the thana.

Sulagna Banerjee had known of her son's fascination with Drishti, but had dismissed it as no more than a crush. In the aftermath of her husband's death, she thought he was getting on with business rather well, even though he had been spending longer and longer hours away from home. But the night Tara had gone missing, she knew that he had been at Surya Apartments, and for some reason, he had not returned home. She had called to check up on him, but he said he had not gone to the empty flat at all that evening as he had worked late, sleeping on the couch at work. This had happened before as well, when pressure of work was high, so she suspected nothing.

But when he didn't return the next night as well, she knew something was wrong. In the morning, she called on the office landline, and when she learned he had not been in at all that day, she feared the worst.

She waited one more day, and then went to the flat at Surya Apartments. She rang the bell, once, twice, but he didn't answer. She dropped in on Drishti to see how she was doing, and it broke her heart to witness her grief. So she tried again at the door of her own flat, knocking and knocking, not too loudly for fear of alerting the neighbours, till Palash finally opened up. She found Tara ill, running high temperature.

'He didn't want any harm to befall her,' she said, hoping this would offset some of the horror of what he – they – had done. 'He asked me to take care of her.'

She nursed Tara as the child battled a fever and stomach bug. She knew they couldn't consult a doctor, but she told her son which medicines she needed and she handled it herself. She sent Palash to get new clothes as well. And then, when Tara was better, she demanded that her son set things right.

The ransom effort was concocted only as a means of returning Tara to her mother, Sulagna told the police. But when Palash didn't follow through, she decided that it was time to take charge of that too. She insisted that he find a car, and that they drop off the girl outside her home. She would give him time to get away; that was all she could do for him now.

And she stuck to her word: she still wouldn't reveal where Palash was. All she kept saying was that she had protected Drishti's child from any real harm, and now Drishti should find it in her heart to forgive hers. That she could have reduced Tara's misery, and Drishti's, by at least ten days if she had brought the child back as soon as she discovered what her son had done, didn't matter.

Three days later, there was the first sign of Palash when he made a cash withdrawal in Paharganj, in Delhi. The bank alerted the police immediately, but it was still too late: he was gone by the time the team arrived. But having identified where he was broadly, they were able to intensify efforts. It was close to the railway station, and the police surmised that he had arrived by train and had likely checked himself into a hotel nearby. With the risk that he would flee Delhi being all too real, they acted fast. They found him twelve hours later, less than a kilometer away from the ATM, holed up in a cheap hotel with a suitcase full of clothes and a small digital camera.

Once he was arrested, Palash was quick to assert his innocence. 'Tara was wandering about, afraid and alone, in the middle of the night. I simply took her into my home. How is that kidnapping?' he said.

When pressed about why he didn't come forward when he realized the hunt was on, or even the next morning, he clammed up. 'Drishti is not fit to be that child's mother. She is not the woman you think she is. She is not the woman I thought she was.'

And that was all he would say.

Closed Door

Palash would watch as Drishti came back late at night, night after night. It was much later than his mother thought prudent, or, more to the point, decent. In fact, it wasn't till Sulagna mentioned it several times that he had really noticed Drishti at all. But soon, he began to wait up for her. Usually she wouldn't return till after midnight, at the earliest. Sometimes alone, sometimes not.

Once in a while, he would be able to hear music from her flat: the band practicing or a party happening. He would lie in bed and strain to listen. A few times, when he knew she had a male friend over, he thought he heard her cry out in pleasure, three floors up. Nights like that, it was hard to get to sleep.

He got to know the faces. So when she brought a friend he had never seen before, it caught his attention. They didn't go upstairs. They hovered just outside the building, outside his window. They sat on the bench next to the children's park, the lights out at that time of night. Palash could see them only in silhouette at first, but gradually, his eyes adjusted and he saw a little more through that window, one little corner of the curtain pushed back. Drishti and the man seemed close, and then there was no doubt about it, despite the darkness. They were kissing, and he couldn't help himself. He was pressed against the glass by that time, protected by the night, pushing the curtain further back than he had ever before dared. In that moment, nothing else mattered. He reached for the drawstring of his pyjamas.

By the time Drishti was on her back, he was sure she was putting up a show just for him. He couldn't see her face, but he knew her eyes were turned to his window; as she gasped, she smiled to see his pleasure too.

After Tara was born, for a long time, the late-night returns stopped. But then he started seeing more of her, as his mother slowly was taken in by first the child and then, strangely, Drishti. It started when Palash's cousin was visiting with her own child, and Tara and his niece were both at the playground. Drishti had started speaking to Sulagna, and suddenly, it was as though she had forgotten all those things she used to say about her. And then Drishti became a visitor to his house, all the time, close enough to touch.

But then, life changed again. His father fell ill and they had to move away. They saw less and less of Drishti and Tara, he even less than his mother. He had almost managed to put her out of his mind, particularly when his parents decided to arrange his marriage.

But then she started performing again, and he was ensnared once more.

How he hated that bar, riddled with teenagers with more money than sense, the silly swaying with the lighter when they liked a song. He would stand at the back and burn through a pack of cigarettes as he downed first two beers and then one whisky. Drishti was always in a rush to leave in those days. He always played through the scene of walking up to her and saying something, but he never did. He was always in the shadows, not hiding, but confident that she would never see him. Because she never did. There was always some other man with his hands on her, and as disgusting as he found it, he couldn't look away.

So he started going back to the complex, on the pretext of looking for a tenant for the house, and then he would wait again, as Drishti returned late at night. Just like the old days.

And then, one night, he saw little Tara wandering about on her own. The tiny girl in a white nightgown, silent tears running down her face. He opened the door and she walked right in to his arms. He picked her up, smoothing the tears away, and closed the door behind him.

Epilogue

Ahana took a week off from work the day after Palash Banerjee was arrested.

She had finally announced the news of her impending engagement in office. It was also the excuse she had given for the leave, but that wasn't the only reason.

After a few days of franctic activity following Tara's return, Ahana was back to her old beat, covering the launch of a new boutique in town. It was a big one – one of India's leading bridalwear designers was opening a flagship store. She interviewed the designer, sipped cocktails with the socialites, returned to the office and filed her story. And it was as though she wasn't even there.

Once it was all over, she thought she'd catch up on some sleep, but she ended up bingeing on the news. Then finally,

Palash's face slowly dropped off till she believed she might even be able to forget what had happened.

Suddenly, with time on her hands, she was also speaking with her fiancé, at least once a day, sometimes more. The conversations were pleasant enough, but Ahana felt as though she was under water and everything was reaching her in a slightly muffled, slightly warped form. She was afloat, but at the same time, drowning.

And then the day was finally upon her. It was an evening engagement, at the community hall in Surya Apartments. Ahana spent the morning at home, and then, after lunch went to the salon to have her hair done and her sari draped. Two of her cousins flitted around, making suggestions, urging her to have her make-up done as well.

'I've already done it. And anyway, there is no time now,' said Ahana.

Then Priyanka walked in. She had chosen the salon, the owner was her contact through work, and she had come to make sure Ahana was being given the princess treatment. But she took one look at Ahana's face and knew better than to say anything. The draping was already over, and Ahana was watching her hair being rolled into curlers.

She still felt as though it was all a fancy dress ball, like she was getting prepared to step on to a stage for a performance, and after a few hours, it would all be over.

Except it wouldn't be – it would be just the beginning.

Priyanka managed, in her uniformly charming manner, to send the cousins back to the house without too much of a fuss. And then she sat down next to Ahana.

'What are you doing, girl?'

Ahana would have spoken, but she had a lump in her

throat and she didn't want to ruin the make-up that had taken her an hour to get just right.

Instead, she shrugged.

'If I didn't know any better, I would not believe this was the happy face of a bride-to-be,' said Priyanka, looking at her in the mirror.

Ahana took a deep breath before she trusted herself to speak. 'It is only the engagement.'

'You aren't happy.'

'If I don't know that, how could you possibly be so sure?'

'You'd know it if you were happy.'

'Are you happy?'

'No.'

'Then?'

'I am not happy about being slightly hungover today, at my best friend's engagement. I am not happy about not being able to fit into last year's jeans. You are not happy about making a life-long commitment to someone. These are slightly different things.'

'Well, it's done.'

'No, it's really not.'

And then the blowdryers went on and conversation was no longer possible.

Ahana knew she'd feel love, or something like it, in the early days. Many arranged marriages she'd seen had begun that way. Ahana could always convince herself of anything if she tried hard enough. For a while at least. Just like her first job. Just like her MBA. So she'd get married, leave the city, discover a new adventure. When the novelty wore off... what did she know? Maybe it wouldn't. Maybe by that time the love would be real.

They were late getting back, as Ahana's mother had predicted before her departure. But there was nothing to be done for it.

The traffic was backed up, and the two kilometers home took twenty-five minutes, with her mother calling every five minutes to check on their progress. She knew this was being done at her father's behest. The groom's family had already arrived, she informed them. The feeling of dread in Ahana's stomach grew bigger and bigger as they inched along the road.

'Should we get out and walk?' asked Priyanka.

'Not in these heels,' Ahana said.

Finally, they pulled into the drive and Ahana walked straight to the party hall. She should have been rushing, but her legs felt like lead.

The door was open, and she felt herself watching the scene from afar. It was like a movie in which a suicide bomber walks into a crowded space in slow motion: you know people will get hurt, but the only one guaranteed to be blown up was her.

Ahana looked at Priyanka, still earnest and unsmiling, and realized her friend wasn't about to make it any easier for her.

She scanned the room and saw him sitting there. He looked good – very good in fact. He was nice too – clever and funny. He turned to her and smiled. She didn't know if she smiled back.

Her mother and aunt stood up then. 'She's come, she's come! Blow the *shankh*!'

The room erupted with the sound of the conch and ullu. Without waiting for them to stop, she crossed the room to where her father stood.

Her mother was staring at them, fear writ large across her face.

Ahana stood there, feet already in agony, hairpins digging into her scalp.

She was uncertain of what she was about to say. But she knew then that she would find the words.

Prologue

The Loss of Tara

What happens when we lose a child?

What happens when those entrusted with the child's protection stand accused of the most abhorrent acts imaginable?

What happens when a whole town stops to watch?

On 13 June 2002, Tara Sengupta, age four, went missing from her own home, her own bedroom. Kidnap or murder – what had become of the girl in the middle of the night was a mystery that took the nation by storm. A girl who happened to be the daughter of a single, celebrity mother.

The aftermath of the tragic events wrecked several families. The town that watched, open-mouthed and ugly, emerged unscathed, and walked away nonchalantly, as it always does.

What about the disappearance of Tara brought out the worst in us? It was a scandal to be sure, but at its heart it was an intensely personal tragedy. Coming at a time when the 24-hour news cycle was just emerging, when India was getting a taste for sensational news. After decades of dry Doordarshan, it had discovered the painful pleasure of watching the crises of others from a safe distance. But there was more to its hunger for blood, something sinister and frightening to those who watched closely.

The case had all the ingredients of a hit: tragedy, love, sex, money. It occurred in an upmarket Calcutta neighbourhood which made it feel as though it could happen to anybody, anywhere. But even though Drishti Sengupta, the tragic mother, was People Like Us, she was also Drishti Sengupta, singer with a salacious past, sufficiently different to set her apart. It was everyone's worst nightmare, but at a comfortable distance.

This book is a factual account of the events that unfolded. As the newsmen played judge and jury, I too became a part of the story, and it has stayed with me in ways I did not expect. Which is why when I received a request from the most unlikely of sources to write this book, it gave me pause. Was I ready to open up the wounds of all involved again seventeen years after the fact? Was I willing to relive and recreate the horror of 2002 in 2019?

As I took a closer look, however, I became convinced that there was a need to tell the story, for despite the hysteria of the time, the chilling crime had been largely forgotten by the public. But for those involved, it had never gone away.

If the frenzy during the hunt for Tara was bad, they wouldn't let go, even with her return.

Was Tara, not yet five, raped? The answer was no, according to forensics and police. But the expert panels on TV had other ideas, and breathlessly explored every single possibility.

It was finally enough to chase Drishti from the city. After Palash's arrest, it became clear that the attention was not going to go away any time soon. It was also clear that Palash would not see a trial for possibly years to come.

With Tara's statement recorded, Drishti and Tara left town. A dear friend of hers in Australia opened her home to them, and it seemed far enough away from everyone to be a safe haven. While she was there, the country captivated her, and she decided to make the move permanent. She returned to India to wait for the immigration process to follow its course, and to wrap up her business. By that time, the phone was no longer ringing. The gaze had shifted and she and Tara had been mercifully forgotten.

Until August 2017, when another child, Varun Agarwal, went missing. Palash had been out of jail for three years, having served his sentence for kidnapping a minor. His prosecution had seen inordinate delays, following which several justice campaigners had championed his cause, and finally secured his release.

The disappearance of another child from his home, with shocking echoes of Tara's case, prompted Palash to be invited into news studios. The very channels, the very anchors that had vilified Drishti now resurrected Palash – a convicted criminal – as an expert consultant to tear apart another crime.

Palash grabbed the opportunity to attempt to rewrite history. He insisted that he had done his time, and now he wanted the truth to be known. There was a film being made about his life, he said, which would shed new light on what had happened all those years ago.

And that is when Tara called me. I had moved on to helm a newspaper in Doha. Over the years, my relationship with Drishti and her family had deepened. Tara, now twenty, was finishing university, and said that before anyone else had a chance to hijack the story, she wanted the truth to be told. Her truth.

With this immense burden of trust on my shoulders, my first task was to try to talk her out of it. But she would not budge. Drishti was wary at first – having lived through the scrutiny once, she didn't want to poke the bear again. But Tara worked her way through both our concerns, with a determination she owns so completely and without apology. Just like her mother.

Tara had no doubt that if Palash's film ever got made, he would paint her mother in the most unfavourable light. Not to mention, possibly revive claims of his own innocence. He had reverted to some version of a story involving Sumita, the maid who had been thoroughly investigated, had cooperated with the police, and had ultimately been exonerated. If she had been guilty of anything, it had been of negligence, and though the courts had not tried her, the scandal chased her away from Calcutta to Delhi, where she changed her name and still lives to this day.

She refused to be interviewed for this book, saying that her daughter knew nothing about the affair and that she wanted to keep it that way. But Tara remembered it all. Leaving the house – the door had not been bolted, and she had learned how to open the lock months ago – wandering down to the ground floor and finally out into the lawn.

She was not, as some had suggested, sleepwalking. Her story has remained unchanged over fifteen years: she had called out for her mother in the bedroom, and when no one came in, she had gone out in search of her.

How much of this is true memory and how much has been built over time into a narrative that Tara can make sense of, is not clear. Tara is aware of this. However, she is unwavering on the moment that Palash opened the door to the ground floor flat and she walked in, and the terror she felt when she realized that Didun wasn't there, and her mother wasn't coming as had been promised.

Tara said she may not have been able to articulate all of this as a child, but that didn't mean her memories were not hers, that they were not true. And I, most wholeheartedly, had to agree.

And so this book was born. It is the tale of many people who found themselves embroiled in this painful episode. A crime, but also more. It is Tara's story, and Drishti's. It is the tale of Tara's grandparents. And of Vidyut too.

After the kidnapping, Vidyut went back to the States, and within a year his marriage was over. For the next few years, he would fly to Australia to spend the summer with Tara – and Drishti. In 2005, Tara's baby brother Akash was born. Vidyut then moved to join them in Melbourne.

Every year, on Tara's birthday, Vidyut asks Drishti to marry him. Every year, she says no. And then, they all go out for ice-cream.

Acknowledgements

Dirty Women is an idea that was born a lifetime ago. It refused to go away, despite being neglected and ignored for years. It was finally completed and given a shot at catching some daylight by Anish Chandy at Labyrinth Literary Agency. Thank you for that, Anish. And also to Greeshma Gireesh for being the first reader and providing valuable feedback.

The entire team at Roli has been a rock through the most challenging time in recent history. Thanks to editorial director Priya Kapoor and commissioning editor Chirag Thakkar for greenlighting this book. They've truly made the publication process a pleasure. Managing editor Neelam Narula and copyeditor Sreejata Guha both lent their critical eye to the manuscript and strengthened it greatly. And a very special shout out to cover designer Gavin Morris for creating the piece of art that clothes this volume.

Dirty Women has been an intensely personal project from the get-go. My daughter, who, like Tara, has tried to feed me sand on many an occasion but has always accepted defeat graciously, is at the heart of it. Seeing the world through her eyes has changed me, mostly for the better, and caused me to question so much of my experience navigating the world. I wish for her a life in which she can be herself without fear, knowing that she always has a safe space to land.